Praise for
A Hundred Other Girls

"The most delightful, absorbing, and hilarious book I have read in ages! An automatic favorite—there is nothing like this anywhere. Iman Hariri-Kia has that rare talent that comes along once in a decade."

—Christina Lauren, *New York Times* bestselling author of *The Unhoneymooners* and *The Soulmate Equation*

"Juicy and fun. I loved it!"

—Cat Marnell, *New York Times* bestselling author of *How to Murder Your Life*

"Slick, astute, and clever as hell, this book literally is the zeitgeist. Between the biting cultural commentary, heart-thumping plot, guffaw-worthy zingers, and ultra-vivid characters, reading *A Hundred Other Girls* felt like watching a Gen-Z *The Devil Wears Prada* on a big screen... Take it from a former beauty editor: it's more realistic than you might think."

—Amanda Montell, author of *Cultish: The Language of Fanaticism* and *Wordslut: A Feminist Guide to Taking Back the English Language*

"I couldn't put this book down. I loved experiencing New York and the publishing world through Noora's eyes."

—Ashley Hesseltine, *Girls Gotta Eat* podcast

A Hundred Other Girls

a novel

IMAN HARIRI-KIA

For my eight-year-old self.
We did it, bitch!

Copyright © 2022 by Iman Hariri-Kia
Cover and internal design © 2022 by Sourcebooks
Cover art by Sandra Chiu
Internal design by Ashley Holstrom/Sourcebooks

Published by Sourcebooks Landmark, an imprint of Sourcebooks
P.O. Box 4410, Naperville, Illinois 60567-4410
(630) 961-3900
sourcebooks.com

Library of Congress Cataloging-in-Publication Data

Names: Hariri-Kia, Iman, author.
Title: A hundred other girls : a novel / Iman Hariri-Kia.
Description: Naperville, Illinois : Sourcebooks Landmark, [2022]
Identifiers: LCCN 2021037098 (print) | LCCN 2021037099 (ebook) | (trade paperback) | (epub)
Subjects: LCGFT: Bildungsromans. | Novels.
Classification: LCC PS3608.A7375 H86 2022 (print) | LCC PS3608.A7375
   (ebook) | DDC 813/.6--dc23
LC record available at https://lccn.loc.gov/2021037098
LC ebook record available at https://lccn.loc.gov/2021037099

Printed and bound in the United States of America.
LSC 10 9 8 7 6 5 4 3 2

Vinyl Magazine

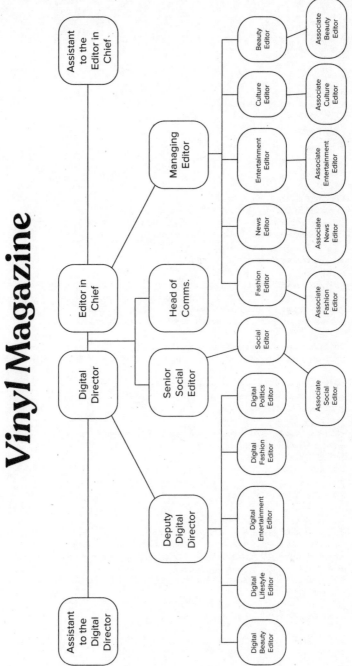

Chapter One

There's a special place in hell reserved for men who manspread on the subway. Take this one guy: midthirties, hair slicked back with so much gel you'd think he was speeding off to audition for the revival of *Grease* on Broadway. But given his clean-cut gray suit, leather briefcase, and the pace at which he's whispering into his earpiece, he's most likely in finance. My guess? Investment banking or trading, based solely on the size of that Rolex hanging off his left wrist. I roll my eyes as he allows his right knee to meander a few inches wider, effectively taking up three whole subway seats. This is what I do when I'm anxious: I people watch. As a native New Yorker, studying different human species in the wild fills me with an odd sense of inner peace. It's like camping in the desert and staring up at the stars—it reminds me that the world is so much bigger than me and my anxiety.

I suddenly notice an elderly woman without a seat, clinging to one of the ceiling handlebars. Since Goldman Ball-Sachs is too distracted to give up an inch of space on the bench he and his junk have claimed as private territory, I offer her mine. She graciously accepts and I smile at her. "Honey, you should really fix that gap between your teeth," she tells me, her voice dripping with a thick Staten Island drawl. I stop smiling. New Yorkers are fucking crazy—myself included.

Ladies and gentlemen, we are being held momentarily by the train's dispatcher. This is a Brooklyn Bridge–bound six local train. The next stop is Wall Street. Stand clear of the closing doors, please.

I check my phone. It's 1:42 p.m., which means I only have eighteen more minutes to get to South Street Seaport. I was planning on arriving ten minutes early, but that's clearly no longer in the cards. Why do I even try to be on time when the universe so clearly has a vendetta against me? I flip open my camera and check out my reflection. My long, black, curly hair has gone totally frizzy due to the July heat, so I pat it down using a little bit of saliva, my thumb, and my forefinger. I straighten my gold nameplate necklace, which says *Noora,* written in Farsi. Noor means *light*—as in, if I don't get my ass off the six train in the next eight minutes, I'll never see the light of day again.

I catch the banker dude looking at me looking at myself out of the corner of my eye. At first, I think maybe he knows me from the internet. My blog, *NoorYorkCity,* has around twenty-two thousand followers on Instagram. Substantial, considering it's mostly an internet black hole where I post incessant rants about the current state of our country along-side pictures of my riskier outfits. My sister, Leila, is always telling me I need to step up my "aesthetic" to look like I care less about how many followers I have. She's a publicist, so she probably knows what she's talking about. I usually just tell her to fuck off, though.

All of a sudden, I see a bright flash and realize the banker douche was actually just taking a sneaky picture of me fixing myself in the mirror. Great. That's all I need—to become a viral meme. I'm about to go tell him where he can stick his phone when the train suddenly jolts and resumes moving.

I decide to stay put and review my interview talking points instead.

When Leila first told me her coworker had gotten a tip that the assistant to Loretta James, editor in chief of *Vinyl* magazine, had quit without giving notice, my entire body went numb. I've been reading *Vinyl* ever since I started getting an allowance as a kid. When a new issue came out each month, I'd use my entire ten-dollar allotment on a copy of *Vinyl*, an Oreo Hershey's bar, and a Diet Coke from the corner bodega. I even collected them, convinced that one day they'd be worth a fortune. My mother, unfortunately, hadn't seen it that way; she'd called it hoarding and threw out nearly every issue when I left home for NYU. As my good-luck charm today, I've brought along the only copy she'd saved.

For as long as I can remember, I've wanted to be a writer. And yeah, I know. There's no money in writing today—magazines are dying, newspapers are selling out, and journalists are more interested in becoming celebrity editors than prolific authors. But that's not me. I still maintain that magazines like *Vinyl* saved my life. You see, my parents were immigrants, fresh off the boat from Iran, so to speak. And while my mom and dad were able to give me a lot of things—an education, a stable home, and a whole lot of love—advice was not one of their strong suits. They're from a different culture and a different time and very good at talking *at* me but not necessarily *to* me. I was essentially raised by three pillars: Leila, young adult novels, and magazines. I always had my head in between pages, reading back lines until I had them memorized. *Vinyl* became an older friend. It taught me how to properly insert a tampon, select which political philosophy I subscribed to, and differentiate between an orgasm and an organism. Reading showed me the way forward during a time

3

when I felt stuck between worlds: girlhood and womanhood, Iran and America. I've always vowed to one day become a writer myself and devote my life to my readers because, well, I was the reader. Actually, I *am* the reader. That's why I started *NoorYorkCity* in the first place.

"You *have* to apply," Leila said. "You can finally put that English degree of yours to good use. Can you imagine never having to explain what an Oxford comma is to another Brearley brat ever again?" No, actually. I can't. Ever since graduating in May, I have been tutoring Manhattan private school kids, which actually means writing their essays for them while they bitch to me about their friends with fake IDs who go to Paul's Baby Grand on Wednesday nights. "She, like, buys a table just so she can sit there and film herself getting bottle service and put it on her Insta story," Eliza, one of my fifteen-year-old pupils, once complained to me. "It's honestly lame. Like, we get it. Your dad's a prince in Saudi Arabia or whatever. OH MY GOD, oops!" Her hand flew over her mouth. "Isn't that where you're from?" I explained to her that my family is from Iran, but I was actually born in New York Hospital, several blocks away from where she lives. "Oh, sick," she said, relieved. "So you get it then."

Put plainly, the job sucks. But as long as the kids get As, I get paid a *ridiculous* amount. Plus, it's left me a lot of time to write freelance pitches. Not that those have been getting me anywhere. No one has ever responded to me, save for that *Vice* editor who wrote back to ask if I'd ever been published anywhere other than my "online diary." I cringe, remembering how angry the email had made me. My hands begin to shake, and my chest tightens. Why did I ever think I could apply for a position like this? *Vinyl* is the magazine responsible for publishing last month's deep dive into the history of sexual misconduct during New York Fashion Week, for Christ's sake. Last week, I wrote a blog post comparing my postgrad life to a charcuterie board. Why the *fuck* did I convince my grossly underqualified ass to apply?

I snap out of my spiral just in time to realize we're pulling into Fulton Street station. I run out of the train and up the subway steps, pushing passersby out of my way. I'm careful not to let the heels of my tiny Manolo kitten mules get stuck in the crevices of the cobblestone streets. My body is clad in a slinky vintage slip, which was originally white with some sketchy discoloration when I found it at Beacon's Closet, but after I tie-dyed it in Leila's bathroom, it was reborn as a certified *lewk*. The dress feels like me: undiscovered potential. The right person just has to recognize it.

I turn the corner on Varick Street and arrive at the Shifter & Pearce Publishing (SPP) Tower. It's one of those buildings I've probably passed a hundred times over the course of my life but have never really *seen* before. It's made of old brick, probably about fifty floors, with large windows and beautiful veranda detailing, the kind that makes every room look like a Renaissance painting. It's dripping with old New York charm. When I close my eyes, I can hear the clacking of typewriters and the barking of newsroom reporters in the 1920s. I can smell the smoke from their cigarettes wafting out onto the sidewalk. This is what I love about this city. Every neighborhood has its own history and personality, every block has its own language and people, and every building has its own story—one constantly being edited by the pedestrians who dare to enter. And when they exit for the very last time, they leave the ink wet for the next unsuspecting tenant. Now it's my turn to scribble something in its margins.

I enter the lobby with my shoulders back and head held high, strutting like a *RuPaul's Drag Race* contestant toward the turnstiles that block off the elevator bank.

BEEP.

An alarm goes off, and a large security guard approaches me. I notice he's wearing novelty Superman socks underneath his uniform.

"ID badge, please."

"I...I don't have one," I say. He grunts impatiently.

"Come with me."

I follow him to the security desk. He asks if he can search my purse then hands it to his colleague to run through a black, bulky machine. I feel like I'm in line at JFK. Who knew SPP would require as much security as the White House? He hands back my purse and asks for a copy of my driver's license. I explain I don't have one of those either. Hey—I'm a New Yorker, remember? I never learned how to drive. He wants to know who I'm here to see.

"*Vinyl* magazine, please," I announce proudly. He nods.

"The fashion magazine."

"The *culture* magazine," I correct him.

He takes my photo and prints a visitor pass for me. I quickly snap a picture of it and send it to Leila, in case this is as far as I get, then thank him for his help. "I like your socks," I say before returning to the turnstiles, this time passing through with ease. When I turn to wave, he finally cracks a smile.

The elevator bank looks straight out of the Matrix—sterile, glossy, and white. I press thirty-two on a touch screen pad. One of the elevator doors immediately opens, and I get on. I'm joined by an older woman in a fluffy red faux-fur coat and white tennis shoes. I don't recognize her face, but she has an air of importance to her. At the very last minute, a man rushes in. He's dressed a bit too casually in jeans and a T-shirt, which reads HOWARD UNIVERSITY. I can't help but notice how perfectly the sleeves frame his biceps. He sees me noticing and smirks. I blush and turn to stare at the double doors.

The elevator pings open, and Fur Coat Lady gets out. I step forward to check the floor. Somehow, we've made it all the way to forty, missing thirty-two entirely.

"What the fuck?" I accidentally say out loud. Howard Man laughs.

"Let me guess," he says. "You didn't check what elevator you had to go to when you hit your floor?" I shake my head. "Well, I suggest you get out quickly and try again. These are smart elevators." I check my phone. I have exactly two minutes. I run out onto the fortieth floor, my cheeks bright red, my forehead beading with sweat.

"What's your name?" he asks, just as the doors close.

"Noora," I say to absolutely no one. The hallway is empty and silent. I quickly press the number again, making sure to check my assigned elevator this time. Luckily, one arrives in seconds, and before I have time to stress, I'm here.

There's a giant neon *Vinyl* sign hanging on the wall and a millennial-pink velvet couch sitting in the hallway waiting area. Books are arranged by color, and pillows are embroidered with empowering, punchy catchphrases like "dress like a feminist" and needlepoint illustrations of vaginas. Someone with a buzzed head and an entire sleeve of tattoos is waiting for me while wearing overalls, cowboy boots, bright-red lipstick, and a huge smile.

"Noora, right?" I nod. "Welcome! I'm Saffron, and my pronouns are they/them. I'm *Vinyl*'s Digital Beauty editor, and I oversee everything from makeup, hair, skin, yada yada, to physical and mental health, sleep, wellness, trauma, etc. You're Loretta's new assistant, right?"

"Not exactly," I respond slowly, confused. "I'm here to interview for the position."

"Right, but like, basically. Didn't you already phone interview with HR? And take the edit test?" I nod again, feeling unsure of what to say. Saffron says, "See, so you're in. Loretta wouldn't waste her time meeting you if you weren't top of her list. Plus, she needs someone ASAP. I don't know if you heard, but her last assistant didn't exactly leave things—how do I put this?—neatly. Usually she'd be the one meeting you out here, but she kind of just left. I volunteered because I actually *like* meeting new people. I'm low-key from the Midwest. Plus, I needed to take a break from editing this story." Their eyes widen. "PTSD, you know? Heavy stuff."

They lead me through the glass doors and into the bullpen. I'm greeted by a sea of cubicles separated by two large offices. At first glance, it looks like any other place of business. I'm hit by a wave of disappointment, followed by a pang of annoyance at said disappointment.

"So, where to begin? This is where all of Editorial sits—Art, Sales, Audience Development, Branded Content, everyone else, they're all on different floors. You'll meet them eventually." I sort of shrug, pretending to know what they're talking about. "All the offices lining the walls belong to more senior people, like our Digital deputy editor and Print's managing editor. Oh, also, for some reason, PR gets an office here too. Our head of Communications is Daniel. Wait till you meet him, he's a riot." They point at the biggest office, the one closest to us. The glass is frosted, so I can't see inside. "That's Loretta's office, but her last meeting is running late, so I'm just gonna give you a quick tour."

We walk through a wasteland of deserted desks, all kept in pristine condition. The cubicles are all bare-bones, with no photos or decorations to indicate their owners, just cutouts from magazines, Venus ET Fleur flower arrangements, diptyque candles, and copies of *Vinyl*. It looks like a fake IKEA template of what a magazine office *should* look like.

"This is Print's half of the office, where their Beauty,

Fashion, Culture, and News editors sit," they continue. "Plus, all their associate editors, of course. But they're hardly ever in. They only come in for meetings or to write their issue pieces. Then they leave to go to events and shit." They roll their eyes and keep walking.

"It's all so…clean," I remark. Saffron snorts.

"If by *clean* you mean *creepy*, sure. They're super formal. Plus, they're all much older. We're talking, like, in their thirties, *at least*. They've been here since the dinosaur age. Well, not *here* here. But at some brand or another at SPP. All these Print people, they just move around from magazine to magazine." They're talking so fast that they have to pause for a second to catch their breath. "They're not exactly think-outside-the-box types. You'll see when you meet 'em."

Strange—I always imagined a print magazine's offices to be a little more *Vogue* than WeWork, but this feels as impersonal and transient as one of the Universal Studios lots. I'd pictured thin white women in stilettos carrying large stacks of paper and being barked at by bosses draped in giant fur shawls and oversize sunglasses. The reality is a lot lonelier, sterile. It's as if the staff has been picked off one by one, like in *Survivor*, until there's nothing left but a pile of bones, unopened boxes, and sharpened No. 2 pencils.

We continue walking through the floor. I can hear a murmur coming from down the hall. Curious, I pick up the pace and turn the corner. I stop short, shocked. Suddenly, I'm standing in what can only be described as an elevated dorm room. There's a plush pink carpet lining the floor and velvet beanbags that look straight out of an Ariana Grande music video. Lizzo is quietly playing through someone's phone speaker. Each chair is packed with a young writer in colorful clothing, some clutching gravity blankets and stress balls, others with giant headphones or AirPods glued to their ears. Bottles of kombucha and CBD oil are sprinkled across desktops. There are twinkling lights hanging from the ceiling, alongside an old HAPPY BIRTHDAY banner somebody forgot to take down. Every single wall is covered in photographs and stickers, like a Pinterest board come to life. It's a blur of succulents, highlighter, and perhaps most notably, laughter. Yes, on this side of the floor, people are actually *talking* to one another. Saffron catches up with me and grins.

"Welcome to the Digital team. Here we have Alex, our Politics editor; Crystal, our Fashion editor; Lola, our Lifestyle editor; Seb, our Entertainment editor, and then all these lovely ladies—Staci, Gwen, and Amanda—are on Social. Guys, this is Noora. She's kind of, sort of, probably Lily's replacement."

Upon hearing her name, Lola stops typing mid-JUUL pull and blows a *giant* puff of smoke in my face. She's tall and thin, and isn't wearing a drop of makeup, nor a bra. The blasting July air-conditioning makes her nipples look like two pencil tips. I try to focus on her perfectly symmetrical face instead.

"What's your sign?" she asks, her dark-brown eyes burning a hole through my forehead. I open my mouth to respond, but she cuts me off.

"Dude, don't take this the wrong way, but you seriously need to chill. This isn't *The Devil Wears Prada*. We aren't going to give you an Anne Hathaway makeover. And your *real* star sign, I mean. None of this *horoscope* bullshit," she clarifies.

"Virgo rising, Cancer moon." I clear my throat. I fucking hate this part. "Gemini sun." I roll my eyes, waiting for what always comes next.

"Ooh, cheeky!" she cheerfully exclaims, giving me a mischievous look and raising her eyebrows. "I'm keeping an eye on you. Who knows what your second personality is like?" I can't help but laugh.

"You don't want to find out," I reply. It's silent for about fifteen seconds. Shit. I can't believe I've been here five minutes and have already made an enemy—of the Lifestyle editor, no less. I might as well see myself out the do—

"Word," she says, before taking another drag of her JUUL. I exhale—I passed the test. Everyone goes back to typing suspiciously fast and ignores my presence.

"And then, of course, there's my desk." Saffron parks and shows off their collection of anti-fascist stickers, a crystal lamp (made of *real* crystal), and enough loose beauty products to sink a ship. There are so many packages and shopping bags swallowing their desk, I can barely see their laptop.

"Oh, you think this is bad?" Saffron asks, following my gaze. "Come with me. I'm going to blow your fucking mind."

We walk down the hall and approach what appears to be a janitorial closet. Saffron pulls a key chain with a giant pink pom-pom attached out of the front pocket of their overalls, and they give me a devious wink. On the count of three, they dramatically throw open the door. Rows and columns of beauty products organized by brand line the walls. It looks like a window display at Barneys. Every section is color coded and pristine, and each display rotates like a carnival ride. Goody bags are thrown all over the floor. There's a single pink chair sitting in the corner. It looks like a Wes Anderson film. I catch myself holding my breath.

"As you probably guessed, this is the beauty closet," Saffron says. "This is where all the products on my desk will eventually end up going. If slash when you get hired, you'll probably be the one to help me organize everything and hold the annual beauty sale, like Jade's assistant Kelsea does." They plop down on the floor, and I follow suit by taking a seat in the chair.

"So." They grab a tube of Glossier Boy Brow and start meticulously applying. "What did ya think of the team?"

"There are so many of them!" I practically squeal, no longer able to mask my excitement. This time, it's Saffron's turn to nod.

"Yea, well, we can't skip out on work! We publish, like, ten stories a day, you know?" There's a bit of contention in their voice, but I don't want to pry—it's too early for that. So instead, I scan the room, in search of a welcome distraction. My eyes land on the box of tissues nestled underneath my chair.

"Wouldn't makeup-remover pads or wipes be more effective?" I ask jokingly. Saffron giggles.

"Oh, those? Those are for crying," they explain. "This is *the* best spot in the office for crying. Whenever you want to cry here, just let me know and I'll give you the key! I'm in here, like, twice a day."

I stare at them, not sure what to say. As far as I can tell, working for the *Vinyl* Digital team is like living in a millennial amusement park. What could they possibly have to cry about?

Saffron's phone buzzes. They look down and furrow their newly minted brows.

"Shit—Loretta is ready for you."

Chapter Two

*Loretta James is wearing a vintage-looking kimono that prob-*ably costs more than Leila's rent. She's paired the robe with black combat boots (her signature), and a shirt that reads: *If girls could kill*. She moves like an old-school film reel: hypnotic, nostalgic, and a little bit on the nose. As I walk in, she takes the pen she's been chewing out of her mouth and sticks it in her tightly wound bun. Her hair is electric red, the color of ketchup—unpoetic, I know, but the perfect descriptor. I can see it's graying at the roots, despite the money she most likely spends trying to hide her age, which, coincidentally, I couldn't find online no matter what keywords I searched.

Her office is pristine and minimalist, like a Rothko come to life. A giant framed *Vinyl* cover from the late '80s hangs on the wall behind her desk. She's got several big plants scattered around the room, but they're all slowly withering in size and color. I wonder the last time they were watered—presumably the day her assistant walked out and never came back. There's a single photograph sitting on her desk. It's a still from her wedding, a close-up shot of her and her wife staring into each other's eyes. As I take a seat across from her, she looks at me with that same intensity. She wrestles her jaw open to reveal a wide, inviting smile. I clear my throat.

"Ms. James, first off, I'd just like to say, I'm such a huge fan," I begin, choosing my words carefully so I don't come off as too much of a kiss-ass. "I've been reading *Vinyl* since I was a girl, and it's truly changed my life in more ways than one. I used to hide a copy underneath my pillow every night when I went to bed then read it in the dark after lights-out. In fact, I have you to blame for my poor eyesight."

I pause for effect, and Loretta lets out a small laugh. She keeps staring at me like a friendly alligator. My mouth feels dry.

"Anyway, I admire all of your philanthropic efforts so much. The bra burning you initiated across campuses in the early nineties? Brilliant. That spread of queer celebrities at home that documented them following their everyday routines, making coffee, feeding their cats? Truly iconic. And that recent article you published online about artist royalties and streaming rights was just—"

"Enough about me," she says, scanning my body up and down. I suddenly feel self-conscious, and TBH, a little bit chilly. Why didn't I wear a bra today? "We're here to talk about you."

With that, I launch into my whole spiel. I tell her I'm a first-generation Iranian American who was born and raised in Crown Heights, but that I now live in Chinatown on my older sister's couch. I recall writing news clippings when I was a young girl, and sending my favorite authors fan mail— Judy Blume, Meg Cabot. I go on to talk about attending NYU and further exploring the city I'm so in love with, so inspired by. I don't mention that living at home had a little something to do with it. I wouldn't want her to think I'm desperate for anything, including money. I recount how hard I had worked as a journalism major, all the internships I completed at publishing houses, the freelancing I did for mediocre magazines like *Iron Home* and *The American Family*.

When I arrive at the present, I reluctantly explain I've been tutoring English. Loretta glances down to her phone, and I feel my throat seize. I've totally lost her. I knew my résumé would leave much to be desired, but I was banking on allowing my passion for writing and *Vinyl* to shine through and fill in the gaps. Instead, Loretta swallows a yawn.

As I wrap up my TED Talk, I notice her smile beginning to waver. She's looking past my head and off into the distance. For a split second, she feels like just your average human, someone I'd spot on the subway and assign an entire narrative to. Perhaps her son had just gone off to college on the West Coast or her husband had cheated on her with his secretary. Her eyes are so expressive—a translucent, murky gray. She has the look of someone who lost something or someone vital, a woman missing a piece of herself. I'm not sure I'm the person who can give her what she needs. But I so desperately want to be.

"Look, I love your enthusiasm, kid..." She quickly glances down at my résumé. I assume she's double-checking my name. "...Noora." I guessed right. "But I need to be up front with you. Can I tell you a secret?"

Did I just hear that right?

"Of course! Anything!" I respond with a little too much enthusiasm.

Loretta inhales sharply. "As you've pointed out, I know a lot of things," she begins. "I know the history of the Stonewall Riots in vivid detail. I've memorized Martin Luther King's entire March on Washington speech. I can recount every annual Met Ball theme because I've attended every single one since its conception. Hell, I can even tell you what Gloria Steinem is like in person, because she's a very dear friend. But you know what I just can't, for the life of me, figure out?"

I can't tell if she's genuinely asking me a question or adding dramatic flair.

"Um, why people make mukbang videos?" I try.

"No," she says with a sigh. "Well, sort of, I guess. Since I don't have the faintest clue what you're talking about." Her shoulders droop slightly, causing her kimono to drag on the floor. I lean forward in anticipation.

"Young people. I just can't understand today's young people. Gen Y or Z or Gen LMNOP or whatever you're calling yourselves now. Truly, I don't have a clue how to give your generation what it wants."

I sit there a second, soaking up the silence.

"I'm sorry, but that's not true," I blurt out. "You have done so much incredible work catering to my generation over the past few years! Your coverage of the midterm elections? It was like my bible. Seriously, when I was in college, my home page was your site. And what about all the investigative pieces you've been publishing lately? The interview with that scam artist that every single other platform picked up? Or what about the music streaming rights piece that every—"

"Okay, sure." She cuts me off again, this time visibly flustered. Her face is flushed, and her left knee begins to jitter. "Those were lucky one-offs. But on the day-to-day, our issues aren't selling to the right demographic. In fact, they're not selling at all. These are dark times, Noora. Can you understand what I'm getting at?"

I process her words. She's warning me. But about what, I'm not sure.

"Just tell me what you need."

She blinks twice. That smile is still slapped across her face, but somehow, it now looks more like grimace.

"What I need? I need an assistant who can whisper all the right things in my ear. I need someone who will run to my side, day or night, for the good of the cause. I need someone who is willing to pledge their sword, or rather, their pen, to fighting for me and the magazine's success. I need a *warrior*."

She's tapping her left foot so furiously, it feels like the entire building is beginning to shake. Loretta James is single-handedly starting an earthquake below Fourteenth Street. I begin to respond, but for the third time, she interrupts me.

"Noora, how many Twitter followers do you have?"

"I, uh." This is awkward. "I don't have a Twitter account."

"Oh." Loretta's mouth hangs open in shock. "What kind of aspiring journalist isn't on Twitter? How do you expect to connect with the industry? How can you promise me you'll have your finger on the pulse of what's hot?"

"I HAVE A BLOG," I practically scream, this time cutting *her* off.

My brain begins to buzz. I'm having a SaulPaul-esque revelation. I finally realize what Loretta is looking for. She doesn't need an assistant. Serving the reader is not her primary concern. An aspiring writer can offer her very little. What she wants is a Gen Z state representative. Someone who can explain what TikTok is to her team. A young savant who can show her how to properly use Snapchat. She needs a woke wunderkind.

"I have a blog. I'm a blogger. With a pretty good following."

Loretta immediately perks back up. She sits straight, pushing her shoulder blades together like a company member of the New York City Ballet. Her head bobs as she nods, which seems more threatening than encouraging.

"A blog?" she asks curiously. "Are you, then, an influencer?"

It takes everything I have to keep from cringing.

"Well, I wouldn't call myself an influencer," I explain slowly. "I have about twenty-five thousand followers."

Okay, I fudged the numbers a bit. Sue me.

"Oh," she says again, disappointed. "That's not that many."

"I know." I need to ride off the high of the last two minutes. "But I know things. I know how to analyze data—how to check to see what people are searching for, what they're interested in reading. I can analyze KPIs—you know, unique visitors—and optimize content to make sure it searches well. And when it comes to targeting audiences, I know exactly how to engage your prime demographics. I'm basically, like, an influencer whisperer. It's a small network. We all know each other."

I'm straight-up talking out of my ass, but what else am I supposed to do? She's slurping up my bullshit like an Aperol spritz. I watch her bouncing in her seat as if she's rolling at Coachella. I can hardly believe this is happening. *The* Loretta James is confessing to me—a broke, unfortunately hairy recent college grad with no real career prospects—that she's out of her depth.

My brain finally catches up to my mouth, which has been practically running off to Queens. "Plus, I am, like, at the forefront of every movement right now. I've organized peaceful protests for Black Lives Matter. I've actively collected signatures for the #TimesUp campaign. I donate to Planned Parenthood every single month. I marched for our lives."

I hate that I'm using real philanthropic initiatives that I care about as leverage. But, hey—at least I'm not lying. I really *do* care about social justice. Is it wrong to use that to my advantage?

I watch the corners of her mouth begin to ascend. Folks, Loretta James is *beaming* at me. Her knee bopping and foot tapping suddenly come to a halt. She lets out a long exhale.

"I like what I'm hearing. But I need you to know

something, love. We're at war. We're in survival mode, my team and me. And if I hire you as my assistant, I'm going to need more than just your passion and knowledge. I'll do everything I can to protect you, but it will require your dedication. Do you understand what I'm saying?"

I slowly nod my head then transition halfway into shaking it. I have no idea what she's talking about.

"While you work for me, you work exclusively for *Vinyl Print*. I'm saying that under absolutely *no* circumstances—and I mean zilch—are you to take on any projects without my approval. Well, of course, you can write whatever you want to write about on that blog of yours. In fact, write away on your blog! The larger the social media presence you have, the better for the company. But when it comes to your work, I need your focus *here*. Not writing the next Harvey Weinstein exposé for Digital. Here, on my calendar and the Print team's next lineup. All I need is someone who can make my life easier, not harder. Is that so difficult to understand?"

Out of nowhere, Loretta's gray eyes begin to brim with tears. I'm tempted to reach out and give her a hug. They remind me of the New York City sky right before it rains— simultaneously calm and chaotic. I want to offer her an umbrella, a lifeline. I hope we can both weather this storm together.

"Loretta, you have my word," I say, with conviction. "If I were to be your assistant, I would do whatever it takes to prove my loyalty. Anything."

The second the sentence slips out of my mouth, I want to take it back. But it's too late—Loretta's already holding my words captive, daring me to eat them. What exactly am I agreeing to? I've never wanted to be a lackey; I want to be a writer. I crave deadlines and late-night coffee breaks and bonding with sources who later become dear friends. But what other choice do I have? It's either serve Loretta, a veteran publishing hero and literary savant, or get told off weekly by brats who will never know what a "library" is. It's all going to be okay. I'm just doing what I need to do, saying whatever I need to survive. My oath isn't binding. It means nothing.

Loretta's eyes briefly glaze over, but she shuts them tight. When they reopen, she's smiling again, satisfied with my answer. She suddenly grabs my hand and gives it a squeeze.

"Excellent," she says. "So lovely to meet you, darling. What a bright young thing you are! You can see yourself out."

And with that, she stands and gestures to the door. I rise, following her lead. Before heading out, I turn around and dip into a strange half curtsy. I immediately regret it. Why couldn't I have just shaken her hand like a normal person?

"Thank you for everything," I squeak before running out the frosted door.

Somehow, the world has stood still. The *Vinyl* offices look exactly the same way I remember them upon entering. It's as if the last twenty minutes or so never happened.

"How'd it go?" Saffron approaches me, eager for dirt.

"Um," I stutter. "I'm not really sure."

I look down, trying to mask my own tears. But I can feel them coming, hot and wet, flirting with my lashes and caressing my cheeks. What was I thinking? Did I just lecture the editor in chief of a prestigious magazine about growing her own audience? Did I teensplain *blogging* to her? That's like walking into Cirque du Soleil and being like, "Let me show you how to do a cartwheel!"

Saffron walks me back to the elevator bank. As I turn around to exit, they surprise me by going in for a big bear hug. I surprise myself by reciprocating.

"It's going to work out," they reassure me. "I can just feel it. You're one of us."

I thank them for all their help then press *L* for lobby and walk to the appropriate elevator. It arrives and I step in, taking a long look at the entryway one last time.

"Hey, Noora?" Saffron calls to me, just as the doors close. "Follow me on TikTok!"

I ride down in silence, wallowing. I think about Leila, anxiously waiting for word about how the interview went. I hate letting her down. Maybe she'll pity me, since I'm such a complete, utter failure. She might treat me to a night at Thai Diner, my favorite Thai restaurant this side of the East River. We'll get drunk off Moscow mules and people watching, then waddle home, bloated from overeating. All I know is I want to eat and drink this day away until I have to tutor for an entire week to pay it off.

I reach the ground floor and step out of the elevator, making sure to wave good-bye to my new security guard friend, Superman. At first, he tries to avoid my line of sight, stoic like a member of the queen's guard. Then he notices my tear-streaked cheeks and awkwardly waves back. I never even found out his name, and yet, I'll miss him.

As I walk out of the SPP Tower, a wave of anxiety hits me. Or is it a literal heat wave? It's mid-July, after all. The weather only gets hotter as summer drags on.

My mind meanders around the day's events. I hit play on a recap: the pink decor, the unassuming desks, the Digital team's infectious giggles, Howard Man's bursting biceps. It all feels like a blur, a dream I once had. The details are blurry, but the feeling of excitement and taste of nausea remains. In fact, I can even hear Saffron's phone buzzing in the corner of my ear.

Or is that *my* phone buzzing? I snap out of my Netflix special just in time to take the call.

"Go for Noora," I say, immediately regretting it. What am

I, an infomercial? I look down at the number. *Unknown.* I hope I haven't just bought into a scam.

"This is Alyssa from Shifter-Pearce Human Resources," a voice says. The person on the other end of the line sounds so robotic, their message feels automated. "We're calling to inform you that you've been offered the job of executive assistant to the editor in chief of *Vinyl* magazine. Should you choose to accept, you will receive an email with your official offer letter in one to two business days."

"YES," I scream, not caring who can hear. "Yes, I accept!"

"Thank you," the voice says. I feel like I'm on the set of the next *Mission Impossible.* "Can you start on Monday?"

Chapter Three

The noise of New York City traffic is so incessant, it's hypnotic.
People move quickly in this tiny piece of the world, but time
seems to stand still. The July air smells of sunscreen, sweat,
and urine; it's so thick that I can trace its curvatures with my
fingertip, hold it like Silly Putty in the palm of my hand.

   As I get off the six train, mosey my way out of the Spring
Street station, and begin my descent toward Chinatown, I'm
struck by the growing divide the neighborhood encapsulates,
expanding and contracting like a quadratic equation. It's a
blur of culture, profit, and tastemakers. This is where hustlers
flock to—campers who carry dreams strapped to their bare
backs. When I look to my right, I am in the throes of capitalism and mediocrity. Broadway is more than just an avenue;
it's a picket line between Mom and Pop on one side and Big
Brother on the other. Brand names and big businesses litter
its corners, while tourists cling on to their maps and guard
their pocketbooks, afraid of falling prey to the wrong sales-
man. It's claustrophobic and archaic—hundreds of strangers,
marching in synchronicity, moving symbiotically like a wave.
They have no idea where they're headed or why they're
going. But they're sure that whenever they arrive, they won't
be alone.

On the other side of Broadway, you'll find a sort of humble redemption. Nolita transforms Chinatown the way winter's first snow turns to slush. It's quick, organic, and made of the same stuff—the cousin neighborhoods inform each other's existence, like positive and negative space. The shops all cater to locals with inflated price tags and egos to match. Their modesty is performative, but its content is feel-good. There's no better feeling than giving back, other than the knowledge that you're giving back. I, personally, love to be reminded that I'm a good person, that the end won't look like a merciless pit of fire. The restaurants aren't really restaurants, but cafés. The bars are speakeasies. The bookstores are reading nooks. The rats are mice. The tourists are influencers.

I look forward to the stroll from Spring Street to Baxter, where Leila's third-floor walk-up sits. I'm sure many others frequent the same path with similar admiration but with entirely different intentions. This is another reason to love New York: Each and every local attributes certain emotional narratives to neighborhoods, dependent entirely on the formative memories that took place in each back alley or street corner. When we cross paths with certain crevices of the city, it's reactive. They're all subjective as shit, but as I said—New Yorkers are fucking crazy. That old, run-down, graffiti-splattered mecca that sits on Bowery? To me, that's the facade under which I sipped brown-bagged Four Lokos—which I had purchased with my newly minted Connecticut fake ID—with my ninth-grade crush, Christian. We spent that night swapping saliva and lemon-flavored horse piss and promised to stay together for as long as it took to fall in love. But to Leila, it's where she had her first headshots taken by a sleazy Italian "aspiring" photographer who slid into her Instagram DMs then asked her to take off her top in person. Now it's the Supreme flagship store. Tomorrow, it could be nothing at all.

I turn the corner and approach Leila's block. As I slowly walk up the stoop, I pause and wave hello to the owners of the nail salon, Vanity Nails, that sits downstairs. Ever since I graduated and started crashing on my sister's couch, Leslie, the owner, has been giving me free manicures on "self-care Sundays." Honestly, in a city as ambitious and cutthroat as this one, I appreciate the random act of kindness. It's a small gesture that makes a big difference.

I'm practically heaving when I'm done walking three flights of stairs and reach Leila's front door. There's an evil eye hanging above the doorknob, meant to ward off evil spirits. I graze it with my nails for second, hoping it will bring me good luck, then push open the door.

The first thing that hits as me as I enter Leila's apartment is always the smell. Cumin and cardamom, rich and intoxicating, wafts in from the kitchen. Fresh mint from a stale batch of tea lying around on her dining room table waltzes its way to the door. Rosemary, from all the handmade soap sitting in her bathroom, drifts into the foyer. The mélange of aromas evokes old memories. It reminds me of our grandmother's house in Shiraz—the scent welcomes you in and asks you to dance. Leila's external decor is a direct reflection of her internal decor. Translation: Leila's apartment *looks* like Leila. It's tiny, but the space seems to expand for blocks. Art she's collected from all her adventures, her many lives, hangs on the walls: a colorful cartoon scooped up in a Moroccan bazaar, a pair of holographic photos found at a Rhode Island street fair. The throw pillows on her compact, L-shaped couch clash in the most delightful way—some sequin, others leopard print, and a select few faux fur. Everything is loud and careless. It's unintentional conviction in a way that only suits the spontaneous. I could never live like this. I care way too much.

Leila comes out of the kitchen clutching a glass of white wine—Riesling, if I'm not mistaken—in one hand and her phone in the other. She's wearing a full face of makeup and sweatpants. She throws her phone across the room, looks up at me, and raises one brow.

"*Vow*, look at that face." She whistles. "So I take it the interview went well? *Inshallah!*"

I giggle. The truth is, Leila has never interviewed for a job before in her life. She just has one of those personalities that fits into every nook and cranny. Ever since uni (yes, uni—Leila went to Cambridge, *honey*) opportunities have seemingly fallen into her lap. Whether it's an exciting new position at a start-up or an on-set trip to Ibiza, she always seems to be saying yes to the next big thing. In fact, she only landed her current publicity gig after running into her current client in the DUMBO House bathroom and complimenting her shoes. It was love at first toilet flush. Me, on the other hand? My nickname as a kid was *M'Lady No*.

"It was *terriblé*," I cry dramatically, falling into her arms. "They hated me. Kicked me out of the building! Asked me never to return again! Forgive me! Oh, please! Forgive me!"

Leila looks down at me with curiosity, amused. She's used to my theatrics.

"I can't tell how for real you are being right now, but honestly, I'm here for this Oscar-worthy performance," she says with a smirk. "Maybe you're in the wrong industry."

"I'd like to thank my big sister, for helping me land my dream job…"

Leila immediately shoves me away. "BIIIIIIIITCH," she screams so loudly, I'm worried my weekly manicures are about to be off the table. "You fucking got it? Already? *Afareen!*"

She's pacing back and forth, clapping excitedly to herself. I watch her dancing like a toddler, and my heart grows about ten sizes. I love my sister so much. We've been attached at the hip ever since she gave my first makeover at the age of twelve (my facial hair was *begging* for it). When Maman and Baba moved to Dubai to be closer to home (our family had to flee Iran during the revolution), she basically became my caretaker—or, as she would demand to be called, my cool aunt. I can't imagine life without her.

She grabs my hand and drags me to the couch I've been crashing on. Stretching out, she places her head in my lap.

"Tell me everything," she commands.

I start at the beginning, walking her through my day. I tell her about the train delays, the security guard and his Superman socks, and the hot Howard man and the elevator mishap. I describe the pink couches, the spotless Print desks, and Digital's clubhouse. She listens intently, cringing as I recall Saffron's description of the beauty closet as the "best crying spot in the office" and laughing when I reenact my bullshit rant to Loretta. When she finally catches her breath, there's a serious, inquisitive look on her face. It's one that I, unfortunately, know all too well.

"Okay, what's wrong?" I'm not even sure I want to hear the answer—I'm floating on cloud nine and intend to stay here. She pulls on the drawstrings of her hoodie, hiding her face. I know she's about to hit me with some cold, hard facts.

"So you agreed to *not* write for anywhere other than your blog? Even though the entire reason you want to work for *Vinyl* is to become a writer?" Her words are careful but cutting. I pull away from her and nestle into the other side of the couch.

"Right, but only *temporarily*," I say, unsure if I believe it. "Everyone has to start somewhere, right? No one likes an entitled Gen Z wannabe who thinks she *deserves* a byline."

Leila goes to bite her pinky nail but clearly remembers she recently got a gel manicure downstairs. She scowls.

"You need to be careful, Noora. I don't like the sound of this."

I feel my fists start to clench. My mind is doing mental gymnastics. When it comes to what-ifs, I'm essentially Simone Biles.

"Why can't you just be happy for me?" I spit out, my mood entirely turned. Leila doesn't know what it's like to hit rock bottom, to spend 90 percent of your week talking shit with thirteen-year-olds with trust funds and small IQs. Why can't she just let me have this?

"Whoa, whoa, whoa." She inches closer to me, hands above her head. "I am *elated* for you. Truly, I have not been this happy since Lana dropped *Born to Die*. And that's saying a lot." She takes a deep breath. "But from what you're saying, it sounds like there's something sus going on between Print and Digital. You said it yourself, Turmeric or whatever the Beauty editor's name is seemed pissed they weren't in the office. And what's up with Loretta being all insecure in front of someone she hardly knows? Isn't she, like, a feminist hero? Why is she talking down her success? You don't think that's a bit, I don't know, odd? This is just like when that homeless man took a shit beneath seats of the L-train. I can't see it, but I can sure as hell smell it. Something is up."

I don't want her to, but somehow, she's making sense. Loretta *was* acting kind of medieval. Turmeric—sorry, Saffron—was pretty defensive when I brought up Print. But this doesn't mean I'm stuck picking up lunch orders and taking calls for an absentee team when all I really want is to be pitching news angles and features, right? I give in and flop back onto Leila's lap. I grab the glass of wine out of her right hand and take a big swig. She plays with my hair, just like Maman used to do.

"Just promise you'll be careful, okay?" she says, grabbing my hand.

I squeeze three times, our secret symbol from childhood. It means *I love you.* "I promise." I *think* I mean it.

"Good," she says, satisfied. "Now, let's go get something to eat."

With that, Leila leaps up from the couch, grabs her keys from the tiny, tiled bowl sitting on her vanity in front of the bathroom, and bolts out the door. I follow behind slowly, replaying Loretta's words in my head like the soundtrack of the summer.

I need someone willing to pledge their sword.

Her voice echoes loudly in my ear. As the noise clears, I'm only left with one question: Who is the enemy I've promised to fight?

Chapter Four

My first week at **Vinyl** *moves faster than an episode of* Euphoria.

On Monday, I time my commute perfectly, arriving at 8:30 a.m. on the dot. Unfortunately, the rest of the office doesn't appear for another hour and a half, but this provides me with some much-needed time to collect my bearings. I'm greeted by a MacBook Air sitting on my new desk. There's a vase of baby's breath, presumably left by Loretta's old assistant, waiting there too. The bookshelves are empty, save for a single folder marked *receipts*. Of course, she keeps her receipts close.

I unpack my things then get to work tidying up Loretta's office. I fluff the pillows, organize her shoes by color and size, then move them into the walk-in closet in the corner behind her desk. There's no watering can, so I make a note to Amazon Prime one ASAP. Those dying plants need some serious TLC. Once I'm done, I take a seat and wait for Loretta to arrive. She leisurely strolls in around 11:30, her red hair tied up with two chopsticks, rocking her signature combat boots.

"Good morning, Loretta!" I say in an unusually high-pitched voice. She lowers her cat-eye sunglasses and takes in my outfit. Today I've opted for Dr. Martens, mom jeans, and a sheer, translucent dress. The look says *clown but make it couture*.

"Oh, hello, love…" She sounds slightly disoriented, giving me the same manic smile that was frozen on her face during my interview. She turns around and walks into her office. Then I hear a loud shriek. I run so quickly that I get whiplash.

"What did you *do*?!" she screams, flailing her arms.

"I, um, cleaned up," I respond, unable to meet her eyes. "I thought it would be a nice surprise."

"Noora, sweetheart, I'm only going to say this once." She inches closer to me. "*Never* touch anything in my office without my permission. Never speak without being spoken to. Never give your opinion unless you're asked. Do I make myself clear?"

"Crystal." I let out a meek smile. Loretta holds her breath sharply then lets out a slow exhale. When all the air's been expelled from her lungs, she meets my smile.

"Good, good," she says. "So here's the deal. You've been granted access to my schedule and email. If I'm not mistaken, I'm in meetings all day. However, I'd like to meet with Beth, the managing editor, for fifteen to thirty, if you can fit it in. Whenever I have five minutes before my next meeting, I'd like you to knock on the door and give me a heads-up. All appointments are going to buzz up to your phone line. If it's a call, I'd like you to transfer it to me. If it's a meeting, I'd like you to follow this script." She passes me a slip of paper with handwritten instructions on it. "You can't let my day get off track, okay? Think of yourself as my lifeline—if you drop the ball, I die. Oh, also—please refrain from using the bathroom fifteen minutes before a meeting begins. Just in case they arrive early. Got all that?"

I nod, wishing I had taken a voice recording or notes or something.

"What about lunch?" I ask, thinking back to my menial tasks nightmare.

"Oh, I don't really eat lunch," she says with a laugh. "I drink bone broth." Note to self: *Google bone broth.*

Before I can digest everything, her phone rings.

"Quick! Answer it."

I run back to my desk, and Loretta hastily retreats to her office.

"Hello, thank you for calling *Vinyl* magazine," I read off the script. "You've reached Loretta James's desk. This is Insert Assistant speaking." I turn bright red, realizing a beat too late I was supposed to say *Noora* instead.

"This is the front desk. I have a Barbara Potts and Catherine Saks here for you," a voice says.

I check Loretta's schedule. Sure enough, there's a guest appointment scheduled for 12:00 p.m.

"Send them up. Wait, what? Not *the* Potts and Saks, of Saks Potts?! Right?" I pause, waiting for the person on the other side of the phone to respond. "Wait, Superman? Is that you?"

The line goes dead.

The rest of the day goes by with relative ease. Loretta floats in and out of appointments, and I'm there to escort her. Most of them are internal—SPP's upper crust—with a few exceptions. There's one blackout meeting set for 6:00 p.m., which I haven't been given access to. The top-secret meeting is actually a recurring appointment. I'll have to ask Saffron about it later.

My one scheduling glitch goes down around 4:30 p.m., the precise time I've penciled in Beth, the managing editor. She shows up five minutes early, at 4:25 p.m. She is essentially a human unicorn, with hair that is pure white and ironed stick straight. She wears a three-piece suit like an old-school mafioso. When she sees Loretta isn't in her office, she decides to plop down on my desk.

"Let me guess," she says. "You let her go for a smoke break?"

"Oh, no." I turn around to make sure she's actually talking to me and not someone behind me. "She just ran to the bathroom. She should be back in a sec!"

Beth laughs and leans in to whisper, "For future reference, 'the bathroom' is code for a smoke break. We probably won't see her for another twenty minutes."

I feel my heart drop.

"That's not possible," I say, mostly to myself. "She'll be back, I swear."

Beth and I sit in silence, waiting for Loretta to return. Honestly, I appreciate the company. Beth has a warm, inviting presence. Unlike Loretta, her smile feels genuine, calm. She reminds me of my mother—measured yet stern. Her face is lined with wisdom and Botox. But after about fifteen minutes, she sighs and gets up.

"I have to run to another meeting, but let Loretta know I was here," she says, before walking back to her office. Sure enough, Loretta returns five minutes later, reeking of Marlboros.

"Where did Beth go?" she asks, her voice catching in her throat.

"She had to run but said to let you know she was here."

In a matter of seconds, Loretta's face turns as red as her hair.

"*Noora*, now my entire day is ruined," she cries, while confusingly rubbing my back. "Honey, how could you not come and get me from the bathroom?"

I'm about to correct her, to tell her I'm on to her, that I know about her secret habit. But at the last minute, I decide not to. I don't want to upset her further, finding myself in even hotter, deeper water.

"I'm so, so sorry."

"It's not your fault, dear," she says, with a slow sigh. "It's mine, for hiring you. You're not good enough, but that's not on you. I should have known better than to take a chance on an amateur."

With that, she turns around and closes her frosted-glass door. I sit at my desk, hyperventilating, having barely survived the encounter.

By Thursday, *I'm* the one who knows better. I chain myself to my chair (metaphorically, of course) and refuse to let Loretta out of my sight. Wherever she goes, I follow. I'm like a private detective or a BTS fan—I keep my target in front of me at all times.

I fit Beth into Loretta's schedule first thing in Tuesday morning (aka noon), and Beth thanks me graciously. I've decided I like Beth a lot. She has one of those faces that just radiate trust and kindness and plastic surgery.

Loretta goes on to meet with a slew of Print staff, photographers, and salespeople, all before 3:00 p.m.'s production meeting (or *prod*, as the office calls it). The entire Print team comes in to the office for it. For the first time, I get to watch them parade around the thirty-second floor. Sure enough, they're all dressed to the nines in coveted designer items. But instead of the classics—Stuart Weitzman boots, Chanel ballet flats, Gucci loafers—they've opted for up-and-coming brands and newer names. Batsheva dresses. Paloma Wool sweaters. Even the Christopher John Rogers coat that sold out in less than an hour last spring. And, of course, everything is in shades of black (yes, there are multiple), straight cut, and serious. Razor-sharp leather blazers and blunt bobs and no-makeup-makeup, the stench of Le Labo wafting as they strut down the halls. Their department store swagger is a far cry from the Digital team's thrifty feel. Still, they radiate cool, calm, and collected—still very *Vinyl*, if, you know, *Vinyl* readers didn't have student loans to pay off. They honestly remind me more of mannequins than red-blooded human beings.

From the corner of my eye, I spot Philippa Potters walking toward the conference room in a slinky black satin skirt and an oversize white button-down. Damn, I totally forgot that she'd just taken over as Fashion editor of *Vinyl*! Her shoots are legendary—since she was one of the very first women to shoot a major fashion house campaign, she's an icon in her own right. I used to cut out pages of her spreads and tape them all over the walls of my dorm room. She's surely planning something sick for *Vinyl*'s September issue (the August issue has already gone to print, since each month comes out in advance). I wonder who the cover star will be? I slowly trek behind her, then I feel someone tapping on my shoulder. I turn around to find Loretta looking at me.

"Darling, where do you think you're going?" she asks. Her clothes reek of smoke.

"Uh, to prod?" The entire Print staff RSVP'd yes to the calendar event.

"I don't think so. I need you in front of my office, manning the fort." She hands me her laptop, purse, and a stack of papers before walking into the room. I stare at the door, feeling defeated, then sulk back to my desk.

Less than an hour passes before Loretta comes running out of the meeting, startled. She holds up her phone and waves her pointer finger at the screen.

"My email's broken!" she cries frantically. "Someone broke the internet!"

I do everything I can to suppress a snort then explain I'm *sure* the internet is, in fact, still up and running. Loretta asks me to call IT to come and take a look anyway. I think it's a waste of time but nevertheless agree. I dial *5—SPP's technology hub's extension—and put in a request. They promise me someone will be on their way within a half hour.

Twenty minutes pass, and no one shows. I sit at my desk, half-heartedly scrolling through Instagram and trying to figure out how to upload attachments to Loretta's expenses.

"You again."

I look up in shock. I am staring right into the big, brown eyes and firm biceps of the one, the only, Howard Man. Only today, he's not wearing a Howard shirt; he's in a fitted Henley, black jeans, and a pair of suede dress shoes. His hairline is sharp, a tight buzz cut. Where did those dimples come from? I can't remember feasting my eyes on those bad boys in the elevator.

"You're not tech support," I blurt out.

His eyes twinkle. I feel my stomach gurgle. Fuck.

"You just saying that 'cause I'm Black?" he asks, his face drooping. I feel my forehead burning up.

"Oh my God! Of course not! That's not what I meant!"

"Relax," he says, laughing. "I'm just messing with you. But yes, my name's Cal and I work for SPP's IT team. But I'm a graphic designer on the side. I studied software engi-neering at—"

"Howard University."

"Right."

We maintain eye contact for a solid forty seconds before I can't take it anymore and stare down at my boots. I clench my vagina.

"So what seems to be the issue?" Cal asks, gesturing to

Loretta's computer sitting on my desk. For a split second, I had totally forgotten he'd come to the thirty-second floor to do a job. I was a little too busy fantasizing about dragging him into Loretta's office.

"The internet's broken," I tell him, straight-faced.

We both remain silent for five seconds then burst out laughing.

"In all seriousness, Loretta's computer is frozen. She can't access the issue mock-up for prod."

Cal rolls up the sleeves of his Henley and leans in to examine the laptop. I wipe a little bit of drool from my chin.

"Let me try to access this from my server," he says.

I watch as he sets up his equipment, running his finger over the wire, from the outlet to the port. He runs a series of diagnostic tests, squinting at Loretta's screen and shaking his head. I giggle—he looks like a grumpy, old congressman. After a while, he looks up at me and sighs.

"Well, it's clear what the problem is," he says. "This computer hasn't been updated since 2012. Seriously, it's a dinosaur. There are emails on here from the Stone Age. No wonder she can't load anything on the internet! Her hard drive is essentially a storage room that's filled to capacity."

He clicks through Loretta's files, showing me how little space is left. I give it a brief look then quickly look away. I don't want to snoop through Loretta's computer. Well, okay, I kind of want to. But I shouldn't.

"Do you think she'd mind if I backed all of this up to an external hard drive and then wiped her memory?"

"I'd wait and ask her yourself." No way am *I* going to blamed for Loretta's emails disappearing into thin air—this isn't the 2016 election. "Plus," I add, "you should probably explain what a *hard drive* is. Something tells me she isn't exactly tech savvy."

Cal nods and leans against my desk. My arm hair rises. I look like I've been electrocuted.

"Okay, cool. In that case, why don't I give you my number?" He picks my phone up off my desk and enters his digits. "That way, next time there's a problem, you can just text me directly instead of going through tech support. Sound good?"

"Perfect." I text him my name.

"Noora," he reads aloud. "Beautiful name. What does it mean?"

"It's Farsi for *light*."

He gives me a smile and a head nod then turns around. As he walks back to the elevator bank, I can swear the ceiling lights around him begin to dim.

Chapter Five

I wake up the sound of someone softly humming a Billie Eilish song. At first, I think I'm dreaming—there's an angelic light lingering over Leila's living room and a breeze wafting in from the window hanging over the kitchen. Am I still asleep? Does the quiet voice I hear drizzling in from the bathroom belong to someone who works at Shifter & Pearce Publishing? Could it be an imaginary Cal who's come to kiss me awake from my slumber? Or worse, Loretta?

A fabulous, fat, half-naked femme walks into my boudoir (read: Leila's living room) and disrupts my daydream. She's got tiny freckles that crescendo down her chest and a septum ring nestled into her nose. Her bod's clad in only a tank top and boxer briefs.

I let out a sigh. It's just Leila's latest hookup. Last week, it was a handsome but mysterious albino man who spoke little to no English and wore nothing but a tiger-print silk robe. The week before that it was an off-duty mime. She usually sneaks them into the apartment when I'm already asleep, but I always catch them on their way out the door. I know I can't complain—after all, she's the one letting me crash on her pull-out couch. Plus, her one-night stands are usually quite polite. We casually drink coffee together and read the

New York Times daily newsletter. Nine times out of ten, they'll bring up Burning Man.

"Where's Leila?" I ask today's flavor of the week—white chocolate raspberry truffle, if I'm not mistaken. Before she can answer, I overhear the muffled sounds of someone screaming into the phone. The noise is coming from behind Leila's locked bedroom door. I look up, startled.

"Is everything okay?"

"I think so," she says, opening the door to the fridge and helping herself to a carton of milk. "Leila said she had a missed call from work and that she needed to take care of something? From what I gathered, one of the influencers she works with is unhappy with the overall arrangement of her account or something? Or maybe she said *engagement*? Something about the algorithm changing? I'm not sure— sounds serious, though."

She takes a long swig straight from the carton. Ew. I grimace then glance up at the antique clock hanging above the stove.

Shit.

"Okay, well I have to run," I announce to the stranger. "But will you tell Leila to call me if she needs anything?"

I run over to the rack against the couch that houses all my clothes and start pulling out options then throwing them carelessly around the room.

"Sure," she says, now rummaging around the kitchen cabinets for a bowl, holding an unopened box of Lucky Charms. "Wait, who are you again?"

This chick is *seriously* not it.

"Someone who needed to be out the door five minutes ago," I snap.

Sorry, Leila, I have no patience or time to make small talk with your latest "friend" this morning. It's fashion season in New York.

Last month felt like a never-ending episode of *Russian Doll*. I kept going through all the motions of being Loretta James's assistant without ever *feeling* like Loretta James's assistant, partially because I never have a second to stop and catch my breath.

I woke up this morning the way I always do, to an 8:00 a.m. text from Loretta informing me she's going to be in late (shocker) and that I need to push back all her appointments. I email every single guest from the privacy of Leila's bathroom—one day, I swear I'll be able to afford a place of my own—then throw on the outfit I concocted in my sleep and rush out the door.

Actually, I make time to guzzle caffeine like a maniac, hovering over the sink. *Then* I rush out the door.

August in New York is still summer, but sad summer. Everything is excessive and overbearing. The subway is *too* slow, the concrete *too* hot, the air quality *too* dry. The city is swimming with pedestrians who can be divided into two camps: those who mourn for midsummer, and those who pinch their noses and count the minutes till fall. I land somewhere in the middle, taking tastes of both air-conditioned paradise and soggy, polluted walks through Sara D. Roosevelt Park. I like watching the late-summer soccer games. The red, flushed cheeks and scuffed varsity socks. The dissolved sweat turning to salt and melting into the grass.

I'm in the SPP Tower by 9:00 a.m. I've learned to give a subtle head nod to Superman, whose real name is actually Ned. I'm often the only one in the lobby, save for a few other assistants. One thing I've learned rather quickly: Media is nocturnal. This industry likes to sleep in.

I enjoy walking through the thirty-second floor when it's empty—it offers me a rare moment of Zen. Once I get to my desk, organize Loretta's day, formulate my to-do lists, and answer unread emails. Most importantly, I take out my brand-new watering can and deliver the elixir of life to Loretta's plant babies, whom I've affectionately nicknamed Thelma and Louise. I make sure not to touch anything else. I learned my lesson the first time.

Around 10:30 a.m., the Digital team and a few stragglers from Print make their way in, gripping cold brew. I peer over my cubicle wall to count how many people surround me then wave to Beth, who can see me through the glass door of her office. She smiles and waves back. I appreciate that. In fact, I appreciate her.

Saffron has made a habit of stopping by my desk to debrief right after they get in. Today, they ask about Loretta, and I have an absurd story to tell them. Last night, Loretta literally asked me to fight sixty Uber cancellation fees. She has a two-star rating and insists a broken app is to blame, but I think it's because she makes every driver wait half an hour. Then Saffron tells me about what they're working on. Last week, it was an STI glossary. Today, it's a photo spread reclaiming birthmarks and blemishes. They're also really stoked about this new Beauty Politics column they're launching soon. Apparently, they've hired some big-shot freelancer for the job. They practically beam while describing their back-and-forth email exchange.

Around noon, I head to the beauty closet to reapply my Fenty highlighter before heading to the SPP cafeteria on the off chance I'll run into Cal at lunch. Nine times out of ten, it's a pipe dream, but today, I'm waiting in line at the salad bar when I see him strut through the back door, chatting to a coworker, a hoodie carelessly thrown over one shoulder. Our eyes meet, and he gives me that dimpled smile that always makes me swoon. I consider going up to talk to him but don't want to lose my spot in line (these Shifter Pearce bitches take their salad so seriously, I call them Shifter Fierce. I'm genuinely afraid of them). But by the time I'm ready to cash out, he's gone. I've once again missed my opportunity. We pass each other like ships in the night. Or like Staten Island ferries.

The idea of accidentally on purpose crossing paths with Cal gives me, at the very least, one thing to look forward to each day. I haven't needed him for a tech emergency since late July's server fiasco, when he had calmly explained to Loretta what the problem was and somehow convinced her to move all of her information to the cloud. ("I hate flying," she had complained. We both *died* laughing.) Don't get me wrong, there have been many snafus since then—the Uber cancellation fee mishap, to start—but nothing warranting contacting the IT department. Honestly, I've considered making something up just so we can make small talk and I can stare longingly at the nape of his neck.

Anyway, the latter part of my day consists of scheduling external meetings and internal tête-à-têtes. This might sound relatively simple, but Loretta is *so* frantic, she borders on batshit. She's constantly adding in her own personal appointments—lunch with her wife, an hour-long brainstorm with her therapist—without giving me notice. Then, if I can't reconfigure the schedule to fit, she'll start *crying* and ask me to prepare résumés for my replacement "just in case." I usually do, although she never gets around to actually looking at them.

I can never schedule anything during the recurring blackout period reserved for her top-secret meeting that I still know nothing about. I've attempted to press Saffron for details, but turns out, they're in the dark as well. Very sus.

I have other responsibilities too. Although I don't attend prod, I'm responsible for exporting the Print staff's pieces from the content management system (or CMS) so Loretta can give her notes. She refuses to do any of this on a computer because she claims it makes no sense and gives her a migraine. When she's done, she hands her edits back to me and I input them into the CMS then reroute the workflow back to the appropriate editor. It's all very, very confusing.

In the evening, as the rest of *Vinyl* Print and Digital filter out of the office, I get started on Loretta's expenses, which are composed of everything from five-hundred-dollar dinners at Cipriani (she claims they're "networking dinners"), facials from Rescue Spa (they keep her looking on brand!), and a new flat-screen sent straight to her Park Slope town house (so she can "keep up" with the competition). I go through her receipts folder, driving myself mad trying to match charges to each tiny, fraying piece of paper. I also sift through her email, printing Uber, Lyft, Juno, Via—you name it!—receipts. The entire process takes a week, on top of my daily responsibilities. I can't remember the last time I left the office before 9:00 p.m. I keep telling myself that everyone starts at the bottom, that I'm lucky to be here. That one day, it will all be worth it. But Leila's not so sure. She has started calling me her *rooh*. That's Farsi for *ghost*.

But my number one priority is managing Loretta's Fashion Week schedule. When she first told me about this specific assignment, it sounded like a literal dream. I'd be RSVP'ing to fashion shows, calling in samples for street-style looks, arranging car pickups to and from the venues. It's basically the next best thing to attending New York Fashion Week myself. (That's right—you hear that, middle school bullies? This awkward, hairy Middle Eastern gal is officially Fashion Week *adjacent*.)

Two weeks into the task, however, I've learned that New York Fashion Week is about more than fangirling after

Anna Wintour and salivating over whatever Jacquemus puts on the runway. Just like everything *Vinyl* related, Loretta's attendance is purely political. With the rise of social media and Instagram capital, Fashion Week has become more of a visually stimulating publicity stunt than a haute-couture circus. The actual logistics, the physical event, no longer matter—it's all about what's left online in the aftermath. Sure, a sunset may be spectacular in the moment. But if it doesn't photograph well, does anyone even care?

Loretta called me on Sunday night, screaming unintelligibly into the phone. It took me a while to gather what she was so upset about: she's been invited to sit *second row* at Sandy Liang this year. According to Loretta, this is a fate worth than death. Her words verbatim were, "I'd rather be bombed at Times Square."

So this week I've been tasked with working nonstop to get Sandy Liang's team to offer us an explanation and a chance to amend this mistake. I keep pressing Leila to tap every last contact she has, in hopes someone can connect me with someone else who can explain to me why in the hell *Vinyl*'s editor in chief wasn't given the honor of being invited to sit front row at their fall preview. There are whispers that this year's show will take place on the Hive, the newest Hudson Yards architectural development. I've even heard there might be holograms involved. *Holograms.* Is that not the most *Black Mirror* shit you've ever heard? I'm telling you, the Twitterverse is losing its mind.

After sifting through Loretta's inbox with a fine-tooth comb, reaching out to every single person on staff and grilling them about their relationship to Sandy Liang (awkward as fuck), and fiddling with every search phrase imaginable, I've run out of options. Apparently, there is no one on staff at Liang HQ who can provide me with a straight answer.

Of course, Loretta gaslights me for this mishap. "Honey, if I wanted a *secretary*, I would have hired Elisabeth fucking Moss," she keeps telling me. "Now, I don't want to blame you. But I thought you were my assistant. Why aren't you *assisting*?!"

Honestly, I'm not sure what to tell her. I have no idea why this is happening. Someone working this show or within the design house must have a vendetta against Loretta.

Chapter Six

"NOORA, sweetheart, get in here and close the door," Loretta screeches.

It's Wednesday morning, and I've just finished watering the plants. I wipe soil residue from my palms and check my phone—it's 10:00 a.m. What on earth is Loretta doing here at this ungodly hour? I trail behind her, locking the frosted door behind me. She collapses on her couch, fuming.

Side note, her Fashion Week looks have been *killing it.* Today she's in an onyx feather coat, leather cigarette pants, and her signature black combat boots. She looks like a chic dementor.

"I've just received the most horrible news," she says, her forehead in her hands.

"Oh my God, is Sarah okay?!" I walk over to the couch and sit down beside her.

Loretta immediately stiffens. I definitely struck a nerve. She rarely ever talks about her wife, Sarah. Her generation believes in keeping the personal and professional *separate.* Mind you, she usually says this while calling me at 2:00 a.m. on a Friday night and asking me to book her top-secret lipo appointments.

"What? Of course. She's fine. This is much, much worse.

I've just learned *Jade Aki* has been invited to sit front row at Sandy Liang."

I pause, waiting for the *and*, but it never comes. Puzzled, I lean back on the couch and turn to face Loretta head-on, studying her expression.

Jade Aki is *Vinyl* Digital's director, although I've never actually seen her in the office. Saffron says that she's always traveling, doing promotional stuff for the brand. At twenty-seven years old, Jade is known for being a bit of a media prodigy. She took *Vinyl* into the digital age by starting its website when she was just twenty-four. As a fellow first-generation American, I've always looked up to Jade—although I don't know much else about her. Loretta has been the face of *Vinyl* for almost two decades. I've never heard her bring up Jade before.

"I'm not quite sure I understand. Isn't this a good thing? She works for you! Maybe she can help secure a front-row seat."

Loretta squints back at me.

"She's a child," she says. "I was sitting front row the day she was *conceived*. This is an abomination. I want you to get Sandy Liang herself on the phone. Today."

I stare at her, positive I misheard.

"Today?"

Loretta's eyes drill a hole into my skull.

"You know, I'm quite fond of you, Noora. And I want you to succeed here, I really do. But if you're unable to complete this one, simple task…well, I'm not sure I can do anything more to hold your hand. You understand, don't you?"

I slink back to my desk, practically comatose. I feel as if I've been paralyzed. Loretta's venom must have made its way into my bloodstream. As my mind begins to reawaken, I replay the events over again.

I want you to get Sandy Liang herself on the phone.

The next part is where things start to get fuzzy.

I'm not sure I can do anything more to hold your hand.

Am I going to allow myself to get *fired* over this? Over a fucking chair?

I sit up straight, cracking my neck and back. No way in hell am I going down like this.

Time to spring into action. I pull up Loretta's schedule for the rest of the day. Around 1:30 p.m., she's scheduled to sit in a meeting with Daniel, the head of Communications, for about an hour and a half (not sure what that's all about, but still). That's my window. I glance at the timer on my laptop screen—I still have three minutes until the fifteen-minute mark before Loretta's next appointment arrives. In other words, I can leave my desk.

I run to Saffron's sanctuary. They're hunched over, listening to Soccer Mommy, editing a piece about coming out to your friends as pansexual. I urgently tap them on the shoulder.

"What are you doing right now?" I ask, my nostrils flaring.

"Um, my job?" Saffron says with a laugh.

"Any chance you can do your job at my desk? I just need you to cover me for, like, max forty-five minutes at one thirty. Please."

Saffron takes in the desperation in my eyes. They nod.

"Yea, I mean, sure," they say. "I just don't want to meet Loretta's wrath, ya know?"

"I'll be back in time for her next meeting," I promise.

When 1:30 p.m. rolls around, I walk Daniel from his office to Loretta's and close the door myself.

"Aren't you just the spiciest little shish kebab?" Daniel says to me, his English accent flattening his vowels, before entering the room. I roll my eyes. *Racist prick.*

Saffron shows up on the dot and makes themself at home at my desk. I grab my jacket—a slinky little vintage sequin number from the '20s—and run to the elevator bank. When I make it outside, I flag down the first cab I see.

"Where to?" the driver asks. The car smells like a pretzel left out in the sun for too long.

"Grand Street and Kenmare. The Sandy Liang headquarters. And step on it."

The ride takes twenty unpleasant minutes—it should have been ten, but I'm stalled by Fashion Week traffic and influencers taking photos in the middle of the street. I keep refreshing my email, playing roulette with my inbox. I'm both terrified a message from Loretta will arrive informing me of my dismissal and hopeful a representative from Liang's team will get back to me explaining this was all just one giant misunderstanding. I look out the window and people watch to calm my nerves.

New York Fashion Week turns the city into a euphoric zoo, where every single cooped-up animal begins to competitively and harmoniously peacock. Creatures don their most fabulous frocks and strut up and down Houston, desperate to be photographed by street-style photographers and splattered all over the pages of next month's *Vogue*. I watch as a beautiful woman with a tiny, frayed pixie cut wearing a boxy olive-green suit walks straight into traffic. She's probably an off-duty model. My guess? She lives with about seven other women, all of whom look somewhat like her. She glances at her phone and frowns. *Do I have enough money left in my checking account to buy lunch today?* I imagine her thinking. She's about six years shy of becoming a New Yorker. I think Manhattan membership requires ten-year admittance, at the very least. In this jungle, you have to earn your stripes.

The cab pulls up in front of Sandy Liang HQ. The building

is one of those new age, modern developments—a sleek high-rise with views of Lower Manhattan and Brooklyn. I scan the perimeter; there's security hovering by either entrance. There's no chance I can sneak in without being caught and thrown into Rikers. The upside? I'll join the ranks of girl boss Anna Delvey. The downside? Loretta might kill me first.

Reluctantly, I accept there's only one thing left to do: use my remaining thirty-five minutes to stand across the street, waiting like a stalker, on the off chance Sandy Liang might emerge.

I know what you're thinking: *Noora, you're fucking crazy.*

Well, first of all, that's ableist. And, yes, I know I keep saying ableist things, okay? But that's in the past now. I'm not perfect! I'm working on it. Second of all, I'm actually desperate—I'm not ready to lose this job just yet. I can't imagine saying good-bye to Saffron, Cal, and Beth after just weeks of being in their lives. Even Superman! And I won't let myself give up until I've actually written something of value that makes a difference in this fucked-up world.

So I sit on a stoop across the street and stage a full-on stakeout.

At first, nothing comes of it. I kill fifteen minutes swallowing yawns and darting my eyes from the revolving doors to the back entrance. Plenty of characters float in and out. There's an older Latino man wearing a top hat and a three-piece suit, swirling a cane made of marble. I also spy a tiny dog sporting a sweatshirt with a self-portrait stitched into the cotton (I almost break my back trying to get a good picture for my followers). But as I inch closer to twenty minutes, I start to come to terms with the cold, hard truth:

I'm not going to find Sandy Liang. I was never going to find Sandy Liang.

What I am, however, is *so* fired.

My phone starts to ring. Could it be? Have one of her contacts actually come through at the very last millisecond? I answer a little too quickly, desperate for a breakthrough.

"Hello? Sandy?"

"Noora! You little bitch!" Leila's voice blares through my speaker. "Did you borrow my cowhide fringed jacket? The one that apparently used to belong to Stevie Nicks? You know how much I hate when you take my stuff without asking! It's the principle of the thing; if you had just asked, I obviously would have said yes, but now I've just wasted five years of my life looking through my closet for it, only to discover—"

"Leila, I love you, but I literally cannot deal with this right now."

I hang up the phone then slowly stand and collect my things. Out of the corner of my eye, I catch a flash of long, black hair. It's moving quickly down the crowded street. I stand up and chase after it.

The hair is attached to a body dressed in head-to-toe black and carrying a briefcase. Could it be?

I follow the hair through side alleys and backyard dumpster dives. In fact, I trace it all the way back to Chinatown. As the smell of roasting duck begins to seep through my nostrils, I turn the corner and suddenly, I'm face-to-face with the hair. I look up.

The hair is attached to a middle-aged Chinese woman. She hands me a menu.

"We have lunch special," she says, waving me into her restaurant. I feel my knees buckle.

"Maybe next time."

I cab back to the office, cursing myself out for feeling hopeful. I imagine telling my parents, breaking the news to my Mom all the way in Dubai. She'll pick up and, before I can get a word in, give me the gossip: which cousin is getting married to which lifelong nemesis. What silly television show my retired father can't stop binge-watching (it's currently *The Crown* on Netflix). "Maman," I'd rudely interrupt. "I have to tell you something." My eyes brim with tears just playing out the conversation in my head.

When I arrive back at the office, I sulk to my desk. Saffron looks up at me, a triumphant look on their face.

"Your little abode here is actual heaven. I crushed this edit. Like, I actually demolished it." They notice my expression, shrunken and sad. "You, not so much, eh?" I shake my head.

Then, without thinking, I begin to collect my things. I pack up the coffee-table books I brought from home for my bookshelf—*Paris/New York*, *The History of Chanel*, *Vivienne Westwood*—and throw them into my purse. I start taking photos of me and Leila off my bulletin board. I'm just about to erase my laptop's hard drive when the phone rings.

"Hello? Cal? Superman?"

There's silence on the other end of the line.

"This is Sandy Liang calling for Loretta James."

I black out for a split second.

"Hello? Is anyone there?"

I black back in.

"Yes, of course," I tell *the* Sandy Liang. "One second."

I mute the line, run over to Loretta's office, and bang on the door. Thankfully, Beth has joined her meeting with Daniel.

"What is it, doll?" Loretta asks, annoyed.

"IhaveSandyLiangonthephoneforyou." I let the words escape from my mouth as quickly as they can. Loretta stands up straightaway.

"What are you waiting for? Transfer the call!"

I run outside and quickly press *67.

"Hello?" Sandy Liang says.

Shit. It didn't work. I try again—*67. Nothing happens. I check the Notes app on my phone. I'm positive Cal told me that this is how to transfer a call directly to Loretta's line. I must have done this a million times since.

"Noora, sweets," Loretta calls to me from her office. "Transfer the call."

"I'm trying," I call back. *67. Still nothing. What the fuck is wrong with this stupid phone?

"*Noora*," Loretta screeches. "*Transfer the call to my office.*"

"I'm doing the best I can." *67. *67. *6*fucking*7.

"Hello?" Sandy Liang says.

"NOORA," Loretta screams at the top of her lungs. "TRANSFER THE FUCKING CALL RIGHT NOW."

"I AM TRANSFERRING THE CALL," I yell back. "STAR SIXTY-SEVEN ISN'T FUCKING WORKING."

The office goes dead silent. Everyone from the Print team who came into work today stands up and slowly turn their heads to take in the drama. One editor coughs to cover up a laugh. A couple of Digital team members poke their heads from around the corner to watch me get chewed out. I feel my forehead begin to burn.

I just threw a tantrum. I yelled at Loretta James like a spoiled toddler. The entire *Vinyl* staff heard. Sandy Liang probably heard.

"Noora," Beth says to me, quietly. I didn't even notice she had stayed behind. "The transfer code is star seventy-six."

My jaw drops. It's as if my body has been inhabited by Area 51. I pick the phone back up and dial *76. Loretta's phone rings. She picks it up. I squeeze my eyes shut and try to disappear.

"Sandy!" she croons, her voice oozing with faux charm. The door slams behind her.

I can't breathe. My chest feels tight and sharp. I look down at my hands. They're shaking so much that I can no longer hold the phone. My vision blurs. I stand up and run to Saffron's desk.

"Keys," I choke out. "Give me the keys." They throw me the key chain to the beauty closet, and I set off running. I let myself in and collapse on the floor, convulsing in tears. My head is pounding. This is the end—I'm sure of it.

I hear the door creak open behind me. I peer out of the corner of one eye. Saffron is towering over me. They bend down and hold me, rubbing my back in a circular motion, just like my grandmother used to do.

"It's okay," they tell me. "It's all going to be okay."

"I'm dying," I croak back.

Saffron shakes their head. "You're not dying," they say firmly. "You're having a panic attack. It's totally normal. In fact, it's human. You think you're the only one here battling anxiety? Girl, this office is living with demons in our desks and behind our backs. You have no idea how many of us have started taking antidepressants since signing our SPP offers. How many employees left because they couldn't take medical leave. One even had to be hospitalized for dehydration, and what did SPP's HR department do about it? Nothing. And me? I've been this way ever since I was a kid. Do you know what it's like, constantly fighting gender dysphoria, trying to reaffirm who I am every single day? Going on hormones in the middle-of-nowhere bumfuck Idaho? It's painful, it can be debilitating, and terrifying. But no, anxiety isn't death. Because you'll outlive it. For now, just focus on the breath moving like a current throughout your body. Inhale in, exhale out. It'll keep you present. Alive."

I sit still in their arms, hiccuping. The tears staining my cheeks begin to dry. I can feel my heart rate slowing down, too. I look down at my hands. They're no longer shaking. Saffron has cured me.

"Thank you," I whisper.

"Anytime, sunshine. You and me, we've gotta stick together."

They stand up and offer me a hand. I reluctantly accept. I'm not sure I'm ready to face Loretta just yet.

"You'll be surprised," Saffron says, reading my mind.

Curious, I follow them back into the bullpen, fully prepared to be verbally assaulted, perhaps even mauled to death. Instead, I find something much, much creepier.

Loretta is looming over my desk, with that eerie, manic smile on her face. She lights up when she sees me.

"Well, that's done." She smirks. "Jade Oki will never sit front row at New York Fashion Week ever again."

Then, something miraculous and terrifying happens. Loretta James throws her arms around me, pulling me tightly into her bosom. I accidentally sniff her hair. I think we're hugging.

She pulls away. For a second, I think she's going to kiss my forehead. That, or stab me in the back. Instead, she looks down at my scattered desk and frowns.

"Honey, where do you think you're going?"

For once, I don't know.

Chapter Seven

I'm sitting at the table closest to the window at Good Thanks, one of my favorite cafés in the Lower East Side. This sunny little landmark is just a hop, skip, and a fifteen-minute walk away from Leila's. It's also owned and run by hot Australian transplants. I don't know if this is a universal truth or just a New York bubble belief but hear this: Over the past five years or so, Australians have absolutely *dominated* the Manhattan brunch scene. Seriously, every trendy late-afternoon hot spot scattered across this island is an Aussie haven—minimalist meccas filled with altars of acai bowls, overpriced avocado toast, and ridiculously handsome Australian exports sporting deeply bronzed tans and rugged denim button-downs.

On Saturdays, they wear those little beanies that barely cover their ears, and I lose my mind.

The light is pouring out of Orchard Street and bouncing off my laptop screen, causing a glare. I shield my eyes and grin.

It's a beautiful late-September afternoon. The leaves have yet to turn, but the town houses between Park and Madison have decorated their stoops with cobwebs and the Union Square farmers' market has begun selling pumpkins. The sun sets slowly between 6:00 and 8:00 p.m., and its colors melt together like eye shadow pigments or a Monet canvas. New York in the fall is so goddamn beautiful. It's sad August's hot cousin, so to speak. The glow-up is *real*.

The Lower East Side is home to one of New York's most shameless people-watching populations, the Scum Bro (a gender-neutral term, but I digress). Brother to the Williamsburg Hipster and son to the Soho Gallerist, Scum Bros are a mixed bag of freelance photographers, stylists, models, and struggling artists with expense accounts. They dress like Goodwill and Intermix just had a baby—high-end labels tossed in the trash. Baggy, dexterous fabrics. Leather that's been intentionally worn. *Intention.* That's the best word to describe their aesthetic. They are so intentionally uninten-tional. "Gentrifiers," Leila always sneers when she sees them. I, of course, remind her that, technically, we are gentrifying Chinatown, but she just ashes off the comment by emphasiz-ing how little money we have (sometimes, I don't think she actually understands how capitalism works). I could watch them pour in and out of the gallery across the street for hours, rolling their eyes as passing tourists stop to take photos of the art. They would never be caught dead Instagramming someone else's masterpiece. A Scum Bro would much rather Instagram their bloody knee and parse it down with a cap-tion about capitalism. Now *that's* artistic integrity.

Updating *NoorYorkCity* on Saturdays is partially a ploy to push back my "Sunday scaries" by forcing me to reflect on my week with a yawn. On the flip side, it gives my week-ends structure and purpose. I used to look forward to sitting down with a cup of coffee and getting to respond to readers' comments, taking their feedback in stride. But ever since I started working for Loretta, that's fallen a bit by the wayside. Each time I find five seconds to sit still, my phone rings, and I have to get back on my feet again. I hope my followers know how much I miss them, that I'd rather be spending every waking second I have writing and creating for them. When I'm at my most anxious, I wonder if they think I've abandoned them. But I lock those worries in a box and hide it away. There's no time for second-guessing myself. Not now, not ever.

My posts are usually a motley mix of mirror selfies taken in Leila's foyer and street-style shots captured by my trusty personal assistant, the self-timer. You haven't lived until a stranger has caught you posing all alone in an empty subway car. I like to juxtapose those snapshots with existential thoughts and musings, competing philosophies that shouldn't pair well together but somehow do. Today, I'm writing a soliloquy about the history of racialized responses to natural disasters. It's both evocative and depressing as shit. Alongside my discounted GANNI cowboy boots, it'll read like an apocalyptic runway show come to life on the page. No doubt my readership will eat it up. This is the content the internet so desperately craves. It's messy but real.

I'm just about to dive into my breakfast bowl (God bless Swiss chard and chest hair), when my phone starts to buzz. I absentmindedly turn off the volume and go back to scheduling my posts for the week.

I feel at peace. Ever since the New York Fashion Week debacle and Liang-gate (RIP, 2019–2019), Loretta has been in a suspiciously pleasant mood. She's been walking around the office manically smiling to herself, taking only a single smoke break each day. Just last Thursday, she literally told me my hair looked very *nice* (I had tied it back with a black velvet bow). I'm pretty sure it's the first time she's dealt me a superficial compliment.

Additionally, Saffron told me she was seen *holding the door* open for a couple of maintenance workers. This is beyond troubling. Loretta once told me that whenever she approaches a new space, she expects the door to be wide open, waiting for her. Anything less is, according to her ideology, a mark of disrespect. Now she's going around opening doors not just for herself but for *others*? What the flying fuck is going on?

Regardless, I never say no to a gift. And over the past few weeks, I've felt like an *Oprah* audience member.

My phone buzzes again. I let out an audible *ugh* and turn the screen over. Sure enough, I have two new text messages. But surprisingly, they're not from Loretta.

> **Cal (1:07 PM):** Hey little light.
> **Cal (1:08 PM):** Doing anything tonight?

I practically spit out my oat milk latte all over my oversize tweed blazer from the Break.

The last time I had a real conversation with Cal was in Loretta's office, almost two months ago. Since he's been somewhat MIA, I had written him off as a certified fuckboy with great arms. (Note to self: Stop objectifying Cal.) What is he doing reaching out now? Does he need help filing paperwork or picking out an outfit? Or did he actually lose my number by accident? The possibilities are endless.

My mind runs faster than Buzzfeed pumps out listicles. I resolve that the only way to find out what he wants for certain is to—wait for it—respond to his text.

> **Noora (1:13 PM):** Hey there!
> **Noora (1:13 PM):** Got a few things in rotation but nothing set in stone. Wbu?

What a stupid attempt at sounding nonchalant. Of course, I have no real plans for tonight, unless you count staying in, nursing an eight-dollar bottle of merlot, and binge-watching *The Bisexual* on Hulu (written and directed by and starring Desiree Akhavan—we stan a strong, female Middle Eastern artiste). But Cal doesn't need to know that.

I wait for a few minutes then check my screen. He still hasn't responded. I *knew* I should have waited longer to text him back. I fucking hate the politics of flirting, of acting chill. It rocks me to my core that women are expected to strike the perfect balance between uninterested and readily seduced. I'm tempted to throw my phone all the way across the restaurant, but I manage to calm myself instead. That would probably result in having to get up and walk all the way to the kitchen, not to mention getting banned from the premises for life.

The next time I look down, he's typing. *Thank fucking God.* I hold my breath and lower my expectations. I prepare myself for the most mundane, disappointing text message of all time.

Instead, he asks if I have dinner plans.

Did you get that?

Cal-Howard-Tech-Man wants to go on a date with *me*, Noora, glorified "that bitch" and frizzy-haired seductress!

Forgetting the lessons of the past, I quickly text him back and accept his invitation. I suggest we meet at J. Payton's, a charming little eatery and bar in Nolita, right off Spring Street. It's romantic in a nonsensical way, considering I once saw a rat run across a patron's table. But it has that quintessential New York charm. I'm picturing us at an outside table, laughing, my foot casually brushing against his calf. We'll order East Coast oysters and roasted brussels sprouts, and I'll make a subtle joke about aphrodisiacs, and he'll lean in to kiss me, and all will be right in the world. Then we'll spend the rest of dinner and our lives together planning our wedding on a remote Greek island and naming our unborn kids. They'll need to have Farsi names. Maybe Yasmine and Rostam.

We set the time for 8:00 p.m., which gives me approximately six and a half hours to freak out, die, revive myself, panic, *comme des fuck down*, and get ready.

I shut my laptop and rise. *NoorYorkCity* can wait. Hell, New York City can wait. The rest of my life cannot—that begins right now.

I leave twenty-five dollars on the table, thank my server, and rush out the door. A gust of cutting autumn air slaps me across the face then delivers a light peck on the forehead. It's time to seize this day by the pantaloons.

My first stop is No Relation, a vintage shop on Thirteenth and First with a giant selection of vintage denim, rogue slogan T-shirts, and retired motorcycle jackets. I enter the store with my sleeves rolled up high, like Lizzie McGuire about to go bargain hunting with her mom for a second pair of hip-huggers. My chest is huffing like a prize bull, ready take down anyone who gets in my way. Normally, when I go thrifting, I drop off a bag of clothes to donate too. I'm constantly at odds with how to shop sustainably and ethically, trying to figure out how support small business and designers with a fast-fashion budget. For now, thrifting is the only solution—and a passion—but I never want to take more than I can give. So I try to cycle out my closet like the seasons, keeping things fresh and provocative with the racks fully stocked.

I float with ease through a sea of sequins, five-dollar price tags, railway jumpsuits, and '90s Adidas track jackets. This terrain is one I've traversed and conquered before, so I rarely need to stop and gather my bearings.

After hauling a big-ass pile of treasure into one of the tiny changing stalls covered in band stickers and signs that caution against walking out with merchandise stuck up your hoo-ha, I narrow down my dinner looks. I'm between a floral prairie dress with a fitted waist and pointy shoulder pads and a pair of paint-splattered, high-waisted Lee jeans. I would wear the former with a pair of white sneakers and hoop earrings and the latter with a scarf tied around my torso, worn as a top. Since each outfit is priced under twenty dollars, I decide to buy both and decide later. Besides, I've got bigger fish to fry—namely, my hair and makeup.

Now, this may surprise you, but I literally know *nothing* about beauty. In fact, I've been using CVS moisturizer and a hand-me-down mascara wand since I was in the fourth grade. No, I don't have a morning routine and I just learned what primer is, like, last week. Saffron practically punched me in the face when I asked if jade rollers were a type of drug "the kids were doing." *You're, like, 12*, they'd reminded me.

I call Leila, but she doesn't answer. I was hoping she'd be around tonight to help me get ready, but she's been strangely distant lately. She goes out on weeknights and hooks up with rando strangers, opting to stay over instead of coming home. I've seen her take calls at weird hours of the day and get angry over tiny, insignificant things. The other day, she freaked out because an old elementary school friend unfollowed her on Instagram. They hadn't spoken in over a decade.

I check the time. 3:22 p.m. Shit.

There's no time to wait for Leila to resurface. Instead, I give Saffron a call. They live in Bushwick, which is probably just a little too far to haul ass for an entire makeover, but still, worth a shot.

Before I can start to stress about crossing professional boundaries, Saffron answers on the first ring. I *knew* I could count on them.

"What's up, honey buns?!" they shriek into the phone.

I recap my day in one fell swoop. When I'm done, my story is met with a round of applause on the other end of the line. Saffron is *so* good at gassing me up. I ask if they want to come over to Leila's and help me get ready. They tell me they're planning on taking a Reiki class at 4:00 p.m. but could come over after. Classic. Saffron lives with their partner, a tattoo artist, in a loft-style studio space. I've never seen it in person, but they've shown me about a million pictures on Instagram.

"I'll bring over a million products and paint your face," they reassure me. "Cal will feel like he was hit by a taxi."

My phone feels hot against my cheek. I look down to see my screen flashing.

"One second, I have a call waiting. Lemme put you on hold."

I've got so many shopping bags in my hands that I have to use my pinky finger to swipe up and change the line.

"Hello?"

"Oh, good, you answered," Loretta says.

I stop dead in my tracks. It's still Saturday right? Time hasn't magically fast-forwarded two days, correct? Why, oh, why is Loretta James calling me midday on a weekend? I feel brunch coming back up my esophagus.

"H-hi Loretta, is everything okay?" I use all my might to will her to reply, "Wrong number!" and hang up.

"Sweetie, I've decided to take a last-minute trip to Los Angeles tomorrow." I can hear her twisted smile formulating in her vocal nodules. "Then I'll be staying to visit friends and take meetings. I'll be out of office for about a week, so I'll need you to reschedule in-person appointments as soon as possible."

My shoulders shrug in relief. Honestly, this could be a

good thing. A week of Loretta-free bliss sounds too good to be true.

"I'll also need you to book me a first-class round-trip ticket using the company system," she continues. "Which, of course, you'll check me into then send over my boarding pass and add all the info to my calendar. As well as the car that will take me to and from the airport, which, by the way, you must book as well. Also, can you call all the usual spots—the Beverly Hills Hotel, Chateau Marmont—and see if you can get me a media rate? I do hate to pay for hotels, love. Can you get this all done within the hour?"

I look down at the spoils I'm still carrying. It's probably around 3:30 p.m. If I run home now, I might have time to fulfill all of Loretta's requests before Saffron arrives with the goods.

"I'll certainly try."

"Good, make sure to try hard enough, because when you're done, we'll pack," she exclaims, giddy.

"Pack?"

Is she allowed to use me, an executive assistant, to help her pack a suitcase on a Saturday? I'm not getting paid overtime for this. I'm barely getting paid *under*time. The only reason I can afford to shop and eat is because I take the subway everywhere, don't pay rent, and have virtually no friends to hang out with other than my sister.

"Meet me at 32 Eighth Ave." She hangs up, leaving the dial tone buzzing.

I'm about to call Saffron back and give them the bad news. Then it hits me.

32 Eighth Ave. That's not the SPP Tower's address.

I'm going to Loretta Jones's town house in Park Slope. Straight into the den of the devil.

Chapter Eight

Loretta James lives in a palace of alabaster. The ceilings wear crown moldings, and the fireplace is glazed in a deep bronze filler. Her front door is painted a fresh coat of azure blue, and each of her five (five!) street-facing windows are vacant. The block is lined with London plane trees, sprouting from concrete soil, arms stretched out to the heavens, ready to receive. A chandelier once owned by a Russian oligarch hangs above her dining room table. Each coat gets its own hook.

New York City is filled with apartments, walk-ups, and the occasional abandoned house haunting the end of a friendly neighborhood block. The majority of these lots are placeholders, nothing more than a room with a box-spring mattress and a few stolen glances. But Loretta James does not live on a movie set, nor does she populate an empty promise. Loretta James lives in a home. One day, she'll use a pencil to etch her children's growing measurements into the inside of a closet door. Her family will spill wine on the carpet, fight over politics, and eat too much pecan pie on Thanksgiving.

I walk up Loretta's stoop. Immediately, I'm hit by a wave of nostalgia, a craving for something I've never tasted.

My family's Crown Heights apartment was like a worn, wooden crate full of soil, with budding flowers poking their heads through the surface. Leila and I shared a room until she turned thirteen, our kitchen faucet was always broken, and the pillows never matched. Our apartment housed our family unit, our true home. We had no attachment to chunks of plaster. When my parents announced they were boxing up my childhood and putting the place on the market before their move to Dubai, I felt nothing. Actually, I felt full—full of contempt for my parents for moving so far away. Full of gratitude for a youth so filled with passionately slammed doors and suffocating group hugs. Full of grief that it all had to end. There was not much in my parents' apartment, but growing up, it always felt full.

Entering Loretta's town house feels empty, or rather, lonely. Don't get me wrong, she owns a lot of stuff: a record collection sitting in stacks on the hardwood floor, bookshelves filled with shoeboxes and Gertrude Stein. Her picture frames are mostly empty, save for the one closest to the bathroom, which is filled with a shot of a much younger Sarah. She's sitting on Georgica Beach wearing aviators, tucking a tiny strand of hair behind her ear.

Loretta floods the stairs like a tsunami. I can hear her footsteps drifting in first before I turn around to look.

"Noora? Darling? Is that you?" she calls down to me. "Come upstairs!"

I grip the railing and begin my climb up the spiral stair-case. The walls seem to echo, and I look around to see if anyone else is here, but I know Loretta's wife isn't wandering the halls. Sarah is an OB-GYN and usually on call on the weekends. It's just me and Loretta, all alone in this big, deserted homestead.

When I reach the top, Loretta hands me her phone, turns around, and struts back into her bedroom. I grip it in my palm, caressing it with my thumb and forefinger. The screen lights up. Her background is a Comic Sans–style illustration of Gloria Steinem.

"Are you coming?"

I follow her into her bedroom, which could more accurately be referred to as a *boudoir*. Her headboard is Gothic and ornate, and the bench sitting at the foot of her bed is coated in a dark, plush red velvet. Cluttered hers & hers Victorian vanities are perched beneath the window. A single engraved silver hairbrush sits against the mirror.

"This is incredible," I utter, speechless.

"I know." Loretta's smile and eyes simultaneously widen. She looks like the Joker. We stand in place, staring at each other as I stroke her comforter with my left hand.

"So where's your suitcase?" I ask, breaking the awkward silence.

She raises one brow. "Oh, that old thing?" She waves off my question. "I packed that this morning."

"Then what am I here for?"

It's 5:00 p.m. and I have approximately three hours until I have to meet Cal, primed and highlighted, in Nolita (not counting the thirty-minute subway ride back). I'm starting to think Loretta might just be merely wasting my time for sport.

Does she need a playmate? A dog-sitter? A book club member?

Loretta gestures to the phone still sitting in my hand.

"I need you to film."

The truth slowly dawns on me: Loretta asked me to waste thirty minutes of my Saturday sitting cross-legged on the F train all so I could record an *Instagram takeover* for her.

"Have you heard of them?" she asks.

It takes everything in me to refrain from mocking her.

Apparently, Dickhead Daniel has informed Loretta that her content is only landing with a slightly older, out-of-demo audience. To combat this, he's asked her to pretape a few clips that can later be used as IGTV segments. In other words, she's hoping to turn her LA trip into a vlog. Not that she used that specific word—she most likely has no idea what it means.

I decide not to put up a fight. The sooner we get this done, the sooner I can go home. I sigh and hit record. Loretta takes a deep breath and lights up like the Empire State Building. I accidentally let out a snort so loud that I have to yell, "Cut! Sorry, sorry, take two!"

"Pull it together, sweetie," Loretta says, wiping a bead of sweat from her upper lip. "This is important business."

I suck in my cheeks, count down from five, and begin filming again.

"Hi, readers! You're live on the Instagram with Loretta James, editor in chief of *Vinyl* magazine," Loretta says, doing her best Kegel-clenching impression. "I'm about to fly out to LA for a very exciting industry event. But first, I want to show you folks at home what I'm packing." She extends one long, frail index finger, coated in red nail polish, and curls it in a come-hither motion. "Come along, kitties!"

It's almost too painful to watch.

We go on to film for another fifteen minutes. Loretta walks me through her pre-packed suitcase filled with La Mer products and "comfort clothes," aka 100 percent cashmere sweat suits and Golden Goose sneakers. I roll my eyes—there's no chance readers can actually afford to pack like this. But I guess that's the point? Perhaps to a random stranger living in Minnesota with a navel piercing and a coupon to Chili's in their wallet, Loretta's life is aspirational.

"And CUT," Loretta says. I snap awake, having accidentally zoned out after minute eight. "Play it back!"

We sit down on the bench at the foot of her bed, and I hit

play. Slowly, I watch as the muscles of Loretta's face tighten into knots. Then she turns her head away, as if I'm showing her a scene from *Saw V*.

"Turn it off!" She breaks down into tears. "It's a goddamn disgrace."

"What's wrong?" It's already been twenty minutes. I need to speed up this process, like, yesterday.

"What's wrong?" Loretta throws her hands in the air like a preacher, wailing. "I look *old*, Noora! I look like a decrepit, old hag!"

"That's simply not true. Look at your complexion! Your facial lines barely move as you talk. You don't have a single stress line! And your roots have been dyed to perfection."

She waves off my comments as if they're mosquitoes.

"I need you to try again."

My heart drops—I don't have time for this. Loretta frowns, noticing that my upbeat "can do!" attitude has taken a decline.

"Okay, what's wrong, my sweet?" Her vocal tone turns from sour to pure sugar. She sounds like a concerned teacher.

I sigh. "No, really, it's nothing."

"Come on, honey. Out with it."

"I don't want to bore you."

"Noora," Loretta says, approaching me.

She lays one manicured hand on my shoulder and turns to meet my gaze. Her expression is maternal—warm, even. Up close, I can see her more clearly: the vein popping ever so slightly in the middle of her forehead, her dilated pupils. She's scared. Underneath all her frustration, layered like a winter coat, lies deep-seated fear. An insecurity that she's no longer what she was once. That's she's not enough.

"You can talk to me, you know?" she says, "In some ways, you remind me of my younger self. A plucky thing, I was.

Full of ambition and distractions, in equal measure. What's distracting you, Noora? You can trust me."

She pats my shoulder like it's a miniature poodle and, for some reason, I find it endearing. Maybe opening up to me makes her seem, well, I don't know. More human, less android? This is, after all, *the* Loretta James. The publishing legend. There's a reason I wanted to work under her, to study her every impulse. I'd always hoped she'd be more of a mentor to me, molding my writing into its truest potential. Perhaps, I was too quick to judge her. Too harsh. She is, after all, under a lot of pressure. And right now, we're having a moment.

"It's just..."

"Go on."

"I have a date tonight."

Loretta narrows her eyes. It's amazing, watching her entire face, voice, and demeanor all transform in a matter of seconds. If her performance weren't directed at me, I'd be a captivated audience member.

"Well, that's a shame," she says. "You know, Noora, I really wish you hadn't told me that."

Moments pass.

Loretta stares at a single spot at the wall, furiously shaking her head. It's as if her body might involuntarily combust.

"Now we have a classic catch-22, don't we? Because, you see, I feel for you, I really do. But this is your job. And I think I've made the parameters of your job perfectly clear. So you can go on your date. In fact, I want you to go on your date! But there's a task that needs to be done. And it's *going* to get done. And if you don't stick around and do it, I'll have to find someone who will. You don't want that, do you?"

I feel a tiny tear escape my duct and slither down my left cheek.

"No, I don't."

"Good," she says, smiling once again. She leans over and wipes the tear off my face with the bottom of her thumb. "Now, let's try that again."

We record the entire takeover and watch it back two more times. After each take, Loretta breaks down in front of me. She hates how flat her hair looks but is also disgusted by its volume. I matte her face to perfection with a compact, but then she cries out that she needs to look "dewy." Her voice sounds too high-pitched and squeaky then low like Elizabeth Holmes. She alternates between telling me I'm a disappointment and like a daughter to her.

After the second take (third in total), I ask to go to the bathroom. Once I'm sitting on top of the toilet, I send Cal a quick text informing him that I'm not going to make it. But before I get the chance to press send, Loretta bangs on the door and asks what's taking so long.

Are you smoking in there? She wants to know.

How could I be so wrong? To think, even for one second, that Loretta and I are one and the same? That's the last time I lower my guard around her. I'll never be so naive again.

I quickly shoot off the message and run outside, barely pausing to look at my reflection in the Victorian-era, gold-plated mirror. Put politely, I look like the shit I didn't have time to take.

Around 9:00 p.m., I walk out the door of Loretta's town house. I've filmed her Instagram takeover six times, brushed through her knotted red hair five times, reapplied her Chanel Rouge lipstick four times, messed around with different lighting schemes three times, sat through outfit changes twice, and, somehow, only cried once.

When we finally got it right, I collapsed on Loretta and Sarah's bed, momentarily forgetting where I was. I looked up at the wall. There's a framed photo of Barack Obama hanging above her bookcase. She has a pair of Gucci mules wedged next to *We Should All Be Feminists* by Chimamanda Ngozi Adichie. Loretta came up behind me and patted me on the head like a Pomeranian.

"Good girl," she crooned.

It's now dark outside. Pitch-black, actually. All the streetlights on Loretta's block appear to go out at 8:00 p.m. on Saturday nights, most likely for the kids or to ward off wayward partygoers. As soon as I'm surrounded by the cover of nightfall, I break out in big, gigantic sobs. My body shakes with each wave of misery. People stop in passing to ask me if I'm all right, and I offer a tiny smile and a nod. I look down at my phone and find I have three messages.

> **Cal (7:56 PM):** Happens.
> **Leila (6:42 PM):** I found your coworker Saffron outside the apartment? You didn't mention that their head is shaved and they've got like a bajillion tattoos. Kind of hot TBH. Are they single??? Anyway, I let them in and made a pot of chayee. They said u were supposed to meet them here? Wru? Is everything OK? Call me.
> **Saffron (4:33 PM):** Yo I'm at your front door where r u?

Oh my God. Cal hates me. I totally spaced about Saffron. It's official. I'm a blue-check verified, capital C-U-N-T.

I call back Leila. She unexpectedly answers on the first ring.

"Noor? You good?"

Between the snot pouring out of my nose like Niagara fucking Falls and the mascara-stained tears painting my cheeks, I can't get a word in edgewise. I just take a seat on the sidewalk and cry into the phone. I can hear my sister's concern grow on the other end of the line.

"Meet me at La Esquina," she says. "I'm on my way."

Leila hangs up and I follow suit. Without another word, I pick myself up and solemnly get on the subway.

La Esquina is my and Leila's happy place. From the outside, it's a nondescript taco stand sitting on the far end of a tiny park on Kenmare Street. There's a red LED sign extending over the ceiling that says THE CORNER in big, bright lights, right in front of a billboard that usually boasts YSL ads (or just SL now, I suppose). The interior consists of a sole worktable to order your meal and a series of barstools, facing an open window into the heart of Nolita. Every surface imaginable is covered in stickers—free stickers, band stickers, Fuck the Man stickers. There's an impressive display of vintage Coca-Cola bottles featured behind a sheet of glass below the counter. During the warmer months, you'll find scattered lime-green and pink tables and chairs sitting outside. A fake greenery, like a virus of vines, lines the scaffolding above. It's a secret plastic garden.

Even more discreet is the dark, smoky speakeasy that sits beneath the taqueria, which reeks of sex and cigarettes and sounds like the cheap mumblings of elevator music and chatter. The first time I discovered it was by drunkenly wandering past bathroom signs and into a false kitchen. It served as a good reminder that nothing is ever as it appears, so best not to judge from appearances. Also, knowledge is *always* power. All you need to know is the password.

When we were little, Leila and I used to celebrate small victories with tacos at La Esquina—a top grade on an English paper here, a DFMO with a hot but snotty collegiate boy there. We'd perch on the stools facing the street and divulge confessions to each other over minced meat and ceviche. As we got older, the tortillas and guac transformed into margaritas and sangria. But we kept coming back, time after time, year after year. It's where Leila whispered to me that she thought she might be bi—then gay, then pan, then queer. Each admission was made between tears and salted rims. We'd fight then hug, leaning into both our differences and our similarities. There's something about blood mixed with tequila and cilantro that can heal even the deepest of wounds.

As I get off at Spring Street and make my way down Mulberry, I can feel my cheeks begin to air-dry. I pick up the pace, speeding past tourists taking photographs of Little Italy and nano-influencers sharing a glass of wine outside Ruby's. I turn the corner, power walking through Petrosino Square, and see Leila sitting outside, waiting for me. She's dressed in a pink power suit and chunky loafers. I can tell she's stressed by the speed at which she's hitting her vape pen. When our eyes meet, I start running.

"Whoa, slow down there," she says, leaping up to hug me. I collapse into her arms. She smells of nicotine and kai oil. "Tell me everything."

I sit down and begin to unload. As I heave word vomit on to the table, it occurs to me just how long it's been since Leila and I had a proper heart-to-heart. I walk her through my crush on Cal, Liang-gate hell, and the mysterious blackout meetings. I stumble briefly, tearing up once as I describe Loretta's manic mood, changing as rapidly as the racks at Zara. It's hard to put into words, but I try. I outline her vendetta against Jade, her obsession with technology and understanding the "youths." The mysterious war she keeps alluding to. When I finally finish, I land on a sentence that catches me off guard.

"I'm going to quit."

The second the words come out of my mouth, I know they're true. I can already feel a giant weight, all the pressure that's been suffocating me for the past two and a half months, begin to lift off my shoulders. I imagine what it would be like to sleep through the night without waking up in a pool of sweat, terrified that I missed a text or email from Loretta.

Leila loudly clears her throat, waking me out of my trance. She's biting the corner of her cheek. That's never a good sign.

"Noor, I have something to tell you," she starts. "Promise you won't be mad?"

"Promise."

"You want the good news or bad news?"

"Good news."

"Well, Willow *totally* hooked it up." She pauses for effect, grinning. I have zero clue what she's getting at.

"Sorry, Willow whomst?"

"Willow! You met her, right? I think you guys, like, had coffee one morning recently?"

I shut my eyes and try to concentrate. Then it hits me.

"That femme you hooked up with? Like, a couple weeks ago?"

"Yes! So, she's kind of an up-and-coming Instagram model type thing. She's been doing a ton of concept shoots for Central Saint Martins kids—you know, the ones Rihanna tapped for Fenty—and Lim loves her. He's using her for his Paris preview. Anyway, she gave HQ a call and put an end to the whole Liang debacle!"

I can't fucking believe it.

Actually, I can. Of course, Leila saved the day—she always does, always has. But that rando septum piercing chick with zero manners and a penchant for swigging from the carton?

That's one plot twist I didn't see coming. I guess you never know who you're sharing a bathroom with.

"I don't even know how to begin to thank you, Lei." I throw my arms around her and give her a squeeze. Her body immediately stiffens.

"Um, I have a few ideas," she continues. "So, don't freak out, but I may have gotten a little, eensy-teensy, teeny-weeny, tiny bit fired last month."

My jaw drops. Leila pushes it back up and closes my mouth.

"Basically, you know that gala I helped organize? Puppies for Penelope, with all the golden labradoodles and that one retired acrobat from Cirque Du Soleil who had the eye patch, at that Meatpacking District roof deck pool? Well, everything was going so great. Like, so, so great. Next-level perfect, Noora. All the puppies were doing that little synchronized swim we taught them, and the venue had a line practically wrapped around the block. I mean, I was about to get *promoted*, really. Until, you know. Penelope had to take a quick pee and may have found me bending over the bathroom sink, hooking up with her, er, husband. It's the bastard's fault, when I really start to think about it. He didn't tell me who he was or anything. Plus, he swore he locked that door. I asked him to check. Twice! And, besides that, it was, like, a hell of an event. For the record books, I swear. But try telling my boss that."

I can see Leila's on the verge of tears. It's a strange sight. Growing up, she never cried—not even when our *baba bozorgh* died. She's the most confident person I know. I swallow my own tears.

"How bad is it?" I'm almost afraid to ask.

"Well, I have a little bit of money saved. But you know personal finances have never been my *thing*. And for some reason, things just aren't falling into place the way they normally do for me. I've reached out to, like, fifty firms and nobody has so much as done me the courtesy of responding to an email. And these are places that used to beg me to even consider joining their ranks, let alone beg to apply. It's going to take a bit longer to find a new gig than I would have liked, Noora. I think I may need to consider switching industries or reinventing myself as a pop star or something. Maybe I've run out of good karma or used all nine of my lives or I don't know. It's like I've been blacklisted."

She's avoiding making eye contact with me. I can tell whatever she's about to say next is hurting her as much as it has the potential to hurt me.

"I know things are shit right now, and I'm your big sister, and I'm supposed to protect you from narcissist monsters, and I'm sorry. But I'm going to need your help with rent, at least until I find my next gig. The thing is, I'm already a little late on this month's check. Our landlord pretty much has no chill. And..."

"And?"

"And I give it a couple more weeks, maybe a month, tops, before he makes good on his threats. But if you quit your job now, we're probably going to get evicted."

I slouch back and feel the weight of her words crushing my spine.

"Will you promise me you won't quit your job? At least not for the time being," she pleads. "I need you, Noor."

My entire life, Leila has never let me down. It's time for me to lift her up.

"I promise." I'm not so sure I mean it.

Chapter Nine

I keep my promise to Leila. On Monday morning, I wake up at the crack of dawn and haul my ass to the SPP Tower, even though it kills me. Something I didn't account for when Loretta told me she was going to be traveling to LA for a week: the time difference. While, yes, it is nice to have her physically off my back, I forgot Loretta is omnipresent, and the time difference only exacerbates that fact. On Sunday night, she was sending me text demands until 3:00 a.m., forgetting that it wasn't midnight in New York. I slept about three hours, max. If Dickhead Daniel or anyone else fucks with me today, I swear to God, I'll pull a Renata Klein and run through the halls destroying everything in sight.

When I get to the office, I'm overwhelmed by the quiet. Don't get me wrong, the Digital team continues to laugh and chitchat as loudly as the tourists in Times Square, but for the first time, I find their mumbling somewhat soothing. Without Loretta around to poke and prod at everything that I do, *Vinyl* appears to be a much more tranquil setting. The equation is so simple, I can't help but shake my head.

Just subtract one person and solve for X.

With Loretta in meetings nearly three thousand miles away, I'm free to go about my day with ease.

After cleaning up her office (I touched everything, just to feel the thrill) and comp table and marking what will get sold back to the RealReal, I head to the cafeteria and take my time picking out my lunch. I settle on a poke bowl (they have a sushi chef come with fresh fish and prepare it each day) and walk toward the register.

I look up and see Cal crossing the room, all the way from the opposite quadrant. I give him a smile and a wave. In return, he quickly nods his head, a 'sup nod, then continues walking and chatting with his fellow tech team members.

My stomach drops. He *definitely* hates me for blowing him off. But what can I do? I'm Loretta's henchman, forced to serve at her leisure.

I pay twenty dollars ($20!) for my poke bowl and retreat to my floor.

I resolve to spend the rest of my day updating *NoorYorkCity*, since I was so rudely interrupted over the weekend. As soon as I log into the URL and begin messing around with my last blog post, I hear footsteps turning the corner toward Loretta's office. I look up and come face-to-face with a rhinestone-littered shadow and a dark-black lip.

"Saffron, please, please don't hate me too." I think of Cal and his occupied eyes from earlier.

They roll their eyes. "Bitch, I could never!" they exclaim. "I am mad at you, though. For hiding that *fabulous* sister of yours! Seriously, she was wearing this amazing power suit, and she made me the most delicious pot of fresh mint tea, and it was all so sexy, I thought I might propose. Anyway, when you stopped answering your phone, I assumed Loretta was so far up your ass, you'd gone into a coma. Was I right? Speaking of, where is that sparkling ray of sunshine?"

"It's a long story," I moan. "But, long story short, LA for a week. No idea why."

"I am literally laughing out loud," they say, without even cracking a smile. "Wait, if Loretta's out of the city, then what are you working on?"

"Uh, nothing." I shield my computer. Truth is, I've been keeping my blogging background a bit of a secret from everyone at work. I don't know, I guess I'm worried that my frequent typos and love of alliteration won't meet the *Vinyl* golden standard. Or maybe I'm afraid of being rejected, told I'm not talented enough—mediocre, middle-grade. I'm terrified of being told I'm nothing special. I guess there's a nagging voice in the back of my brain whispering, *If you're not going to the best, then why be at all?* When Saffron asked why I have so many Instagram followers, I told them it was because Loretta had tagged me in one of her posts and given me a major boost. They had just nodded and said, "Finally, a perk!"

"Bullshit," Saffron says now, practically grabbing my laptop from me, yanking it out of my hands. They lean in and squint at the screen then proceed to scroll in silence for nearly a minute.

"Noora, what the fuck! This is, like, really sick. I had no idea you were a content creator!"

I let out a faint giggle. "Is that PC for *blogger*? 'Cause I can take it, I promise."

"I'm serious, lady." They're scrolling through my site, clicking in and out of posts. The sound their fingers are making as they press down on the touch pad is practically *feeding* my anxiety. "Excuse my hyperbole, but this is insanely cool. Who takes these photos? And who translates your copy into fucking Farsi?!"

As I explain that I write, edit, photograph, *and* translate *NoorYorkCity* all on my own, I can see a thought bubble forming above Saffron's head.

"What are you doing today at four thirty p.m.?"

"Literally nothing. Today, tomorrow, the entire week. I'm managing Loretta's life from afar and three hours ahead."

"Great, you're coming to the weekly Digital meeting with me."

Before I have a chance to rebut and explain I've been banned from canoodling with Digital, Saffron turns around and runs back to their desk.

Technically, Loretta said I'm not allowed to *write* for Digital. She didn't say anything about attending meetings, right?

When the time comes, I meander the corner toward the Digital nook and plop down in one of those inflatable, translucent beanbags I thought they stopped making in 1999. I land on it like it's a trampoline, briefly bouncing back up again.

Around 4:29 p.m., the rest of the Digital team begins to take out their AirPods and turn their desk chairs around to form a circle. I'm shocked to see Jade gliding down the hall, entering the ring. I had assumed her deputy, Mila, would do the honors of conducting the service. In fact, I had no idea she was back in the office—a product of being shoved in a corner, all the way across the hell. Sorry, I mean the hall.

It's the first time I've seen Jade IRL, and honestly, I can't tell if I'm impressed or disappointed. For one thing, she's tiny: Her frame probably fills up five feet, maybe an extra inch or two. Loretta could quite literally step on her with one of her combat boots and squash her like a roach. Also, her thin, black hair is chopped into a short, unkept bob underneath her chin, a haircut that says, "I don't have time to touch this shit, nor do I care to." At first glance it looks as if she's wearing a sweat suit from ASOS or Topshop, but when I look closer, I can tell that she's dripping in seven hundred dollars' worth of athleisure. Her chunky sneakers are Balenciaga, and her sweatpants and matching zip-up hoodie are from Kith. Even her tiny sports bra peeking out from underneath displays a small Supreme logo. Her skin looks sweaty but is most likely coated in serum. She's wearing a Livestrong-style bracelet on her wrist that says, *Made in Japan* (*Esquire* says she's Japanese American) and a dainty gold necklace that has *give a shit* written in Sanskrit on it.

She practically floats above us, and the rest of her team applauds her grand entrance. She must have just landed from Milan, where she was wrapping up fashion month. There's a tall, blond chick trailing behind her, taking notes on her phone with one hand and sipping on a kombucha with the other. This must be the other assistant Saffron told me about that day in the beauty closet. I think her name is Kelsea.

"Alright, alright, alright," Jade begins, emulating a drunken Mick Jagger. "What's up ladies, gentlemen, and nonbinary honeys?!" More cheers. "It's so good to be back with y'all. I swear to goddess, I hate industry events almost as much as global warming, but if I have to show face in the front row of a fashion show in order to get people to support stricter gun regulations, then that's what I'm going to do. Who's with me?"

A few people *literally* stand up to applaud this time.

"Anyway, what have I missed? Who wants to start this week's rundown? I want to hear both timely and evergreen pieces. Alex, you want to take it away?"

Alex, the extremely quiet, nerdy-looking, tall, white, and lanky Politics editor sits up in his seat. I notice he's slightly leaning his weight on a chic wooden cane, his limbs involuntarily contracting as he steadies himself to a stand. Just as he pushes up his glasses, Jade interrupts.

"Wait, so sorry there, Alex. Forgot to mention one thing.

Last week we broke a *record*. September marked fifteen thousand KPIs on our site. *Fifteen*. Seriously guys, I could cry, but I'm not going to. This really is a testament to all your hard work. Pieces like last month's article about Trump crowning himself king of the fuckboys really made this possible. You guys are changing the world. I'm just lucky to be a part of it."

The whole room erupts in cheers. A couple people high-five. Others lean in for hugs. I sink deeper into my balloon chaise, wondering if they've even noticed I'm here. Once the noise clears, Alex begins again.

"So, this week, we're going to look into whether conservative legislators are planting moles in migrant caravans. I have a source on the ground who is promising cutting-edge stuff. We're talking, like, wheels-up action."

Jade nods, impressed. Alex stops scratching his stress rash on his inner elbow then steadies his cane and slinks back down.

Next, Crystal, the Fashion editor, rises. She's dressed in a tiny beret and even tinier sunglasses. Her hair is divided into tiny braids and her shirt reads, *BLACK & BEAUTIFUL*.

"Okay, so I'm thinking, with Halloween right around the corner, we get a head start on all the appropriators by running a piece on the colonization of turquoise in the use of silver jewelry. As y'all know, I'm Afro-Indigenous and a descendant of the Zuni, and the way my people's designs have been repackaged and marked up should be considered a motherfucking hate crime."

So I guess we're allowed to curse at these things.

"We can photograph Indigenous models in pieces made by actual surviving tribes. It'll be a cultural reset."

The whole team snaps for Crystal's breakthrough. I hesitantly snap along. Lola, the Lifestyle editor who gave me my stamp of approval on the day I interviewed, takes this as her cue to go next.

"Right…" Lola speaks so slowly that I feel like I'm stoned out of my mind. Now that I mention it, she might actually be. "For Lifestyle, I'm thinking bathroom products. But not just ones you can, you know, use to clean and shit. I'm thinking bathroom products you *can have sex with.*"

Jade's eyes widen.

"Whoa," she says, patting Lola on the back. "That goes hard. Saffron, would there be any overlap with your vertical? Since you usually cover most of our sex stuff?"

Saffron rises. I beam with pride. They are by far the coolest editor on staff.

"Before I begin, I just want to introduce everyone to Noora."

All heads turn at once, and I can feel everyone's eyes piercing my soul.

Don't throw up, Noor. Whatever you do, don't you fucking throw up.

"She's Loretta's new assistant, but don't worry, she's chill. She's a Middle Eastern American content creator living in Chinatown."

The circle members all give me steady nods of approval. Content with my embarrassment, Saffron moves on.

"Okay, so for this week, I'm thinking of speaking with an all-American family anonymously—like, three generations of American—and asking each of them about their earliest childhood trauma. Thoughts?"

Jade sucks in her cheeks, thinking.

"I think it needs to be fine-tuned, but has potential," she finally says. "Bringing attention to mental illness is important, but I don't want to publish straight-up trauma porn. Just make sure to consult a therapist, okay?"

Saffron nods then gleefully takes their seat. That only leaves Seb, the Entertainment editor. He's a Mexican guy wearing a flashy paisley button-down. The circle lets out a few *whoops* as he gets up.

"Welcome back to my channel," he begins, pausing for laughter. "Okay, so with awards season coming up, I was thinking we run a series about how Hollywood is full of flat-earthers! I got a tip that, like, at least Nic Cage is a legit flat-earther. Also, the Olsen twins. Swear on my dog. Like, you can't make this shit up."

Jade *laughs*.

I'm sorry, what did he just say?

"We're going to have to pass on that angle, I'm afraid," she tells Seb. "But, as always, love your enthusiasm."

With that, the meeting starts to slowly dissipate. Jade spends the last few minutes chatting with members of Social about their analytics, and I get up to begin to journey back to my desk. I run my hand up and down my arm and discover I have goose bumps. The last half hour was electric—Jade has a magnetic energy. And to witness the way her team, the people who work under her, worship her? Well, I've never seen anything like it. I can't even begin to understand why Loretta hates her so much. She's probably just jealous.

I barely get four feet away before I feel a light tap on my shoulder. I turn around and find Alex, Mr. Shy Guy Politics editor, staring at me, stepping on my foot with his cane. He looks nervous and agitated, sweating from the tip of his philtrum.

"I just want to say I really appreciate you joining us today."

"Aw, thanks, Alex," I say, touched. "It was a pleasure."

"Also, I'm totally against the Muslim ban," he says bluntly. "I think the Islamophobia in this country is disgusting."

I feel as if I've been knocked down by a wave. Maybe I misheard?

"Oh, yeah, totally." I give as vague of a response as I can muster. This *sagtooleh*.

"As Politics editor, please let me know if you ever want to write your story for us," he says, sort of bowing his head. "Like, if your dad was a cabdriver or something. It would be an honor to give you a platform to speak your truth. So often, narratives like yours are marginalized."

Before I can open my mouth to call this kid a racist sack of shit, I hear someone behind me clear their throat. Saffron. Thank fucking God.

"Hold that thought," I say to Alex before turning around and walking away. "Saffron, amazing timing."

"Ha, sorry, what?"

Standing before me is not, in fact, the genderless monarch of spice themself, but the tall blond with perfectly coiffed hair, wearing skinny jeans, Stan Smiths, and a leather jacket. It's none other than Kelsea, Jade's assistant.

"Look, we haven't met yet, but we're going to need each other." She scans me up and down, as if looking for a piece of lint or a lost contact. There's something about Kelsea that feels *so* familiar. She just sort of looks like a high school student's fake ID photo that was taken at CVS.

"Sure," I tell her, unsure how to respond appropriately. She gives me a sweet, assuring smile.

"What are you doing for lunch on Wednesday?"

Chapter Ten

Kelsea chews with her mouth open. I grimace as tiny chunks of her avocado toast fly out from beneath her tongue and onto the tiny wooden café table at Gotan, a trendy café in the financial district filled with freelance tech bros. She uses the back of her gel-manicured hand to brush the crumbs from her face and smiles. There are still seeds stuck between her teeth.

"You look very familiar," she says, her voice dripping with a thick Long Island accent. "Did you go to Michigan?"

"Nope, I went to NYU."

"Are you a Persian Jew? Do I know you from temple?"

"Nope," I say. "Not Jewish."

"Ooh, were you a Kappa?" she asks, getting excited. Why are all sorority sisters always so glaringly predictable? Talk about boring.

"I didn't participate in Greek life. It wasn't really a 'thing' at NYU. The school is so big."

"Right, right."

I watch her forehead scrunch up as she racks her brain for other possible connections. She's wasting her time, though—I know for a fact she's probably confusing me with one of the million Iranians living in Great Neck, a mere twenty-minute drive from her hometown in Long Island. Us frizzy-haired Middle Eastern ladies all look the same to some people.

Kelsea suddenly snaps her fingers. The sound is so jarring, I flinch.

"I got it! What camp did you go to? Point O'Pines? Tripp Lake?"

Oh God. As a born and raised New Yorker, I'm familiar with primarily Jewish sleepaway camps. In fact, I used to beg my maman every summer to send me away to one, but she always said no, claiming she couldn't bear to part with me for three whole months. Looking back, the fact they basically cost half a year's worth of college tuition might have had something to do with it. But I didn't understand that at the time. All I knew was that over half the girls in my class came back to school every year with colorful, spray-painted camp swag, a new squad of best friends, and a series of songs and cheers they'd perform between classes and at lunch period. I learned a few of them too. Just to blend in.

"Vega," I finally say to shut her up. She looks smug.

"I knew I'd get to the bottom of it! Anyway, thanks for grabbing lunch with me. It's so nice to have another assistant in the office. I've been at the bottom of the food chain for so long, I feel like a freaking cow!"

I don't feel like explaining to her that that's not how the food chain works.

"It's been interesting," I respond, like a diplomat. "Loretta is a legend. Working for her is an honor and an incredible opportunity."

Kelsea rolls her eyes, looks around to make sure we're alone, then leans in closer.

"You can tell me the truth," she whispers. "We're all friends here."

"Well…"

As much as I'm dying to unload, I don't know Kelsea. Actually, I definitely *do* know Kelsea, in that I know so many girls exactly like her. I'm sure she landed her job because someone on the SPP board is, like, her godfather or something. She's privileged and acknowledges it, but that's the extent of her self-awareness. She gets her hair blown out once a week. When she was thirteen, her mother made her get a nose job. She never told a soul. But none of that means I can trust her.

"I won't tell anyone, I swear." She pries, slowly breaking me down.

"She's..."

"Go on."

"She's a psycho," I finally spit out. Kelsea claps her hands excitedly.

"She's totally bipolar, right?!"

"Well, I wouldn't say that." As much as I can't stand Loretta, I don't want to go around diagnosing people with a real mental illness. I don't fuck with that. "She's not exactly *mean* to me. She's actually kind of nice, but in a scary way. Like, she tells me she loves me and calls me *sweetie* and stuff, but I have no doubt she'd fillet my corpse and feed me to her Instagram followers. When she's on a high, she can make me feel like the most important person in the world. But then she crashes and reminds me of how replaceable I am. She literally makes me look for my own replacement sometimes!"

"Get out!" Kelsea screams. She's absolutely living for the drama. "Do you think she just gets off on being a bitch? Is it all just one giant power trip?"

I think for a second.

"Honestly, no. I think it comes from a place of insecurity. She knows the industry is changing, but she isn't evolving along with it. The internet is her kryptonite. And she breaks down. Like, all the time. But it's definitely taking a toll on me."

"Aw, you poor thing!" she cries, clutching the tassel of her Balenciaga classic city bag and giving it a twirl. "I don't know how you're holding up! Can't you, like, not pee? You're not allowed to use the bathroom fifteen minutes before a meeting, right? That's a *Bon Appétit* recipe for a UTI!"

"You have no idea." I laugh.

I uncross my legs then recross them again in the other direction. Today's early-October weather calls for a big, chunky fisherman's knit sweater and a midi-length kilt I thrifted from Beacon's Closet two weekends ago. I've polished the look off with creepers, to give off that *schoolgirl gets devoured by Beetlejuice* vibe. I can't wait to upload it to the blog along with a poem about universal healthcare.

"Wait, how do you know that?"

"Jade told me! We're super close, even though I'm technically her assistant," Kelsea explains. "She's only twenty-seven, so I'm basically her little sister."

Huh. I had just assumed Kelsea had been close with Lily, Loretta's last assistant.

"How does Jade know so much about Loretta's management style? Does HR send out a newsletter detailing her most ridiculous demands that they're somehow a hundred percent okay with?" I joke.

"No, dude," Kelsea says, giggling. "'Cause she started as Loretta's assistant! You knew that, right?"

I literally freeze midbite. Poached egg yolk dribbles down my chin. I can hear forks and knives clanking against midcentury plates.

"I'm sorry, what?" I couldn't possibly have heard that right. "But they hate each other!"

The second the words come flying out of my mouth,

I want to take them back. I *know* that gossiping with the assistant of my boss's sworn enemy is not what I should be spending my Loretta-less week doing, but I can't help it! It's my Gemini sun—sometimes, the other half of my personality takes over and I completely lose control. I call her Shabnam, and she's a total snake.

"Okay, so, I'm going to tell you everything, but I'm trusting you with my *life*," Kelsea says. I can tell by the solemn look on her face and the speed at which she's tapping her Rag & Bone heeled booties that she's serious. "Here's a little *Vinyl* history lesson for you, one you won't find on Wikipedia.

"In 2013, SPP execs came to Loretta and told her that her numbers for the quarter were down and basically black-mailed her into launching a website—told her she'd lose her job if she didn't find another way of bringing in money. Remember, this was basically the Stone Age. Instagram had just launched. Blogs were still frequented daily by die-hard fans. Tumblr girls were fucking hot and VSCO girls probably weren't even born yet. So Loretta was, like, no. *Vinyl* is above the internet. It exists only in print. It's for the elite. *Vinyl* Print is haute couture and bringing it into the digital age would make it off-the-rack. You catch my drift?"

"So she refused to do it?" I ask, trying to follow along.

"Right. She wouldn't—and TBH, couldn't—do it. And SPP had her head on the chopping block. They were going to replace her with someone younger, hipper. And Jade, who was her assistant at the time, knew this was all going down because she had access to Loretta's email. Like you do. And she can code—her parents made her learn when she was, like, twelve years old or something. You know, because she's Asian or whatever."

I try to brush off the microaggression because I'm interested in what comes next, but Jesus.

"So Loretta asked her for help?"

I mean, if Loretta was willing to help Jade get promoted, maybe there's hope for me yet.

"Not exactly," Kelsea says with a devious grin. "You know Loretta—she's so erratic. SPP needed someone dependable, and Jade knew that. So, one night, when she was working late, she marched right up to the office of Grace Simms, the creative director of all of SPP. And although no one knows for sure what happened that night, the very next week, Jade was announced as the new Digital director of *Vinyl*."

My stomach churns.

"So she went behind Loretta's back?"

Kelsea scoffs, as if I've personally offended her.

"Not even! She saved Loretta's *job*. SPP was going to fire her and a find an editor in chief who would run both Print and Digital. Loretta's pride and ego were getting in the way of seeing what was best for the future of the brand. Jade stepped in because she knew Loretta was committing career suicide, and Jade is, like, the most empathetic human ever. She couldn't let her do that to herself. As Loretta's assistant, you should know better than anyone that she can be her own worst enemy."

She has a point.

"Still, isn't doing precisely the *opposite* of what your boss wants and then benefiting from it a little shady? I mean, she literally stole the website from under her, right? Sounds like Loretta was just looking out for what's best for the brand. How can you know *for sure* that Jade was doing the same, when she was handed the keys to the kingdom as a reward for her Brutus-like betrayal?"

Kelsea's eyes narrow. I can tell I struck a major nerve. I guess I severely underestimated how loyal this chick is to Jade's camp.

"Loretta does *not* care about what's best for *Vinyl*," Kelsea says sharply. "You said it yourself: She's just scared of the change that comes with accepting a world run by digital media. Because it makes her and her brand of white feminism outdated and irrelevant."

Whoa. Harsh. Especially coming from someone I may have mistakenly misjudged as being white feminist herself.

"I mean, clearly Loretta is not as out of touch with the age of virality and Gen Z as she thinks," I say, playing devil's advocate like it's motherfucking Candy Crush. "*Vinyl* is as relevant today as it was ten years ago, thanks to pieces like the music streaming rights deep dive, which consistently put us on the map. Not many brands are saving pieces like that for print anymore. They're more in line with something like *Jezebel* or *Vice*."

I look over at Kelsea. Her pale skin has turned bright red, and she's flaring her nostrils. I can practically see steam coming out of her ears. She looks like a cartoon character.

"That was Jade's piece, Noora! Don't you see? Everything cool, innovative, edgy about *Vinyl* comes from Jade. She ideated that piece, found the freelancer, did on-the-ground reporting, courted sources, the whole nine yards. She worked on it for over a year, sending it back for over fifty rounds of edits. Fifty! And when it was finally ready to publish, Loretta got word and scooped it up, publishing it in the June issue. And what's worse is that she didn't even *attempt* to give Jade credit for any of it. She's been lapping up the praise like the pussy that she is, because Loretta James only cares about Loretta James."

I digest my food and her information. Kelsea continues.

"This was going to be the Digital team's Deep Throat moment, Noora! Jade should have been nominated for an ASME Award. She should be in first class right now, drinking champagne and to flying to LA this weekend to accept on all of our behalf!"

I sit back in my chair. Honestly, I hate to admit it, but Kelsea's story checks out. I think back to every single time I've brought up the streaming rights piece to Loretta, how she's always flinched and promptly changed the subject. I thought she was being dismissive of her own accomplishments. Turns out, I was confusing humility for *guilt*. She's been walking around for half a year, taking credit for a piece that she did nothing but copy and paste. No wonder she's been forcing herself to look more digitally savvy, filming awkward Instagram takeovers before jetting off to LA. She's probably terrified of being found out.

My chest aches. I raise one hand to my heart, as if to check to see if it's actually broken. I knew Loretta was capable of a lot of devious shit, but I truly believed that, at the end of the day, she would put everything aside for the magazine. How could she let her pride get in the way of what's right? I think back to the many years I've spent idolizing her, the fan mail I used to send to the SPP offices, foolishly believing it would find its way into her manicured hands. My shoulders shudder. I guess it's true what they say: You should never meet your heroes. They'll only disappoint you.

Then it suddenly clicks. The takeover. Loretta hasn't posted it yet.

"Kelsea. Loretta's in LA right now. You don't think she's there for the ASME Awards, do you?"

Kelsea springs into action.

"Oh my fucking God, that narcissistic witch! She's going to accept an award for a piece she didn't even touch. This is going to crush Jade!"

Her body begins shaking. Worried she's going to burst out in tears in the middle of Gotan, I reach over and pat her shoulder. It's an oddly intimate moment for two people who hardly have anything in common except their job titles.

"I'm so sorry, that's awful," I say sincerely. "I wish there was something I could do." Kelsea looks up from the dirty plate she's been tearing up into and looks me directly in the eye.

"Well, maybe there is," she says. "You have access to all of Loretta's emails, right?"

I don't like where this is going.

"Technically, but I don't, like, read them or anything."

Kelsea clutches my hand as if she's about to propose.

"Look, Noora, we are at war." A chill runs down my spine as I hear Loretta's words echoed back to me. "But it's a cold war, where information, above all else, is currency. This is about the past versus the future, good versus evil. And you're a smart girl. Saffron said you're a content creator, right? You know that no matter how long Loretta prolongs this, Digital is going to win at the end. We have longevity and momentum that Print lost years ago."

I wish people would stop calling me a content creator.

"But at the end of the day, don't we all play for the same team, so to speak?" I ask, wondering when this got so Lancastrian. This must be *the* war that Loretta has been alluding to for months. And here I thought it was just one long, twisted analogy. "We all work for *Vinyl*, right? We all love the magazine!"

"This isn't about love, Noora," Kelsea says. "It's about power." She squeezes my hands so hard, they almost fall off my wrists. "It's going to be our heads or theirs. On a spike."

I contemplate her words, unsure of what to do or how to feel. On one hand, Loretta hasn't exactly been my champion. In fact, she's treated me like her wench. But on the other, I swore on oath of loyalty to her. And when I give someone my word, I usually mean it. Usually.

But Shabnam? That bitch has never kept a promise in her life.

Screw it. I'm not doing it for myself or even to hurt Loretta. I'm doing to for the magazine. For Print. For the readers! And I'm just a lowly assistant, really. What good does that do at the end of the day? I'm exercising the tiny bit of power I have, and even then, the odds that it'll make a difference are practically nil. And it's not like I'm hurting anyone. Not yet, anyway.

"What exactly are you looking for?" I ask.

Kelsea smiles.

"The holidays are coming up. What do you know about the December issue?"

Chapter Eleven

Okay, so I peeked. I'll admit it. I'm sorry! I couldn't help myself!

Here's how it went down.

After I left lunch with Kelsea, I couldn't stop thinking about it—the December cover star, Kelsea's mission. Sure, I haven't been sitting in prod meetings, and the team hasn't begun working on the actual copy for the issue yet (we literally *just* wrapped up November).

But I'm sitting on a gold mine—Loretta's email—which contains billions of dollars' worth of intel, and for some reason, my selective "morals" have been preventing me from prying and getting rich *real* quick. What's the harm in a couple of meandering computer clicks? The touch of a button has never killed anyone. But then I think of Loretta's fallen face when she finds out, and I'm sure I'm going to be sick. That, or I'm close to throwing my laptop against SPP's bulletproof windows.

I spent the next two days at work twiddling my thumbs, trying to distract myself from thinking about the task at hand. I scoured LinkedIn, looking for potential job opportunities for Leila to apply to. When she stopped responding (usually after the fourth or fifth message), I'd move on to asking Saffron to give me extreme home makeovers in the beauty closet. But after several swatches of mismatched foundation and a superglue mascara incident, even that lost its allure.

Finally, I decided to get organized. I made headway with Loretta's expenses, color coded her file cabinet, added more information to her calendar, and structured it for the rest of the month. Having her away in LA has been, frankly, a breath of fresh air—I've been texting her before and after every meeting and remotely calling her cars, which means I can't lock eyes with her as she calls me *love* and expresses her disappointment about the model of the vehicle.

But today is the ASME Awards. I can't stop thinking about it. Obsessing over it. She still hasn't added in anything on her calendar for that night, but she does have a very suspicious manicure appointment around noon. She never gets her nails done, because "real feminists aren't afraid to get down and dirty." And yet, folks. *And yet.*

A few times each day, Kelsea will Slack me, asking if I've made my decision. The first couple of times, I said I was still mulling it over. Eventually, I stopped responding altogether.

I wonder if Jade, who once very much stood in my shoes—or rather, sat at my desk—ever had to make a similar impossible decision. To pick sides between a publication and the person attached to it, that she loved and respected all her life, and the future she knows it deserves. I imagine that's what she must have been considering when she made the decision to betray Loretta and throw her hat in the ring for head of Digital. She was once Loretta's secret weapon. Now, that very same weapon, which Loretta molded from scratch, is being used to stab her repeatedly in the back.

On Friday morning, I decide to stop at Maison Kaiser, a quaint French coffee shop that sits in the heart of Lower Manhattan between Leila's apartment and the six train. I need to grab an extra dose of caffeine to finish off the week (sometimes, my three cups chugged over the kitchen sink just don't cut it).

I open Instagram and begin mindlessly scrolling. Between fall runway looks from Paris Fashion Week, memes of cats pretending to play chess, and photos of all my college acquaintances getting engaged—actually murder me—I almost miss a post of Leila's from two days ago. I swear to God, these algorithm changes make literally zero sense.

It's a picture of Willow and Leila at Cubbyhole, a historic LGBTQ+ bar in the West Village. They're leaning up against the jukebox, their fingers subtly caressing each other's thighs. The lighting makes them look like two sexy space aliens. I giggle and throw it a Like. Looks like those two might be getting serious.

I absentmindedly flip through my Instagram story from yesterday—I swear, I'm, like, the funniest person alive—when I notice a pattern. Whenever I click on the option to view those watching my story, *Cal's* username, TechBr007 (I know), is at the very top of the list.

You know what this means? He's totally orbiting me. You know, when the person who ghosted you continues to haunt you on social media.

I quickly jump to my Safari app to look up whether someone's name appearing first in your line up means they're one of your most frequent viewers. But before I can type anything into the search bar, my phone lights up with a notification. It's an email from Beth.

Beth Bennett 8:17 am (1 minute ago)

Hi Noora,
Can you stop by my office before EOD? We need to
talk.
Best,
B

I feel my heart drop. She knows. She totally knows about my lunch with Kelsea. How could she have possibly found out? Unless, of course, Kelsea told her? I chug my cold brew like a white frat boy at a kegger, then bolt toward the train.

Throughout the duration of my ride downtown, I keep replaying my talking points.

I never agreed to spy on Loretta.

I don't know anything about why Loretta's in LA.

I love my job and am grateful for the opportunity and would really, really like to continue submitting myself to this tempestuous torture chamber each day. Or something like that.

I walk through the double doors of SPP, mouthing these points to myself over and over. Superman gives me a look. I must look like I'm talking to myself. Whatever. Maybe I really *have* lost my mind and I'm in desperate need of an intervention. That or a Xanax prescription.

As I exit the smart elevator onto the thirty-second floor, all I can think about is Leila. I imagine her face—the desperation in the way her forehead wrinkled, her cheeks deflated—when she asked me to keep working. I can't disappoint her. I can't be the reason we end up couch surfing or sleeping in Central Park.

I knock on Beth's door around 5:00 p.m.

The second I enter her office, I feel my heart rate

accelerate. The walls smell of lavender and basil, the lingering incense of the tiny garden I've heard she keeps outside her Westchester home. There's a jar of hard caramel candies that sit on her desk, the kind you can only find at a reception desk or in the musty, old pocket of a grandmother who just got home from bridge club, next to two unopened bottles of Dom Pérignon. Her smile is soothing. It sends a shiver that runs down my spine, similar to the one I get when someone plays with my hair.

"Sit down, Noora."

I twiddle my thumbs, thinking about what I'll say during my exit interview. Actually, scratch that. Knowing SPP, I probably won't even get an exit interview. Beth leans forward in her chair like a good therapist.

"*Vinyl* loves to gossip. You know that, don't you?"

"Yes." I gulp. "I'm learning that."

"Word travels fast here. Rumors spread like a nasty virus."

"I know."

I'm *so* getting fired.

"But you're new and still learning." Beth extends her hand and pats my shoulder. "You still have time to rise above it."

She moves her hand off my shoulder and begins playing with the Star of David necklace hanging from her neck. I fixate on it too. I think back to all the bat mitzvahs I wasn't invited to, some held at extravagant venues like the Natural History Museum or Cipriani Midtown. That's growing up in New York for you. You don't get to take home any bat mitzvah swag, but boys *will* give you the gift of reminding you that you look like their hairy uncle.

"You get to decide what kind of reputation you build for yourself in this industry, Noora," she says. "I trust you'll make the right decision."

Beth stands and gestures to the door, signaling to me that

our meeting is over before it even begins. I smile and do the same weird little curtsy again. She looks mildly amused.

Was that it?

As soon as I'm at my desk, I let out a sigh of relief. I'll live to see another day. And while I'm not sure how exactly Beth found out that I had been approached at enemy lines, I'm not going to waste time trying to change the past when I just got a second chance at a future.

Ping.

I look up to see one new incoming Slack. I check my notifications. Sure enough, it's from Kelsea.

Kelsea (9:43 AM): Look at Loretta's IG. R u in or out?

I open Instagram and refresh my feed. Loretta's added the video I spent my entire night recording. Watching it is painful. She's edited it so each clip lasts around five seconds and tied them together with "What's Up?" by 4 Non Blondes.

I'm about to x out when the video changes to a new slide. This one, I don't recognize.

It's a selfie of Loretta speaking directly into the camera. There are palm trees behind her, swaying in the wind. Her lips are painted plum, and she's talking with her hands like an orchestra conductor.

"Now, my darlings, I'm finally here in LA, getting ready to attend the ASME Awards. It is my great honor to announce that *Vinyl* has been nominated for best feature of the year. I've come to the Golden State to hopefully accept the award on the magazine's behalf. What a thrill!"

I click out of Instagram and promptly drop my phone. My arm hair is standing up as straight as a country music festival.

She's actually going to accept that award. Kelsea was right.

I stare at my laptop screen for what feels like a millennium.

The last shred of optimism I have left starts to sour, leaving my insides filled with acid. This time, I'm sure I'm going to be sick. Loretta, this magazine, the entire fucking Shifter & Pearce Tower all feel like a massive lie.

For a split second, I picture Beth's face—the concern in the crease of her forehead, the levelness of her voice wavering as she warns me to keep my friends close but my enemies at a distance. I can't help but want her to respect me, to be proud of my choices. She's like the angel hovering above my padded shoulder, willing me to do the right thing. But then there's the devil, with a face so dark and clouded that I can't quite tell who they are. Loretta? Is that you? Are you gloating about your victory as you destroy this magazine's legacy through lies and deceit? My brain snaps back into focus. I guess life has handed me lemons. The question is: Am I going to make lemonade or spike it with vodka?

Fuck it.

I glance around the office to make sure nobody is watching me, then turn around and double-check that there are no security cameras secretly recording me from behind. All clear. Holding my breath, I open Loretta's email and type *December issue* into the search bar. Last week's run of show is the first thing to pop up. Before I can second-guess myself, I click into it.

It takes me two seconds of scanning the page to figure out who the cover star they've recently signed is: Zendaya. Yes, *the* Zendaya. The manic pixie powerhouse of my dreams. She who only needs one name, like Beyoncé. Or Jesus.

I mark the email unread and x out of her inbox as quickly as I can. Afraid I'll chicken out, I immediately message Kelsea. She responds within seconds.

Kelsea (10:02 AM): Let the games begin.

Chapter Twelve

The war begins. Print draws first blood, but Digital is quick to go straight for the jugular.

It's been two weeks since I officially kneeled and pledged allegiance to Jade's forces. Well, not officially. I guess I'm more like a covert operative. But I've definitely double-crossed Loretta, an irreversible action I know I can't take back, even if I wanted to. Although she doesn't know it yet. Actually, Digital hasn't even *used it* yet. I'm beginning to wonder why Kelsea even needed this information in the first place.

Loretta won the ASME, of course. In her acceptance speech, she made no reference to Jade or the Digital team's contributions to the story. She briefly thanked the freelance writer who actually conceived and birthed the words onto the page. But mostly, she patted herself on the back. She expertly acknowledged all the young whistleblowers who are fighting the good fight, risking their own security to go on the record. What's more, she recognized all the young readers whose thirst for knowledge and dedication to the truth motivated *Vinyl* to pursue the story, even when it would have been easier to pay a kill fee and move on. She comes off as a saint, purer than the Virgin Mary.

I watched the clip of her acceptance speech at 3:00 a.m. on YouTube. The time difference made it nearly impossible to keep my eyes open, but I swallowed every word. My stomach churned. *What have you sacrificed, Loretta?* I thought to myself between taking hits of Leila's vape pen. Apparently, Daniel *and* the head of Art were both seated at her table. Malala was there too.

Since getting back to the office, she's been in a smug mood. Her ego imitates her new inner mantra—she won this round, and she knows it. She struts the halls between meetings as if she's stomping on the Digital staff's necks and paychecks, daring them to get one step closer to her.

Jade, on the other hand, has gone the petty route. Upon Loretta's return, she has straight-up *refused* to set foot in a single conference room if there is even a slight chance Loretta might stop by to listen in. She moves with an army of editors around her to ensure she never so much as makes *eye contact* with anyone on Print. Kelsea is at the helm of her battleship. I wonder if Jade knows about the choice I made, that I'm secretly on her side. All I know for sure is that right now, she won't even look me in the eye.

Among the masses of those who refuse to acknowledge my presence is Beth. She seems irritated by my mere existence, often floating quickly past me on her way in and out of Loretta's office. I tell myself she's just distracted, stressed out by being so close to both war zones. But the grimace she makes whenever walking by my desk makes me feel like she knows about my treachery. And she believes I chose wrong.

The entire office is up in arms. Jade found out the head of Art was seated at Loretta's table at the ASME Awards and that Daniel was the one who talked her into doing the video series, so she refuses to meet with either of them face-to-face. For a week and a half, nothing gets done. Stories go up on the site at half speed because editors have to wait for days for their design requests to go through. Prod has also become as intimate as a small council meeting. Our numbers are dwindling so much that I couldn't help but suspect something's gone awry.

So I slip up and check Loretta's email again. Somehow, committing a crime is way easier the second time around—like how stealing lip gloss from CVS is less scary when you know the alarm won't go off the second you walk out the door.

According to my research, the Print team has been having a lot of trouble getting Zendaya's people on the phone. They haven't yet scheduled a day for the cover shoot. The Entertainment editor claims her publicist won't nail down a time and day to conduct the interview. The entire Print staff is unraveling. We are now entering crunch time, and if we don't shoot this cover ASAP, we won't be able to go to print in time.

But somehow, Loretta remains unfazed. She's still riding off her victory over Jade. The stench of her arrogance is difficult to ignore, like cheap perfume.

Last Wednesday, Beth decided she'd had enough. She called a cease-fire between L and J, forcing both of them to come to the table and negotiate. I gave her a prime team meeting spot: an hour in the afternoon, right before Loretta's secret blackout period. She still attends those, every week, without fail.

The meeting was supposed to take place in neutral territory: the Shifter-Pearce cafeteria. This was a genius tactic on Beth's part—the people moving in and out of the lunchroom meant there would be many, many witnesses. That removed the possibility of extraneous screaming and tantrum-throwing. Although it did increase the odds of an unsavory food fight.

Loretta begrudgingly agreed to attend, after much

prodding from Beth. I've noticed that Beth is pretty much the only person Loretta will listen to at this point. Beth and Sarah appear to be the only two souls on earth whose opinions matter to Loretta. This gives Beth tremendous power.

I walked Loretta over to the meeting at 3:59 p.m. on the dot. We took our places at a quiet, sunny corner table. A maintenance worker whistled as he walked by. I could hear the audible crunching of a woman eating Lay's potato chips at a nearby countertop.

Five minutes went by. Then ten. Fifteen.

Loretta went from looking mildly annoyed to majorly pissed. After about thirty minutes, she stood up and stormed away without a word. Beth and I exchanged our first look in over a week. It's a face of grave concern. I stirred nervously in my seat.

Jade *stood Loretta up.*

This can only mean one thing: Something big is in the works. Has to be. Otherwise, Jade wouldn't risk threatening Loretta like this. It's almost as if she's daring her to get sloppy and make a wrong move.

Loretta responds by doubling down on Print's efforts.

Ever since the failed peace negotiation, spearheaded by Beth (who has now seemingly given up on getting the two to break bread), Loretta has been presenting me with more and more seemingly impossible, technologically savvy tasks.

We're livestreaming at least once a day. Loretta wants *Vinyl* readers to see how pitch meetings work (or rather, fake, televised pitch meetings that are basically *SNL* skits). She asks me to film her walking down the hallway on her way to off-sites and pretending to eat her lunch. I'm surprised she hasn't had me follow her into the bathroom to record her taking a shit! The only two places that are decidedly off the record are her smoke breaks and internal meetings—especially her blackout dates. Everything else has basically become a reality show. The only silver lining is that every time I'm featured in her stories, *NoorYorkCity* gets a shit ton of traffic. I think I'm up to forty thousand followers now. I guess there really is no such thing as bad press.

Loretta's efforts aren't in vain. I've noticed her social numbers have gone way up. She's almost at one hundred and fifty thousand followers, which is still a far cry from Jade's five hundred thousand (as she keeps reminding me) but basically proves Daniel's strategy is working. Although he's been sort of on me about the "composition" of her clips. "Shish," he keeps complaining. "You need to help her find her light." He reminds me of an angry little British colonialist cartoon.

And then all hell breaks loose on a mid-October afternoon.

It's that time of year in New York City right before daylight savings turns back the clock. The days are growing desperately shorter. The sky lingers a little darker; people drift in and out of the streets with a little less energy and acting a lot more somber than they were at the start of the season.

Vinyl Digital is fully at the helm of Halloween content planning. Saffron is shooting Halloween-inspired beauty clips almost every day—DIY looks for Marianne Williamson, a hilarious red-tape look inspired by the Mueller Report, Kim Kardashian studying to be a lawyer. Crystal also commissioned a phenomenal think piece about why slutty Halloween costume sources like Yandy and Spirit Halloween don't sell enough options for fat women. All women should have the right to sexualize costumes like Dora the Explorer and Ruth Bader Ginsburg. Spooky season has led to considerably heightened morale.

But Loretta's ASME chess move is no secret. She keeps the award on display, right at the front of her desk, so it's impossible to miss. It's so incredibly gauche.

What happens is this: Loretta is stuck in an hour-long meeting with Art (I know from experience to leave some leeway for her other appointments), which I decide is an opportunity to go hang by Saffron's desk and congratulate the whole team on their wins. I get caught up in a conversation with Lola about South Street Seaport and SPP Tower.

"I just hate coming to this neighborhood each day and passing so many Starbucks," she complains. "It makes me sick. What happened to small businesses? To locally roasted beans? This area of Lower Manhattan is so gentrified, you'd forget it was built by immigrants who passed through Ellis Island with nothing in their pockets but big dreams. Now what's left? Condos and Sweetgreens. When is SPP going to wake up and smell the stink of dirty capitalism? Why don't we move shop to some place a little less touched by the middle class, like Bed-Stuy?" She rolls her eyes and continues scrolling through TikTok.

"But wouldn't SPP moving to Bed-Stuy, in fact, *contribute* to the gentrification?"

Lola looks up for a second. She nods, mulling over my words. "Right on," she says.

Our conversation is interrupted by a hoarse shriek. It's Seb, the Entertainment editor.

"It's up, you guys! It's up!" He claps with excitement. The entire cluster breaks out into applause. I push through the rest of the bodies to catch a glimpse of the action. The second I'm close enough to the computer screen, I stop dead in my tracks.

This is *not* happening.

Without saying a word to anyone, I bolt straight back to my desk. Saffron trails behind me.

"What's going on?" they ask, confused. I don't bother pausing to answer.

I reach my desk. As I suspected, Loretta is still meeting with Art. She hasn't seen it yet, but in about fifteen minutes, she will. I solemnly take my post.

I've hardly been sitting for more than a few seconds when both Beth and Daniel come running toward me.

"Have you seen this?" Beth points frantically at her phone. I nod.

"This is a fucking PR nightmare," Daniel says. "And the worst part is—she actually looks *hot*. And not just to the heteros. How am I going to explain this away? Just say that the two most important departments at *Vinyl* are in some sort of pissing contest?"

I sort of shrug. "It's not like I have any real power here, Daniel."

If only he knew the truth.

The three of us sit outside Loretta's office, sharing deafening silence, as if waiting for a hurricane to hit or a bomb to detonate. Instead, all we can hear is Loretta laughing about foliage puns and ad layouts. I breathe out a quick sigh of relief. She clearly hasn't seen it yet.

Daniel taps his foot anxiously. Saffron clears their throat. We collectively jump, having forgotten they were even here.

"Let me see it again," they whisper to me. I pull it up in a new window and turn over the laptop to them. I can't bear to look.

GEN Z-ENDAYA & the Followers
of Tomorrow's Leaders

Below the headline there's a gorgeous photograph of Zendaya posing by the Gowanus Canal, disposal bins and graffiti painting the background like a vignette. The pictures were taken by Ryan McGinley and probably cost a small fortune. But below the headline, above the key image, sits the dynamite that will be used as a catalyst to burn Print to the ground.

As told to Jade Aki.

"Focking bloody 'ell," Daniel mutters to himself.

I turn to Saffron and widen my eyes, willing them to read my mind. I wish we could run to the beauty closet to debrief, but Loretta could be out of her meeting at any minute. I'm not allowed to leave my desk.

"Did you know about this?" I whisper.

"No, Seb and Jade have been keeping this airtight," they whisper back. "I just knew they had someone big. Why are we whispering?"

"Because Z was supposed to be *our* December cover star!"

"I know! Kelsea told everyone, like, a couple weeks ago."

"*What?!*" I ask, shocked. "Why didn't you say anything?"

"I honestly forget," they say. "You know I don't care about celebrity stuff. What's the big deal, anyway?"

"The big deal, Saffron, is that this will go one of two ways," I explain furiously. "Zendaya will either refuse to do the cover now, because why would she offer *two* exclusive interviews to *Vinyl* in the same fucking month? Or, let's say she doesn't back out, Loretta will still come off looking like an idiot for letting Jade beat her to the scoop. It'll be yesterday's news."

"We can all hear you," Beth says sharply. I shut the fuck up and sink into my seat.

This is all my fault. I knew picking a side of this fight wouldn't be easy, but I guess I just didn't expect it to feel so shitty. Was this really the answer? Print is going to have to scramble to find someone big for their holiday issue. They'll have to spend so much more money. SPP won't be happy. This was a dirty, dirty move.

Plus, there's one question swimming around in my mind that keeps popping to the surface. One even more terrifying than the question of what Print will do now.

How will Loretta retaliate?

Suddenly, a cry rings out from the other side of Loretta's frosted-glass door. We all grimace.

"I think she's seen it," Beth says. "Who wants to go first?"

Before any of us gets a chance to answer her, Loretta sticks her head out from behind the door. Her red lipstick is smudged. She taps the glass manically with her fingers.

"Noora, I need you to move all my meetings for the rest of the day and call an all-hands huddle with Print. Beth, Daniel, get in here." She looks up at Saffron for a second and snarls. "Do I know you?"

Saffron shakes their head and bolts. Probably best not to engage.

"And love," she says, before slamming the door. "Do. Not. Move. An. Inch."

I sit still, contemplating my fate. Loretta is going to try to find out who spilled the beans about Zendaya. If she ruffles the right feathers, she might find out it was me. If she has Cal go through my computer history, she might even be able to find out I went through her email. I'll be fired on the spot. Not only would I disappoint Loretta, my parents, and Leila—who is literally relying on me to bring in an income right now—but I'd really be letting down myself. Writing has always been the only thing I've ever wanted to do. It's basically the only God I believe in.

I was four years old on 9/11, just starting kindergarten. I had Ms. Sheila for a homeroom teacher, and my parents had bought me a *Powerpuff Girls* magenta backpack in a desperate attempt to help me fit in with my peers. The ride from Crown Heights to the Upper West Side took over an hour, without traffic. There were many bumps along the way, and I often threw up my breakfast immediately once I arrived at class. The day the towers collapsed, I was the last kid to be picked up. Public transit was shut down. I had to walk home—through the Central Park, down Fifth Avenue, across the bridge. I remember clutching my baba's hand and watching as the smoke swallowed the sky. From afar, it was beautiful, peaceful.

Two things changed that day: how others see me, and how I see myself. No one ever treated me or my family the same way again, even if it hasn't always been overt. We went from being American immigrants to foreign-born intruders. A first-grader asked me whose side I was on during recess. A stranger spit in my father's face while we were crossing the street on my way to the Ninety-Second Street Y.

And I was different too. Paranoid, afraid. Everything felt frightening to me. I developed phobias of frivolous activities. Creaking floorboards became the telltale signs of an axe murderer. *Good-bye* was just another famous last word. I could no longer sleep, so instead I read—every night, in the dark, until it killed my eyesight so much, I had to get glasses. I read tales of faraway galaxies and lighthearted rom-coms with flawed but loveable protagonists. And I read magazines—*Vinyl, Teen Vogue, Seventeen, Nylon.* I read everything I could get my hands on. Words became my allies. Writing became a trusted friend.

I look up at the clock—it's been hours since Loretta turned her office into a war room. I'll probably have to stay late, past eight or nine, to type up notes and tidy the office. Outside the ceiling-to-floor windows of the SPP Tower, it starts to pour. At first, the sound of an October shower calms my running mind and feeds the nostalgia I've indulged for the past hour. But the trickling sound of raindrops against the shatterproof glass begins to place whatever weight it took off my shoulders and place it back onto my bladder. I cross and uncross my legs. The last time I went to the bathroom was this morning—how is that even possible? And why did I drink so much coffee after getting to work?

I'm just going to run to the all-genders' bathroom real quick. It will be quick and painless. No one will even know I was gone.

"Noora?" Loretta calls from behind her office door. "Sarah's bringing everyone dinner. Can you wait till she arrives then escort her up? Thanks, sweetie."

I sit very, very still, focusing every ounce of energy in my body and soul into not peeing. My mind begins to meditate. I focus on my breathing—in and out, as if I'm delivering a baby.

The phone rings, breaking my concentration. I feel my entire body clench then release. My facial muscles begin to relax, as they usually do post-orgasm. Then I feel wet.

Loretta pokes her head out of the door.

"That's her," she says, pointing to the phone still ringing off the hook. "Why aren't you answering?"

Her nose curls up as she sniffs the air around her. I scoot the lower half of my body under my desk.

"Is it just me, or does it smell like *urine* in here?"

Chapter Thirteen

*The very next morning, I march up to Jade's office and con-*front Kelsea at her desk. She hasn't been responding to my texts, Google messages, or Instagram DMs. Yes, I know. I'm borderline stalking her. But I can't help it—she's ghosting me, and I need answers, stat.

"What the fuck was that?" I ask, announcing my arrival.

She looks up from the email she's typing and breaks out into an obnoxiously cheerful smile. Her blond ringlets have been styled into two sections with '90s-era butterfly clips, and she's wearing a light-pink IRO leather jacket paired with medium-wash skinny jeans.

I look down at my own Dr. Martens creepers, velour maxi skirt, and leather blazer. She looks like the Baby Spice to my Morticia Addams.

"Oh, hey there, girlie!" she says, infantilizing me. I hate being treated like an eight-year-old pageant contestant. "Not sure I know what you're referring to."

I grab the collar of her white Brandy Melville crop top and pull her closer to me so she can smell the cold brew on my breath.

"Marty's. In fifteen minutes." I look her up and down, doing my best impression of a mobster. "Or else."

She gulps. I turn around and head to Marty's.

Founded in 1965, Marty's is a dive bar around the corner from the SPP Tower that's practically an institution in its own right. The bars are made of straight-grained, deep-red, glossy mahogany, and the booths are upholstered in velvet and barred off from the rest of the crowd. Slanted walls are lined with framed photographs of famous patrons, like Woody Allen (vom) and Alex Rodriguez. The air smells of peppermint and turpentine, and my favorite bartender, Andy, can make an old-fashioned that's been kissed by Lucifer himself.

At 9:30 a.m., each barstool seat is empty—save for the friendly neighborhood drunk, Phyllis, who's actually wrapping up a late night out. Every early morning can be somebody else's late night, depending on how you look at it.

Kelsea strolls in a couple minutes late. I let out a hiss as she walks through the doors and takes a seat next to me at the bar. Phyllis opens her eyes.

"A little early for this, isn't it?" Kelsea says.

I sip my coffee. "Why did you use that information to sabotage the Print team?" I decide to cut through the bullshit and get straight to the point. "You said you wanted what's best for the magazine. This will *destroy* the magazine! You're not looking out for *Vinyl*—you're looking out for Jade. You just wanted to target Loretta but hurt the entire team in the process!"

Kelsea bats her eyes innocently. I roll mine.

"Okay, whoa," she says. "First off, you seriously need to chill. Second, you knew exactly what you were getting into. And third, this *is* good for *Vinyl*. Loretta is an unreliable leader who is out of touch with our readership. She is narcissistic and egotistical and cares more about her own celebrity than the future of this brand."

She's dead wrong. I had no idea this was coming or what she'd do with the intel. Or did I? I guess, deep down, some teeny, tiny, fucked-up part of me subconsciously hoped she'd pull something like this. But nothing this bad. I thought she'd just, like, plant some heinous rumor about Loretta's temper to Zendaya's agent or mess up the sample sizes for her cover shoot. Not get the cover canceled altogether.

She looks up at Andy and flashes him her professionally bleached white teeth.

"Can I get a glass of fresh-pressed green juice, *por favor*?"

He shakes his head, but she doesn't seem to notice.

"Look, SPP cares about one thing and one thing only: P&L," she tells me.

"What is that? Something to do with clicks?"

"No. Well, yeah, sort of. P&L stands for profit and loss, aka, making money. The second the higher-ups notice a sizeable loss in profit margins, Loretta's in trouble. The holiday issue is going to tank for Print, but with this Zendaya profile, Digital's clicks are going to be through the roof. That means advertisers will be interested and SPP will be impressed. They'll take note because they don't listen to anything but money and nothing talks louder than numbers. Loretta will be out, and Jade will be in."

I stare blankly at Kelsea. This plan is deliberately thought out. It's so intricate, so deliciously evil.

What did she say her sign was again?

"I want to help Jade—I think what Loretta did to her is majorly fucked up—but I won't help you destroy Print," I tell her. "This magazine *means* something to me, Kelsea. This isn't a game for me."

"But it is, isn't it?" Giddy, she claps her hands. "Because the thing is, babe, if you don't keep spying for us, I'm going to go to Beth and tell her what you did. And you'll lose your job. Sounds like the end of a game well-played to me, don't you think?"

"You'll be implicating yourself, idiot," I say. "You set me up."

Kelsea pouts her lips, giving me a look of pity. I want to smack it off her face.

"It'll be an anonymous tip. You won't be able to prove I put you up to it."

"I have the Slacks. The texts."

"No, you don't. You wiped everything because you were nervous about getting caught."

Fuck. She's right. I did do that.

"I took screenshots," I fib.

Kelsea laughs.

"No," she says. "You didn't. You're bluffing, it's so obvious. Come on, Noora. It'll be your word against mine. And who is Beth going to believe: Jade's assistant of over a year, whom she adores? Or Loretta's newly minted lackey who isn't even that good at her job?"

I choke on my sip of coffee, snorting brown liquid out of my nose and all over the countertop. Kelsea uses her napkin to dab at her jacket. She must sense my desperation in some way, know I need the money so I'm not willing to walk away.

This bitch actually set me up. I'm trapped.

"So, essentially, you're using me to deliver clickbait," I surmise.

"Now you're getting it!" She salutes me with her water. "Just pretend you're the brown Nancy Drew, sniffing out the scoop."

With that, Kelsea gets off her stool and walks back out the door. Just as she leaves, Andy resurfaces, holding a glass.

"I couldn't find green pressed whatever, but I got orange juice," he tells me.

I thank him and chug the OJ then use Loretta's corporate card to cover the check. I think she can afford it.

When I arrive back at the office, I'm surprised to find Loretta is already in. I'm even more confused to discover there are handymen in tow, there to assemble a working padlock on her office door.

"Uh, hi." The one on the left is *really* cute and has pecs the size of my head. Damn, I have *got* to stop objectifying the men in this office.

"Noora? Is that you?" I hear a muffled voice from behind the airtight, sealed door. "It's okay, boys. Let her in."

She smiles upon seeing me, taking my hands in hers. Her palms are cold. They feel lifeless, as if all the blood has been drained out and replaced with some sort of artificial plasma.

"We can trust her."

I walk into Loretta's office to find she's seemingly turned it into a bunker overnight. There are rotating cameras set up all over the room, facing every which way. A new vault-like safe has been propped up beneath her desk, with an impressive-looking combination keypad. Blackout blinds have been installed on all the windows. Does she really think Jade is going to send a drone to spy on her?

Actually, don't answer that.

"What's all this?" I ask, taking a seat. I already know the answer, of course, but always good to verbally acknowledge when someone's gone full-blown paranoid.

"I'm taking extra security measures, sweetheart," she says. "From now on, this office will be our headquarters. Entry will be inner circle only. Capisce?"

I gulp, looking around. What's that blinking red light coming from the closet against the wall by the door? It looks like a hanger, and yet, the handle appears to be aimed at her desk. Is that a bug? Are we being *recorded*?!

"Noora, I'm going to tell you something, but you must keep it solely between us," she begins. I nod. "The December issue is hereby *canceled*."

"What does that mean?" I ask. "Canceled, as in, cancel culture? Like, Notes app apology for being racist, canceled? Or, like, not being produced anymore, canceled?"

"I frankly have no idea what you just said," she says, waving off my questions. "But given the current scandal, we've decided to allocate the funds we were going to use for the holiday issue toward something even better."

Loretta flaps her arms around, hardly able to control her enthusiasm. I'm growing more and more concerned.

"We're throwing an Experiences event! For the first week of November. And we're hoping it'll go viral! Even more so than that silly Zendaya story."

"But that's only two weeks away." I think about all the time, effort, and money that would have to go into *really* pulling this off. "Who's running point on this?"

"I am." She glances at the security camera pointed directly at us then lowers her voice to a whisper, as if we're being watched. "Well, *we* are. Actually, make that just you."

Chapter Fourteen

Hold up—do you guys even **know** *what an "Experiences"* event is?

Okay, stay with me for a second. Before the age of social media, events like these never could have existed. Corporate soirees were meant to be private and elitist, behind-closed-doors galas with a black-tie guest list at a five-star restaurant or club. You wouldn't even know they had transpired if not for the glossy pages of society tabloids, the Overheard section of *New York Magazine*. None of that was accidental. Publishing was kept hush-hush with the purest of intentions: to invite envy and inspire intrigue. Curiosity used to be a powerful form of currency, back when knowledge was scarce, and thus, powerful.

Today, that intel is readily available and practically worthless. The internet has rendered access equitable. Everyone has access to the answer to any question at any time, at the tips of their fingers. Social media means we can measure intrigue, and the only way we're able to maintain the attraction is by constantly stimulating the mind. It's voyeurism at its peak. It's performative. Posting on Instagram is essentially exhibitionism without having to take your clothes off. Although, you're welcome to do that too.

Think of Refinery29's 29Rooms. Or the Mu[...]
Cream. Think of a fucking Yayoi Kusama ex[...]
requires tickets bought months in advance and c[...]
around the corner.

What do these events all have in common? They're
"experiential" and meant for the masses. Brands don't throw
Experiences events for the *crème de la societé*. It doesn't matter
who you shake hands with in the foyer or play footsie with
under the table. In fact, what you actually do there doesn't
quite matter at all. The purpose lies in the aftermath—how
it looks the next day on your phone, tablet, or laptop screen.
No one cares if an Experiences event is a "fun time." The
truth is, most include being herded around like cattle, forced
to move from room to room on a tight schedule, with only
a few minutes in between each to snap a picture or two. As
long as it presents as the time of your life, nobody gives a
shit—especially brands.

When Loretta tells me that I only have two weeks to
put together a showstopping Experiences event that will—
must—rival *Vinyl*'s holiday issue in success and piss Jade off
enough that she'll throw up her arms and retreat, I don't
panic. Instead, I allow Shabnam to take over. She knows how
to handle situations like these.

Me? If I were to take the reins, my anxiety wouldn't even
let me come into work the next day.

I make a list of everything we need—an incredible venue,
a sought-after guest list of influencers and NYC cool girls,
and a showstopping "Experience" idea. Dickhead Daniel can
help me with the first two items on my agenda, but I'll have
to come up with the latter on my own. Loretta has made it
clear she wants the mood to ignite "holiday magic." I just
hope it doesn't come out like a DIY middle school science
fair project gone rogue.

During week one, Daniel and I put together a budget and deck of all our venue options. We sift through everything from warehouses in Bushwick to showrooms on Spring Street. The location needs to feel adaptable, so that we're able to pop up quickly—redoing the space, transforming it into a fantasy world—and then strip it back down to whatever it was before. We finally land on the House of Yes, a psychedelic nightclub right off Wyckoff Avenue that used to be an ice warehouse and is now home to cabaret, exotic dancers, disco queens, and circus freaks. Walking into House of Yes is like stepping through a time portal back to the age of extravagance and grandeur. Except, like, much queerer. It's a weird and wonderful paradise and a perfect fit for *Vinyl*.

The guest list is also surprisingly easy to collect. I spend my nights in Leila's apartment scrolling through Instagram and DMing my favorite DJs and activists. (Okay, fine. Leila helps me too.) I invite all of New York's "it girls," sending so many messages that my thumbs turn red and my mind goes numb. But my plan works—within seventy-two hours, I have over a hundred RSVPs, not including SPP staff. I might *actually* be able to pull this off.

But now comes the most challenging part, which could be the undoing of all this hard work: the actual experience. I know anything with the potential to go viral must have one overarching quality: the ability to be photographed well. Our event can't just look *good* in pictures—it has to look positively *mind-blowing* on Instagram. Otherwise, people won't feel compelled to buy tickets for the week it's open in November, and we won't turn a profit. Giving up our holiday issue will have been for nothing. SPP will lose money. Loretta will get fired, and it will be all my fault.

Yes, I'm spiraling.

"I don't really get whose side you're on anymore," Saffron tells me.

We're sitting in the beauty closet, brainstorming. They keep clicking their pen and it's making the most irritating clacking noise.

"I'm not on Loretta or Jade's side—they've both done really shitty things."

It's true. Loretta taking all the credit for Jade's work was wack, but Jade stealing Print's holiday cover star was, in my humble opinion, a totally different realm of fucked up. "I'm on *Vinyl's* side. I just want what's best for the reader, okay?"

They nod and continue clicking their pen. I'm about to ask them to please, for the love of God, stop, when their ballpoint suddenly flies across the room. I can see the light bulb turning on in Saffron's brain.

"I've got it!" they exclaim. "What if you set up an artificial snow machine to *literally* snow on guests? Obviously, it would be fake snow. Just so no one, like, slips and cracks their head open. But think about how *sick* that would look in pictures. And you can project images of mountaintops onto the walls, like Dan did for Serena in season one of *Gossip Girl.*"

Nice. I *always* appreciate a vintage CW reference. Their idea makes a lot of sense too. I start to get excited.

"We can serve fondue and spiked hot chocolate and cider and pass out furry blankets to all the guests. Maybe even rent out yurts for VIPs!" I squeal. "We can call it *Vinyl* Sleighs or whatever! Saffron, this could *actually* work."

Before getting too carried away, I take stock of all the moving parts. We'll have to order gallons of artificial snow from Michaels and figure out how to get it to fall from the ceiling in a way that looks natural, not tacky. We'll need to work with a caterer—maybe Lilia? Café Gitane?—on procuring fondue stations. I can't even *begin* to think about where I'll be able to find a yurt on such short notice. Who would have ever thought I'd need a *yurt guy*? And then, of course, we'll need someone to help us out with the electronics and projections. An engineer of some sort who can deal with the soundstage and lights and anything involving electrical wiring.

Gulp. I know exactly who to call.

The phone rings three times before Cal picks up. His voice sounds rough, hoarse even. As if he just woke up or is getting over a bad cold. I can practically hear his mischievous, toothy smile and see his dimples indenting in his cheeks, solely from his breathing on the other end of the line.

"I thought you'd never call. What's up, Little Light?"

"I need your help with something," I tell him.

He chuckles into the phone. "Of course you do. What can I do you for?"

The night of the event, I wear red, white, and green, in honor of Iran. Red for my people, the sacrifices they have made, all in the name of independence. White representing peace. And green symbolizing vitality, the color of nature, Nowruz: of a great spring, clean slate, and new beginning. And also because I look really fucking hot in green. I sewed the dress together myself, out of fabric swatches from different thrifted pieces, which I collected across three different boroughs. I wear my hair long and naturally curly. It cascades down my back and kisses my hips. My jewelry is bold and golden, like the plated armor of warriors. It's not lost on me that we're still at war.

But tonight, we drink, dance, and most importantly, post.

I decide to bring Leila as my date, for good luck and support. She dresses in a gorgeous leather jumpsuit, one that hugs her curves and makes her look like a young Donna Summer or Googoosh. She *totally* pulled through with the guest list, by the way. As of this week, we were still about thirty-five influencers, actors, models, and party guests away from our goal number of two hundred and fifty. She hit up her entire contact list, inviting everyone in her orbit—old clients, their friends, their enemies. Leila crossed so many lines considering her, uh, reason for being let go, but it worked. The house is packed, and Loretta is pleased. As we enter the venue, I squeeze Leila's hand. She squeezes back three times.

"I love you too," I tell her.

House of Yes looks like *Frozen*'s Elsa went *off.*

There's a light reflecting off the dance floor that makes the surface look glossed over, as if it's made of ice. Flakes of fluff, like cotton balls or the inside of a pillow, both fall from the ceiling and ricochet from the floor. There are tiny white tents, which look like teepees or the *Midsommar* commune, gated off by the right-side entrance. The bar is brewing pumpkin-spiced everything, and the smell of rum is diluting the sweaty, crowded air. And the wall projections? Cal absolutely nailed them. It looks like attendees are dancing on the inside of a kaleidoscope. Virtual snow tumbles down the sidelines like an avalanche. You can see the wind blowing from east to west. If I squint, I feel like I'm sitting in a ski chalet in Aspen or Zermatt. It's hard to believe it's all AI. That the part resembling the most potent displays of nature is actually generated by a computer.

An outdoor terrace nears the entrance that's been tented off for influencers to take photos of themselves, cloaked in faux-fur blankets, with the simulated snow pooling around them. By the time I arrive, there's a line out the door to "experience" *Vinyl's* winter wonderland. It's exactly how Saffron and I envisioned it—simultaneously still and buzzing with energy.

People are so busy taking photos that they're hardly talking to each other. *Perfect.*

I see Loretta and Sarah enter, fashionably late as always. Sarah is wearing a patent leather suit covered in zippers and platform oxfords. Her black pixie cut looks particularly spiky. She looks like an emo Polly Pocket. On her arm is Loretta, dressed in a floor-length, red satin gown with a mermaid tail. Her flaming hair has been blown out and brushed to the side, and her signature combat boots are peeking out from beneath the gown. We make eye contact, and she gives me a warm smile. It's almost as if she hasn't been texting me all day about "photo stations" or I didn't call her Uber here.

"We did it, darling!"

I subtly roll my eyes. Loretta has done nothing but give orders and assume Daniel and I will carry them out. To be fair, she wasn't wrong.

Sarah gives me a quick hug hello then goes to give Leila a firm handshake. Watching her wife approach her, Loretta suddenly becomes aware of Leila's presence.

"Is this your sister?" she asks.

"Pleasure." Leila extends her hand. Loretta looks at it as if scanning for ticks. She reluctantly takes it and gives it a strong shake, looking her directly in the eye and giving her that manic smile. Then, without another word, she grabs Sarah's arm and walks away. Leila lets out a slow whistle.

"What just *happened*?" Leila asks, bewildered. She looks visibly shaken, as if Loretta slapped her across the face.

"Ignore her," I say. "She's weird like that. Let's go mingle. I bet this room is just brimming with young creatives desperate to hire an in-touch-with-Gen-Z, woke, queer, Middle Eastern publicist."

Leila pretends to dab. In her silver lamé jumpsuit, she looks like she walked straight off a movie set. I beam with pride as we stroll around the event. That's *my* sister.

"Okay, let's go network!" she says.

I hate that word—*networking*. It seriously makes me cringe. Like forcing chemistry on a bad first date, I choose to believe that if the opportunity is a good fit, the conversation will flow freely. Just like it did with Saffron. There's nothing more juvenile than this coy game of chess, this back-and-forth, this verbal jousting of *I'll do something for you, but what can you do for me?*

Leila and I do the rounds, even stopping to take our picture and post it to our stories with the hashtag *#VinylSleighs*. The entire Print team has showed up for something that *isn't* a prod meeting for the first time maybe ever. Editors dripping in J. Mendel and vintage Chanel snowsuits, with dashing male models, whom I've definitely seen on Broadway billboards, on their arms. I feel way too uncool to be here, and yet, none of this would exist if it weren't for me.

I see Beth standing in the corner, checking her phone. I'm surprised she showed; I didn't peg her for a party mom. Our eyes meet and she raises her glass. I guess I finally did something right.

No one from Digital showed, of course. I begged Saffron to come, considering this entire thing wouldn't have happened if not for them. But they refused, citing that Jade had called a staff-wide strike of the event, calling it an opportunistic "spectacle." She has a point, but it's working. If it ain't broke, don't break it—right? Even though I think threatening to *fire* anyone who goes and takes a selfie in front of a mound of fake snow is a little extreme, I didn't argue.

The last thing I need is some sort of showdown between Print and Digital causing a scene and bringing in bad press.

"Will you come with me to the bathroom?" Leila asks. Then something else catches her attention. Or rather, someone. "Holy shit, who is that?"

I look up to see a man, clean-shaven, his dark skin glowing under the light of the projections. He's dressed in a straight-cut tuxedo, with a deep-maroon velvet bow tie that would look absolutely heinous on someone who didn't have the confidence to pull it off. The suited look is dressed down by a pair of fresh white sneakers.

I groan.

"That's Cal."

"Oh, my FUCKING God, Noora," she says, freaking out. "Are you serious? *That's* Cal?"

Before I can control what's happening, Leila has left my arm and is marching over to where he's standing, admiring his own handiwork.

"Hello, Gorgeous," she flirts. "Pleased to meet you. I'm Leila, Noora's sister. How come you haven't taken my sister out yet?"

"Leila!" I shout, catching up to her. Man, she moves fast. "I'm sorry about her, she was hit by a cab as a baby."

Cal's eyes are twinkling. Or is that just the artificial snow falling on his ridiculously long eyelashes?

"I'll leave you two to it."

With that, Leila disappears into the crowd. I look up shyly at Cal, hyperaware of the effect he has on me. I try channeling Shabnam, but she dissolves into the butterflies in my stomach, which honestly, feel more like moths. The kind that fucks up all your sweaters.

The song switches to "I'm Not the Only One" by Sam Smith. Cal extends his hand out to me.

"Should we dance?"

I follow him onto the floor, his hand shocking my fingers with an electrical pulse. He gives me a quick twirl, and we settle into a rhythm. I gently lay my head down on his shoulder and inhale. He smells of Old Spice and whiskey.

"Why didn't you ever text me again?" I find the courage to ask, pulling back from his embrace.

"Hey, now," he says, surprised. "If I remember correctly, you're the one who stood me up on a Saturday night."

Okay, fair.

"That's true," I admit. "But only because I was working. And you've been totally MIA ever since, but now you ask me to dance and are five seconds away from letting your hand wander down my spine and cup my ass. Seriously, what are we doing here?"

I can tell Cal doesn't get called out very often. He suddenly looks pale, as if the wind has been knocked out him.

"Look, if I'm being honest, I'm only looking for something casual right now," he says. "I don't know if I gave you the wrong impression, but I just have a lot of stuff going on in my life. It's not you, I just need to really focus on growing my business. I'm trying to launch a start-up, you see. I'm designing an app that will deliver medical marijuana right to your door, like a Postmates for Kush. It's going to be huge. And I just can't get distracted, so I'm not in a place to start something serious, you know?"

This speech. I've heard this before one too many times. The ol' *I'm only casually dating, so I don't want to be your partner, but I will hang out with you at times and places of my choosing, 100 percent on my own terms.* Every woman I've ever met has been in this position; let's call it an almost-relationship. And I know from experience that they're just not for me. No judgment, but I just end up getting hurt.

"Got it." I can't lie, I'm disappointed. "Then why ask me out in the first place?"

"Honestly? I don't know. There's something about you, Noora."

There they are. The moths. The fucking moths.

"From the first day I met you, all frazzled in that elevator, I could tell there's more to you than meets the eye. We're a lot alike, you and I. We're both driven by ambition. There's a darkness inside of you, isn't there, Little Light?"

He inches back toward me, slipping his hands around my waist. I can feel his breath on my cheek, hot and humid. His eyelashes tickle the nape of my neck. Then, he takes both of his hands, rough like a carpenter's, and holds my face, pulling me closer to him. I can feel my heart racing. My brain feels like the spinning pizza wheel on a broken Mac.

Cal is about to kiss me. Me and Cal are about to kiss. I'm going to *kiss* Cal! I close my eyes and lean in. The entire party somehow fades away, until all I can hear are the clicks of the influencers' camera rolls filling up until they're out of memory.

"YOU WHITE, CIS, MICROAGGRESSIVE, SECOND-WAVE, FAUX-FEMINIST, FUCKING LENA DUNHAM–LOVING, ANTIQUE-HOARDING BITCH."

Cal pulls away.

No! I was so close! So close!

Jade has entered the venue. She's dressed in a Fenty lingerie set and Vetements cargo pants. Among the highbrow, old-school Print elite, she looks like a total tourist. Her face is bright red. She's shaking her finger at Loretta while Loretta grips Sarah's hand, as if she's afraid she might get sucker punched. The entire party has formed a circle around them, like a Jake Paul boxing match.

What the fuck?

"You will pay for this. You hear me? You are *canceled*. Finished. I know it was you, Loretta. I KNOW IT WAS YOU!"

Jade turns around and storms out. The ring dissolves, and the DJ continues playing campy Christmas remixes.

"What just happened?"

"I'm not sure," Cal whispers to me. "Everyone's checking their phones."

I run over to Leila, who's holding my purse, and grab it out of her hands. Her face is stoic, dripping with concern.

"It's going to be okay," she says, rubbing my back. I nod, attempting to search Jade's name online. My hands shake and my heart rate starts to race as sweat pours down my back. I can't breathe.

Then everything gets a little fuzzy.

Chapter Fifteen

**BREAKING: Could This *Vinyl* Editor's Problematic
Tweets Be the Undoing of an Empire?**

Vinyl magazine is largely known in the publishing world for taking a progressive stance on social issues. After all, their editor in chief since the '80s has been bra-burner and advocate for LGBTQIA+ rights Loretta James. This magazine has tackled everything from universal healthcare to contraceptive desserts, so the unearthing of problematic, early-2000s tweets from the site's Digital director, influencer Jade Aki, is particularly shocking. Between the homophobic language and the racist commentary, everyone in media is wondering one thing: Could this *Vinyl* editor's tweets be the end of the magazine as we know it?

Let's take a step back. Who is Jade Aki? The 27-year-old digital prodigy began working for the magazine at just 22 years old after graduating from Bard College. Aki's first job in the industry was working as the executive assistant to current EIC, Loretta James. After contributing to the magazine and paying her dues at the bottom of the food chain for three years, Aki made the leap of a lifetime: from grabbing coffee to leading a digital revolution. Aki took over the website in late 2015 and helped James to transform the brand into the woke arena of VSCO girls turned women and allied men it is today. Aki also has a substantial presence on social media, drawing in thousands of followers with her street wear collaborations and commentary about mental health. In fact, Aki has been incredibly vocal about her activism, sharing information with her followers about climate change, immigration reform, and the criminal justice system. This editor has always been more than a shiny new pair of stilettos, which is why we were shocked to learn that the hype beast tweeted a series of highly problematic, offensive messages on a private account, nearly 12 years ago.

Trigger warning: The following tweets may be triggering for members of the Black and disabled communities, as well as for lower-income Americans and those struggling with disordered eating or mental illness.

Aki's tweets were emailed to *Delilah* around 11:00 p.m. last night by an anonymous source, who claimed to be a *Vinyl* employee. The source revealed they were concerned by Aki's judgment in such a senior role, given her lack of experience and problematic history.

Jade Aki @AkAttack69
could math class be anymore retarded if it TRIED?! Me thinks not
11:32 AM -28 Feb 2007

Jade Aki @AkAttack69
Max asked me if I was wearing faux fur and I was
like "What do I look like? A poor?" lol #richasfuck
9:16 PM -07 March 2007

Jade Aki @AkAttack69
Should I buzz my head? Or would that look
SoOoOoOo gay? No homo
3:12 PM -18 April 2007

Jade Aki @AkAttack69
My diet is anorexia
8:00 PM -04 May 2007

Jade Aki @AkAttack69
If I c 1 more juicy tracksuit I'll dead ass slit my
wrists fml
7:25 AM -26 June 2007

Jade Aki @AkAttack69
Deadass I kinda wanna do a tough mudder. But
will that count as brown face? LMAO
4:40 PM -02 July 2007

Jade Aki @AkAttack69
Kk I'll just say it: I h8 Korean food but I love how
they do my nails #notracistcuzimAZN
1:13 PM -10 August 2007

Safe to say 2007 was an unfortunate year for Aki, who
has previously been called everything from the next
Virgil Abloh to the Supreme prophet. Now, the world
certainly doesn't look how it did five years ago, let alone

a decade. Just because someone held certain beliefs in the past in no way means they haven't taken strides to reeducate themselves for the better since. How can we expect people to ask questions if they're scared they're going to be judged and dismissed? As a society, we have to create strides toward accountability, not cancel culture.

With that being said, we here at *Delilah* have only one word for Aki: yikes. If I were her, I'd haul ass to Saint Patrick's Cathedral and repent ASAP.

Delilah reached out to *Vinyl* for comment. The Shifter-Pearce Publishing brand's head of Communications, Daniel Dreyfus, released the following statement:

"Jade Aki has been a valued member of this company for five years. Under the exemplary direction of Loretta James, Aki has been instrumental in expanding *Vinyl*'s digital coverage, reaching traffic goals, increasing monthly KPIs, selling brand ad space, and more. We have spoken to Aki personally, and she has assured us these tweets have all been doctored. There is no record of Aki ever having tweeted these comments in Twitter's archives. Save for these screenshots, no further proof of such commentary exists. We stand by Aki's claims 100%. That said, SPP is launching our own internal investigation and will react according to the results. Our company's mission statement is inclusionary and does not tolerate bigotry, racism, homophobia, xenophobia, or classicism in any way, shape, or form."

Aki herself refused to comment.

So it looks like SPP is choosing to stand by their prized social justice warrior. And we can't say we blame them: The decades-old publishing house has come under fire lately for a lot of backward practices. They've been accused of everything from underpaying freelancers to refusing to use size-inclusive and transgender models. *Vinyl* was the sole progressive star in SPP's portfolio.

Delilah has reached out to Twitter for comment and the social networking company confirmed that Aki did register the user account AkAttack69 from 2007–2009.

UPDATE: While some readers are banding together and demanding full accountability from Aki, acknowledging the racist, classist, and homophobic nature of her tweets, along with a detailed account of how she plans to educate herself and make reparations to the communities she's harmed, others are simply demanding her resignation. "As a person of color and a champion of marginalized narratives, I expected better," one Twitter user wrote. "I acknowledge that people can change, grow, and learn from their mistakes, but should they be put in a position of power and leadership? Probably not." Others were quick to point out that many of those urging readers to forgive Aki for her past indiscretions were not people directly impacted by her tweets. "If you're a straight, cis, upper class white man or woman, please refrain from commenting on this situation," another user wrote. "This isn't your cross to bear."

It took less than an hour of this news breaking for the hashtag #AreYouAKIddingMe to begin trending on Twitter. Readers reactions range from less than thrilled to full-on furious. Many are calling for Aki's immediate dismissal from *Vinyl* Digital. Others are demanding a written apology from Aki, *Vinyl*, and the entirety of SPP, as well initiatives taken to hire a diversity council and inclusion officer on staff. The majority are calling for her cancellation. But consider this:

Just one month ago, Loretta James accepted the ASME Award for reported journalism for a groundbreaking feature that blew the whistle on the music streaming industry and singlehandedly led to an investigation into the rights and resources of recording artists. *Vinyl* magazine continues to do excellent investigative work. Should we give Aki the benefit of the doubt, allowing her to apologize before roasting her on a stick? Look at the bigger picture before jumping off a cliff to join the movements of the masses? Think free thought, led by the mind, not the mouth. And for the love of God, don't allow a single institution to suffer entirely for the sins of one worshipper, no matter how loud her voice or salient her prayers may be. Amen.

Chapter Sixteen

I didn't **mean** *to have a minor meltdown at* **Vinyl** *Sleighs.*
Maybe if I had stuck to water instead of downing three consecutive hard ciders, things could have gone differently. But
that's neither here nor there. All I know is that one second, I
was reading the headline of the *Delilah* article, and the next,
Leila was slapping me across the face and pouring ice cubes
down the front of my dress.

"Snap out of it!" she commanded.

But it was too late—following Jade's violent outburst, the
entire party sort of disbanded. It was as if my Experiences
event had suddenly transformed from a winter wonderland
into "can give you gonorrhea?" and everyone was afraid to
make contact. Loretta was quickly escorted out of the back
entrance of the building by Sarah and disappeared into the
night. I watched lifelessly as attendees quickly deleted the
pictures they'd snapped from the highlights of their stories. I
stayed put while guests evacuated. I didn't dare move while
the cleanup crew moved in or even after the lights went out.
It was as if my body had been mummified, frozen solid from
the shock. Leila stood by through most of it until even she
got too tired and went to join Willow at NO BAR.

It felt like an episode of *Black Mirror*. Somehow, I made

it back from Brooklyn, across the Williamsburg Bridge and into my bed just as the sun begun to rise. I slept until 3:00 in the afternoon the following day, dreaming of Jade's bright-red face and her perfectly manicured fist. When my body finally shakes awake after reliving the previous night's shock over and over again for eight consecutive hours, I reluctantly check my phone.

Ten missed calls. Six voicemails. Forty-two unread texts. *Fuck.*

Daniel called a few times and a left a message asking if I had heard from Loretta or any reporters. He urged me not to comment on the developing story and to wait for the company response that he and SPP's board of directors were working on formulating. *Don't chew with your mouth open, Shish*, his message said. What an *arsehole*.

Delete.

I also have missed calls from Saffron and Kelsea but nothing from Loretta. Odd. I check my texts, Slacks, Google messages, and Instagram DMs. Nada. Did Jade successfully kill her?

When I open my email, I let out a silent yelp.

Sure enough, around seven different reporters from a diverse range of outlets are in my inbox asking if I'd be willing to comment, on or off the record. The Cut even offers me a couple hundred bucks to pen an op-ed about the evening. I briefly consider it then remember the promise I made Leila about keeping my job—a promise that has definitely ended up being more trouble than it's worth.

I check the news coverage from last night. Unsurprisingly, the scandal has completely overshadowed the success of the event. The internet is pissed, the majority of users demanding Jade's removal and an immediate written apology. Several dozen new troll accounts calling Jade an edit*whore* and worse have begun scamming *Vinyl*'s Instagram comments. I see Jade has disabled her own comments—or more likely, Kelsea has disabled them for her. She's also lost thousands of followers, including Hillary Clinton and Lizzo. I guess the truth really does hurt.

I stay nestled on Leila's couch the rest of the day, scared to leave the apartment. Suddenly, basic actions like chewing or getting up to pee feel like they require too much energy. I can't even bring myself to call Saffron or Cal back. Yes, Cal. He called and left a brief message.

"Last night meant something to me, Little Light. Call me."

The funny part is, I can't even bring myself to care.

I think back to that first day in Loretta's office, when she spoke of war. I picture the desperation in her eyes and ask myself why I didn't see that she'd be willing to do anything, whatever it took to hold on to her seat at the table. In trying to protect the magazine and do what's right, I accidentally made everything ten times worse. I exacerbated the situation. By trying to stay neutral, I had somehow played both sides.

Did Jade *actually* tweet those fucked-up things? Maybe. Honestly, I wouldn't put it past Loretta to ask a lackey to plant those comments somewhere in order to ruin her reputation, seek revenge over the holiday issue, and largely, win the war. But she couldn't have done it on her own. Loretta is many things, but technologically savvy she is not. There's no way this was her idea. No, this had to come from someone else's twisted, mangled brain.

On Monday morning, I dress in black. A thick, lace cape and laced-up thrifted granny boots, in honor of Jade's funeral. And, like any dearly departed, I assume she won't show up to haunt her mourners. But still, I choose to honor her in this way. Or rather, honor the magazine I coveted for so many years, which ended up looking more like a Marilyn Minter photograph: a thoughtful vignette from afar, but meaningless up close. Part of me wishes I never got near enough to see it, that I had just remained blissfully ignorant to the mess that is media.

By the way, I still haven't heard from Loretta since the incident. This is highly unlike her. I usually can't last an hour without being pinged to add something to the calendar or answer a simple question. I'm becoming increasingly concerned.

Manhattan mornings are dark and eerie in early November. The trees that line South Street Seaport look vacant, like hollowed-out skeletal remains. All the café chairs have been shuffled indoors, and the park benches sit unoccupied and sullen. On this particular morning, every sign I pass presents itself like a bad omen. A train delay because of a sick passenger. The sight of a couple city rats devouring what's left of yesterday's unconsumed dim sum. Even the tall spine of the Empire State Building, peeking its head above the clouds at a distance, feels uncalled for and cruel. Just another reminder of how small I am. How small we all are.

I skipped updating *NoorYorkCity* last night. When I opened the account, I was spammed by messages and bot accounts, DMing me articles and tweets about *Vinyl* and Jade. The influx of information was so overwhelming that I grew too anxious and had to momentarily delete the app. I hate the term *self-care*, but honestly, I was in desperate need of a social and spiritual cleanse.

As I walk through SPP's revolving door, a chill runs through my entire body. I look up to meet Superman's eyes, but he turns away. Is it because he heard about what happened on Saturday night, the disaster of an event I planned? Or have I grown as paranoid as Loretta?

The entire office feels deserted. It's not just the Print desks that are empty today—most of Digital doesn't show up until 10:30, even 11:00 a.m. When they do, their eyes are red. Everyone looks as if they've been up all night crying. That, or stoned. It's most likely a little bit of both.

Loretta finally calls to let me know she's taking an important off-site meeting and that she needs me to reschedule all her appointments for the rest of the day. She says nothing about the event, and I don't mention Jade, the article, or the tweets. It's just business as usual. Although nothing is as usual these days.

I leave my desk to walk over to Beth's office and let her know Loretta will be off campus for the day. As I turn the corner, I'm shocked to see Jade sneaking into the office.

She's wearing tiny sunglasses that barely shield her eyes, and a Madhappy sweat suit that basically looks like a wearable Snuggie with multiple holes. Her stick-straight black hair has been pulled into a messy bun, and her already tiny body appears to be shrinking with every step. I offer her a warm, consoling smile. She scoffs and runs into her office. Upon hearing the door slam, Kelsea looks up from her monitor and chases after her.

When I was little, I used to count the people who disliked me like sheep. I'd ruminate over each blank stare, obsess over every obsolete whisper. My maman scolded me for my behavior. She told me I mustn't be so desperate to please, to be liked. She begged me to lead instead of mindlessly follow. But I was determined to blend, to fit in as much as humanly possible.

I think that's typical of the immigrant experience, the moral conundrum of being born first-generation American. You're always so hyperaware of your "otherness," of the ways you stand out. What makes you an individual innately becomes your greatest weakness, not a strength. *Unique* becomes a dirty word. People-pleasing is a product of that struggle. My anxiety casts a glaze over the fine finish. I can't help but allow my mind to be preoccupied with those who might hold vendettas against my throat like razor blades. I toss and turn, fixating on how to get each and every foe on my side.

Jade is no different. Even in the aftermath of something so innately horrible, I can't help but want her to like me. Maybe it's the Middle Eastern in me. Or the Gemini.

Frazzled, I relay the message to Beth by leaving a scribbled, half-hearted note on her desk. She skipped out on work today too. Hm. Was Monday optional this week? I had no idea healing from company-wide heartbreak was a reason to call in sick.

As I walk back to my desk, I'm distracted by a muffled whimper. I look around the bullpen. Every single Print desk is empty. Only Alex, Crystal, and Gwen from Social have come in. I glance down at my phone. It's almost noon—where the fuck is everybody? And more importantly, where is that sound coming from?

I follow the whimpering like bread crumbs; they lead back to the beauty closet. When I get closer, the whimpering transforms into straight sobs. I go to fumble with the knob but discover that whoever's inside knew enough to lock the door behind them. With careful consideration, I decide to knock.

"Are you okay?" I say to the door. The crying stops short. There's silence on the other side. "Is there anything I can do?" More silence. Then I hear the lock click back into place the door crack open. I peer inside.

Saffron is sitting on the carpeted floor, surrounded by discarded beauty products and plastic packaging. Their cheeks are smudged with eyeliner and mascara, the Hawaiian button-down stained with tears. They look up at me and begin to cry all over again. I drop to the floor and pull them into a hug. I feel their body fall limp in my arms and give them a squeeze. We sit there, tangled up and intertwined, until I start bawling too. I don't even know why—maybe because of nothing, maybe because of everything.

Saffron pulls away from me, wiping the loose tears from their face.

"Why didn't you call me back?" they ask.

I only pause to cry harder.

"I felt so numb," I say, between sobs. "This is all my fault."

Saffron studies my expression, confused.

"What, why? What haven't you been telling me?"

I take a deep breath and reach for the tissues under the sole chair in the room, the same tissues I joked about the day of my interview. I use one to dry my eyes and blow my nose, then I start at the very beginning.

I tell Saffron about looking through Loretta's email for Kelsea and about Beth's warning. I recount Kelsea giving that information to Jade, the cover star swoop, and subsequent Experiences disaster. I break back down into tears admitting that Leila was blacklisted from her industry and is struggling to find a job, that we're at risk of being evicted. Detailing the war out loud, it strikes me how ridiculous and petty it all sounds. But Saffron doesn't make me feel that way. When I'm done, they simply nod and pat my knee with their right hand.

"You were in an impossible position," Saffron says. "Anyone would have done what you did."

They grab a compact and start dabbing their face, cleaning up the blotched foundation and mismatched contour. Watching Saffron fiddle with their makeup is like witnessing Michelangelo paint the ceiling of the Sistine Chapel.

"Wait, so what's wrong with you?"

Saffron lets out a half laugh. "Oh, besides everything? Let's see. The person who hired me, the boss I idolize, might actually be a homophobic piece of shit. But even if she's not, she might get fired for being one anyway. Who knows what will happen? But in the meantime, the blowback has been…"

They pause and let out a long sigh. I fixate on a piece of chipped paint peeling off the wall.

"…fucking awful. Advertisers are pulling out. I got disinvited from a panel I was supposed to host next Sunday. Industry friends are literally deleting photos of me from their Instagram profiles and unfollowing me on Twitter. And the worst part is, freelancers no longer want to work with us! I posted a callout for pitches today, and, like, two people responded. And one of them said they'd only consider pitching if Jade announced her resignation. Apparently, she's not interested in working for a 'backward bigot.' Her words, not mine."

Saffron hugs their knees into their chest and rocks back and forth. There's something they're not telling me.

"Is that everything?" I nudge.

They rock faster.

"My Beauty Politics column was supposed to launch next week. Remember that freelancer I told you about? It was *Cosette Bylander*, Noora. The writer and civil rights activist who also happens to be a licensed psychologist. Last week, she gave a presentation to fucking *Oprah* and her people. And she was going to write about the politics of 4C hair for *me*. For *my* column. The copy was in. The top edits were done. In fact, I had just sent the piece over to research to be fact-checked."

They pause and take a deep breath. I have a feeling I know what's coming.

"She fucking killed the piece, Noora," they say. "It's over, just like that. Months of hard work, down the drain, in less than twenty-four hours. And I'll never find someone new in time, let alone someone good. I'm totally, absolutely, one hundred percent screwed. All because of Jade's supposedly doctored tweets."

I look over at Saffron shaking uncontrollably and can't help but feel utterly helpless. With my eyes closed, I scan my brain for the right words, but I end up getting lost inside my head. It's a chaotic jumble of mazes and misdirects, until suddenly, I know what I have to do.

"Can it be about body hair?" I ask quietly.

They lift their head up from its nesting spot between their knees and poke their neck forward like an ostrich.

"Yeah, I guess," they say, puzzled. "Why?"

"I'll write it."

Saffron grabs my hands, squeezing them tightly. I can feel myself start to panic, but I shoo away the thoughts. I'll deal with the aftermath later. *One problem at a time, Noora. One problem at a time.*

"Are you sure? I thought you weren't allowed to write for Digital!"

"I'm not," I truthfully admit. "And I'm not."

Saffron takes a beat. We sit in silence together, thinking. I brush my hand up and down the rug burn on my inner thigh.

"What if you used a pseudonym?" Saffron finally says. "You could send your piece from a remote server, from an anonymous email. I'll just tell Jade and the rest of the Digital team that I have no idea who you are, but that the pitch was too good to pass up. They'll never know it was you."

I lean back, considering their proposal.

"It could work," I say. "It could actually work."

Loretta's sad eyes flash quickly in my mind's eye. I gulp.

"What should we call you?" Saffron asks, cracking a smile. I force one back and think for a second.

"What about Bates?" I offer. "C. Bates. You know, like clickbait? It's got a nice ring to it."

They extend their manicured hand, and we shake on it.

"Welcome to the team, C. Bates."

Chapter Seventeen

Have you ever gone viral?

No, I don't mean "dropped in the family group chat" or "making the rounds on Facebook" viral. I'm talking about "messages from strangers," "comments telling you to go kill yourself," a "nine-page spread in the *Daily Mail* with an offensive headline" viral. The type of viral that leads you to spend all night googling the keywords of your article, searching for Reddit threads, scrolling through tweets. Virality that expands your ego and fills the corners of your brain with narcissistic, self-serving thoughts.

Of course, no one knows who I am. No one is talking about me. The only name on the tip of their tongues is one C. Bates.

After promising Saffron I'd take over the Beauty Politics column, I worked on the premier feature for a week straight. Everything else fell to the wayside: updating *NoorYorkCity*, Loretta's expenses and bone broth, even picking up my family's calls from Dubai (and those long-distance minutes are *expensive*). But from the second I sat down at my laptop and typed that very first sentence, I felt something ignite in my body, like a candlewick about to catch flame. This was it. This was what I was always meant to do. The words flowed out of me almost seamlessly, to the point that I began to feel…guilty? Was it supposed to feel this simple, this good, so early on? Wasn't I supposed to wrestle with writer's block, holing up on the couch, shutting out the rest of the world, ignoring Leila as she runs out the door to meet up with potential "connections" for casual drinks? Instead, writing this piece felt as natural as a bottle of orange wine, as organic as the Whole Foods avocados Loretta makes me spread all over her seeded gluten-free toast. Nothing has ever felt so right, so quickly—and the feeling that washed over me after I was done with my first draft was the most surreal level of satisfaction I've ever encountered. Better than blogging. Way better than sex.

I was dedicated to telling the story I set out to uncover: an exposé on the hair removal industry and how it profits off making dark-haired, hairy people feel "less than" and "other," especially Middle Eastern and Latina women. It's a narrative I know all too well. After all, I began waxing and threading off all my hair at the age of eight. When I was in middle school, a peer told me that she found my mustache *confusing*. "I thought only boys had mustaches," she said to me, brimming with innocence. "Are you a boy?"

To get the piece just right, there were so many people I needed to anonymously interview—members of my own Iranian American community, salon owners, ad executives. I was working on an accelerated timeline, which meant conducting phone interviews, transcribing, editing, and writing faster than anyone can ask, "Did you reach out for comment?" But I had two things going for me: First, Saffron is an incredible editor. Like, truly phenomenal. They didn't leave copy untouched with only a few guiding "suggestions," nor did they tear the entire piece apart then rewrite it themself. Saffron edits the way a therapist weaves their way through a session—by asking intuitive questions and allowing me to reach my own conclusions about the best path forward.

Second, everyone is so far up each other's asses and arsenals that no one has even noticed my head is in the gutter.

Print and Digital have both upped the ante on the cold war and given in to the hysteria. The Digital team has begun using a separate server and holding their weekly meetings off campus at an undisclosed location. I also heard from Saffron that editors have been asked to refer to all their assignments, freelancers, and headlines in code, especially over email. They were given top-secret documents containing the new key, which was apparently crafted by New York's top cryptologist. I assume you have to see it to believe it.

For Print, on the other hand, it's been business as usual. By that, I mean hardly anyone has shown up to work, Loretta included. She's been marking more and more blackout periods on the calendar for which I'm not allowed to know the location or participants. I can never predict when she'll stumble in or out of the office and, for that reason, have been leaving her schedule fairly open (read: internal and willing to be pushed around).

Without a December issue to work on, November feels like an empty promise. Print editors have no reason to be present, many opting to take early vacations and two-week Thanksgiving trips to yacht around the Côte d'Azur with their families. At times like these, the classist, cultural, and generational divides between the two teams feel stark and transparent. The Digital team all left early on Friday to attend a climate change protest. The Print team did the same, but to beat traffic on their way to the Hamptons.

Jade has yet to release a public statement in response to the *Delilah* article. However, the private chatter has been as such: Digital stands by her 100 percent and swears the tweets were doctored. They also wholeheartedly blame Print for the sabotage and are calling for Loretta's immediate dismissal. But without any proof of malfeasance, SPP's hands are tied. Speaking of SPP, the company sympathizes with Jade internally but have externally denounced the tweets. They're technically "investigating" the claims with an onboarded contractor, but all things considered, appear to be taking Loretta's side. The Print team is pleased, to say the least.

So I've been quietly plugging away at the column, both day and night. Leila and Willow—who basically lives in our apartment now, FYI—have been bringing me leftover Chinese and Ethiopian food to ensure I eat at least one meal a day. Even though I know the article will go up under a pseudonym, this means everything to me: It's my debut as a published journalist in the magazine I've read since I was a kid.

There were moments during my childhood when I wanted every little thing I have now. Sure, I didn't expect to be paying month-to-month rent in order to sleep on a couch. And, yeah, I never imagined I'd be shuffled around from team to team like an understudy in a Broadway musical. But writing a full-length feature for *Vinyl* might make all these anxiety-inducing battle tactics and full-on sieges worth it—maybe. Just maybe.

When I turned in the final draft to Saffron—at 2:00 a.m. the day before it was due to Copy and Research, because obviously—they immediately called me and put me on speakerphone. I could hear their cat, Bernie Pawnders, whimpering in the background.

"Noora, it's so powerful." Suddenly, it occurs to me that the sound I hear is not Bernie. It's them.

Saffron is *crying*.

"What's wrong?" I ask, alarmed. I hear them loudly blow their nose.

"Nothing, nothing. It's what's *right*. This magazine has made so many mistakes in the past year. But hiring you was not one of them. Are you *sure* you want this to be anonymous?"

"Positive. Loretta would fire me on the spot. And I need to be making a steady stream of income. Otherwise, I won't be able to pay my rent."

I can practically *hear* Saffron's chaotic nodding on the other end of the line.

"Alrighty, then," they say. "C. Bates is about to become a star."

We both hang up and head to bed. It's a Sunday night, and the floorboards in Leila's apartment are creaking because of a heavy gust of wind that keeps slapping against our walk-up windows. The neighborhood, for the first time since I've moved here, has felt eerily still. No police sirens swelling about in the backdrop or yelling from drunk teenagers who stumbled a bit too far down Baxter. All of Chinatown is dead asleep.

But not me. I'm still painfully awake. My mind keeps running through all of tomorrow's possible outcomes like the midterm poll numbers.

Loretta could find out it was me and let me go. Jade could find out it was me and denounce it as absolute trash. My mom could find out it was me and call me to furiously inform me I'll never be allowed back in Iran (which is probably true). I count scenarios like sheep until I'm caught up in a stress dream that lasts until morning.

PING.

I wake up, as usual, to a text from Loretta. I check the time; it's 6:00 a.m.

Loretta (6:02 AM): Did you see this???????? What the F!

I immediately begin to sweat.

Below is a link to C. Bates's first Beauty Politics column. It went live an hour prior.

She knows it's me. How does she know it's me?

> **Loretta (6:03 AM):** THIS WRITER IS "GOOD"? Who IS C? I thought Jade's REP was TOAST?

Phew. Okay, she has no clue who C is. She's only texting me because… she's angry that the article turned out great? Could that be that right?

A warm tingle rushes through my body. Is it wrong to feel happy about this?

> **Noora: (6:05 AM):** Woah. No clue. Will touch base with S and investigate!
>
> **Loretta (6:05 AM):** K Honey. Keep me in loop. This is unacceptable.

I roll my eyes and click into the link to see what all the fuss is about. Then I almost drop my phone.

In the past hour alone, Beauty Politics has begun trending on Twitter. I check my Apple News alerts. Sure enough, there it is on the front page of today's top stories. And according to Google, a bunch of secondary sites have already started aggregating the story.

"Oh my God," I say out loud to myself. "Oh my GOD."

Leila rolls into the living room, rubbing her eyes and spreading her crusty makeup from the night before, which she clearly forgot to remove before falling asleep, all over her face.

"*Khak bar sar,*" she curses. "Noora, what the fuck is wrong with you? What could you possibly be freaking out about this early in the morning?"

"Oh, nothing." I quickly shove my phone into the crevices of the couch. "I had another sex dream about Post Malone, that's all."

"Gross," she says, crawling back into her bedroom and shutting the door.

I haven't told her yet about C. Bates. While I trust Leila with my life, I have no doubt that Willow would find a way of weaseling it out of her. And Willow is just too interconnected to the industry for me to risk it. All I need are a couple of fashion closet assistants gossiping about C. Bates's alter ego.

Wait, I almost forgot. I'm going viral faster than that fucking Instagram egg that got more likes than Kylie Jenner!

I hop into the shower and quickly get dressed. In honor of my secret identity, I'm cosplaying as a covert operative— black cigarette jeans, black turtleneck, a slick, tan trench coat, and chunky, sensible loafers. I let my long, black hair air-dry, even though I know that means it'll blow up faster than a skinny white girl on TikTok. But today I don't have a minute to waste. I need to get to SPP and hear what people have no idea they're saying about me.

When I enter the thirty-second floor, my first stop is Saffron's desk. I had a sneaking suspicion they'd be in early too. I was right. They're sitting at their laptop, dressed in a conductor jumpsuit and Blundstones, staring wide-eyed into the screen, frantically sipping on a cup of black coffee. They look up when they hear me approaching.

"Don't even say it." They cut me off before I have a chance to open my mouth. "I've seen it."

"Okay, so. What the fuck?"

"I know."

"Is this normal?"

"No."

"Then why?"

"I don't know."

"You don't know?"

"Unless..."

"Unless?"

"Unless it's just that fucking good, Noora," they whisper, risking their newly air-dried manicure to bang their hand on the desk.

I look around to make sure we're not drawing too much attention to ourselves. Luckily, it's 8:30 a.m., which means SPP is essentially an editorial graveyard.

Saffron reiterates, "I think the column might just be that good."

The thoughts in my head stop piling up on top of one another, all struggling to overpower the others at the loudest possible volume. Then a wave of silence takes over, which practically hums from ear to ear. The quiet is unsettling yet validating. I feel like I'm sitting in my own incubator of praise.

I've always secretly suspected I may be a good writer. But it had never been confirmed to me, save for a few college professors, my parents, and one particularly clingy ex-boyfriend, until this very moment. Hearing those words fall out of Saffron's mouth tastes sweeter than marmalade. It's as satisfying as finishing a marathon or giving yourself your first orgasm. Utter and complete contentment. Peace. And gratification.

As I'm stewing in my own personal victories, I hear the double doors behind me swing open. Who else would come in two hours early to work at *Vinyl,* especially at a time like this? Was a settlement finally reached?

"Saffron Jenkins."

I hear Jade's voice announce her presence. I immediately step away from the desk, afraid of facing her wrath.

"You've *outdone* yourself this time."

"I take it you've read the column?" Saffron says coolly. Admiration briefly washes over me. Saffron is such a champ.

"Read it? I *devoured* it. It's next-level good. Where did you find such a savant writer on such short notice? Did Cosette end up coming through?"

"Nope! I actually got an anonymous tip from an untraceable email two nights ago. They said they read my callout and wanted to submit a piece for consideration. I took one look and knew it was the one, so I fast-tracked it through the editing process and C&R. But this writer only communicates over email. And privacy seems to be their thing. They've even asked me to pay them in Bitcoin!"

Jade whistles. I look down at my black, lacy quarter-length socks and smile to myself. Saffron is pulling this off quite nicely. Even *I* believe them.

"Damn, okay. Well, I want you to reach out to this 'C. Bates,' whoever they are, and offer them a monthly column, okay? Do your best to talk them out of this anonymity thing. If they continue to produce such top-notch work, we might need to push them to do press."

"I'll do my best," Saffron promises.

Jade gives them an awkward-to-watch high five and retreats to her office. I approach the desk again.

"So, Noora," they tease. "Who exactly *is* this mysterious C. Bates?"

Honestly, I don't have a clue. But we're all about to find out.

Chapter Eighteen

The following Thursday, Leila texts me and asks if I can meet her for lunch. Normally, a question this laissez-faire would to be met with a "ha, very funny" type of response. But because of Loretta's extracurricular off-campus excursions, my schedule has been laxer than ever.

Speaking of which, I was finally able to gain a little insight into who Loretta has been meeting with: consumer goods companies, like Unilever and Procter & Gamble. One of the attendees' assistants let it slip. They called me in a panic yesterday, *on my cell phone.* I only list that number in my email signature in case of emergencies! Surely, accidentally entering the incorrect address for the Carlyle doesn't warrant an emergency. "He's going to be at least fifteen minutes late," the assistant had cried into the phone in a panic. "I'm so, so sorry. It's all my fault!"

Why is Loretta suddenly meeting with giant conglomerates? Of that, I am uncertain. Maybe she's planning on launching a jewelry line with Kohl's or writing, producing, directing, and starring in a movie about her life.

Actually, that last option is *way* too real.

Whatever the reason, it keeps her off my back for most of the day, as well as out of Jade's hair. The less of a chance those two have of crossing paths in the SPP Tower, the better. The entire staff has been collectively holding their breath since the night of *Vinyl* Sleighs. It's honestly created an incredibly toxic work environment. Everybody is walking on eggshells, unsure of who to trust and afraid of what might happen next.

I agree to meet Leila at Bar Pitti, an old Italian café in the heart of the West Village that's known for its infamous people watching. It's difficult to describe the magic of Bar Pitti—it's a tiny, crammed restaurant, with the majority of its tables positioned in open-air seating, covered by a single dark-green awning overhead. There's a line that curves around the block of people waiting for tables, since the current management refuses to take reservations. The menu, which is updated every day with specials handcrafted with fresh-to-order ingredients, is indeed delicious—the pasta is handmade, and the burrata is especially supple. But it's probably not the best Italian food you've ever had in your life and definitely not the best Italian food in New York City. The atmosphere is quaint, the cuisine perfectly average.

So what sets Bar Pitti apart from all other Manhattan establishments? The customers. Sitting at a sidewalk table on any given day, lunch or dinner, is like refreshing your Netflix queue: You never know what will pop up next. One night, I was lucky enough to come across Julianne Moore (a Bar Pitti staple; the owners *live* for her family), Martin Scorsese, and my dude Joffrey from *Game of Thrones*, all in one sitting. There's a dependable mix of low-profile celebrities, actual Italian families that usually span generations, and off-duty models. Leila definitely picked this spot on purpose. She knows I can never say no to a Pitti party.

Strutting through the West Village always fills me with a sense of fated destiny. The sidewalk slopes at a slightly downward angle so you can see the skyscrapers below as you begin to descend into the Atlantic. From above, New York always looks compact and precise, like an orderly recipe for chaos. Many forget Manhattan is an island, but as someone who grew up on the wrong side of the bridge, I never do. I've always suspected that those who scrape their way onto the concrete beaches that line the East River and set up camp below Fourteenth Street are always slightly afraid that one day they'll be kicked off the island and thrown into the water.

But the West Village contains its own mystical alchemy. On this side of the city, the sun always appears to be hitting the cobblestones at just the right angle; every hour is the golden standard. The stoops are lined with ivy, their stairs spiraling as much as their residents. Town houses are painted like resurrected relics from New Amsterdam. If you shut your eyes and open your ears, you might even hear the faint clacking of clogs making their way down Horatio. The closer to the Hudson you traverse, the quieter the world around you appears. Wealthy families dressed alike flock from the neighborhood D'agostino's back to their pieds-à-terre. In another life, I'd inhabit one of those empty windows, and Leila, the other. We'd pick our friends off the pages of the *New York Times* and plan our retirement on another planet. Life would be forgiving and saccharine.

Mid-November calls for heavy bundling, so I'm wrapped up in a long, plaid overcoat, thrifted mom jeans (or rather, old-trucker jeans), and Chelsea boots. The shoes are brand new, scoured from the depths of the Outnet, which means each bottom is slick and slippery, like fish scales. I almost fall several times as I power walk over the unpaved streets and scattered cobblestones.

When I make it to that iconic green awning, I'm pleased to find that not only have I missed the lunch rush entirely, but I've beat Leila here as well. I step inside and am greeted by the aroma of freshly churned tomato sauce. It's warm in here, like stepping inside a witch's furnace. I take a seat at the table closest to the window so I can have the best view of the sidewalk interlopers.

I hear giggling followed by a few very indiscreet camera flashes. I spin around in my seat to find two young girls, dressed in head-to-toe Brandy Melville, Air Force 1s on their feet. Our eyes meet, and the one snapping pictures turns away, embarrassed. The other clears her throat.

"I'm so sorry to bother you, but are you Loretta James's assistant?"

My heart does a quick, Olympic-grade somersault.

"Why do you ask?"

The girls both squeal and clasp hands. "I am so *hype*, I knew it was you! We both follow Loretta on Instagram. We're, like, obsessed with her. She's *sooooo* amazing. Is working for her just, like, a dream come true?"

I hate this question so, so much. There's no right way to answer it without a) lying then vomiting. Or b) telling the truth then ending up a *Page Six* cautionary tale.

I pick option c) the half-truth.

"I've learned a lot from working at *Vinyl*," I answer diplomatically. "They're doing really great work."

The two exchange a side-eyed glance. Clearly, I'm boring them.

"And the beauty closet is sick!" I add.

Satisfied, the girls start squealing again. "Can we get a picture with you?"

I immediately tense up. While Loretta hasn't technically *not* given me permission to be here, I somehow highly doubt that she would approve of her assistant traversing to the West Village mid-workday to rendezvous with her sister. This needs to be kept on the DL.

"I was never here." I wink at the girls. They wink back and refocus on their spaghetti, their minds moving on to their next celebrity spotting.

Wait, was I just the *subject* of someone else's people watching? That's too meta for even *me* to wrap my head around.

"Sorry I'm late!" Leila sings as she runs into the restaurant and takes her seat across from me. She's wearing all white wool, save for her New Balance dad sneakers, and looks like a certified angel. She's quite literally beaming light from her forehead to her crotch. Catching the waiter's eye, she gestures for him to come over. He purses his lips, amused by her showmanship.

"Two glasses of your cheapest prosecco, sir!" She orders.

"Lei, I can't drink in the middle of the workday," I protest.

"Today, you can! We're celebrating!"

Like clockwork, the waiter—who, now that I think of it, definitely had a small part on *Grey's Anatomy* last season—is back with our pseudo-champagne. Leila theatrically starts clinking her glass with her knife. She's using so much gusto that I'm afraid it might shatter all over the table.

"I'd like to make a toast," she begins. I giggle. "To my darling sister, who has worked tirelessly over the past few months to support her rotten, good-for-nothing, failure of a sibling. To Whitney Thompson, the first plus-size model to ever grace the runway, hereby making history more inclusive and changing the industry forever. And, finally, to Jag Models, who will hereby ensure this family never goes to bed hungry or without a roof over our heads."

I stare back at her blankly. She clinks her glass a couple more times, impatient.

"In other words, ya girl got herself a job!"

I start to laugh, which quickly turns to tears. Leila joins me, and we sit there in the heart of the West Village, in broad daylight, holding each other, happily wailing. I take her hand and squeeze it three times. She squeezes back.

"Wait, cheers me, bitch," she says. "Otherwise, it's bad luck for both of us!"

After we sync glasses and take big, hearty sips of prosecco, I unload one round of questioning.

"Who? What? Where? Who wore what?"

Leila's laugh sounds like the chorus of a Rolling Stones song, and all feels right in the world.

"So it's actually a funny story. You know Willow?"

I roll my eyes. "You mean your girlfriend?"

Leila rolls hers back. She waves me off. "You know I hate labels. Besides, we're not exclusive. Last week we had the most scrumptious threesome with this Moldavian homme with the most delightful mustache, which he used to—"

"Don't need to know the details," I say quickly, cutting her off. "Stay focused on the job."

"Right, right, right. So, I was picking up Willow—my friend—from a shoot with Jag, and the second I stepped on to the set, I could see it was all wrong. The lighting was harsh, the clothes were ugly and uninventive, the hair felt so nineties, I almost dry-heaved on the spot. I was like, who is in charge here? That's when I realized they didn't have anyone on-site, assisting the headshots. That's when I had an epiphany: I'd be the most perfect shoot director. I pitched myself on the spot then got to work that very same day. Aka, yesterday. And I got the call this morning. The rest is history!"

My brain swells. Leila has always had the most profound sense of self that I've ever been lucky enough to stand remotely close to. But creating a job title out of thin air? That's next-level boss. Both Loretta and Jade could learn a thing or two from the way she carries herself.

"And you know what that means," she continues. "You can finally quit your job!"

Just like that, the swelling stops.

"I, uh, don't think I can do that right now," I say. Leila raises one eyebrow.

"Noora, you can't be serious. You had a straight-up *panic attack* a little over a week ago. I was standing right next to you. Your sleep cycle is totally erratic, you're on edge twenty-four/seven, and you're never really present. Even when you're physically with me, you're never really here, are you?"

"What?" I tune back into the conversation. Secretly, I was scanning for messages from Loretta under the table. Leila follows my gaze then reaches and grabs the phone from my hands.

"What the fuck! I need that. What are you doing?" I ask, annoyed.

"Proving a point. This job is bad for your mental health, Noora. You have zero work-life balance. At the very least, you should consider talking to a therapist. Or maybe even returning Maman and Baba's calls. Yeah, they told me you've been dodging them."

I stare up at Leila, shocked. This attack seemingly came out of nowhere. What the fuck did I do?

"I can't leave right now, Lei," I say again. "You don't get it. They *need* me."

"Who is *they*, Noora?! Loretta? Jade? Because I'm honestly losing track. Which side are you trying to defend here? Your insecure narcissist of a boss, or the Justin Bieber–looking amateur using you as a fucking mole? Can't you see that they'll discard you when you're done? You wanted to work for *Vinyl* so you could actually write and Jesus fucking Christ, you're not even doing that!"

I'm about to jump in and tell her everything. Explain that I'm C. Bates. That I just showed up on *New York Mag*'s High Brow, Low Brow graph. But I know that would be a mistake, so I refrain. I bite down, hard, on my tongue. It really fucking hurts.

"You don't get it," I repeat. "You just don't get it."

"Is it Saffron? Or that piece of walking meat? Cal or Kale or whatever?"

"Don't call him that."

More silence.

"You're so fucking fake, dude," she finally says. "Just admit it: You *like* the drama. You live for the so-called war or whatever. You enjoy being in the middle of it all, and you're playing both sides like the Gemini that you are. Say it. *Say it.*"

I sit there, silently fuming, and stare down at my glass of prosecco. I can see right through it.

"Whatever masochist bullshit is going on here, I don't want to be part of it." She practically spits all over the table. "Don't come crying to me when they burn you at the stake and blame it on global warming."

With that, she chugs the rest of her prosecco, slams her flute on the table, and walks out the door. I stay put for the next five minutes, stunned, then ask for the check.

"Are you sure you want to leave?" Mr. *Grey's Anatomy* asks. "Fran Lebowitz just walked in and asked for her usual table."

I swivel around in my seat. Sure enough, there she is— sitting in the corner, hiding beneath her signature glasses. Up close, she looks so small.

"No, thanks," I tell him. "I've made enough questionable decisions for one day."

Chapter Nineteen

The last time Leila and I went more than three days without talking, it was because I'd accidentally ratted to Baba about one of her tattoos. She had claimed the cluster of stars surrounding her lower back was made with Magic Marker. To her credit, I knew what I was doing.

It's been five days. *Five.* My calls have all gone straight to voicemail. My texts have been left on read. She's even *muted* me on Instagram. Leila has always told me I'm stubborn, but what she's doing is next level. And yes, I haven't exactly apologized. For fighting with her in public, for stealing the spotlight on a day when we were meant to be celebrating her success. But what am I supposed to say? *Leila, you don't get it. I've started a secret career as a political beauty columnist under a nondescript alias, and it's getting a ton of traction, so I've started to pen my memoir?* That's not an option. Even *I* can hear how out of touch it sounds.

One plus to this entire debacle is that Leila has been hiding out at Willow's (thank God I can still see her Instagram stories), so I've had the entire apartment to myself. Usually that amount of space would mean lighting a few candles, pulling out my favorite vibrator from Unbound, and queuing up a little massage porn. Unfortunately for me, I'm still in the midst of my internet spiral. So, instead, "no parents, no rules" looks a little less like *Sex and the City* and a little more like googling myself over and over without having to shield the computer screen from prying eyes.

By the time Friday rolls around, I've begun seeing my life for what it is: sad. Cooking dinners for one has proved nearly impossible (I always make too much), I have no one to help me fold the couch back up in the morning (Leila usually does it for me), and I've watched so many consecutive seasons of *Love Island* that my brain has begun to decay.

There's no doubt about it: I'm plain old lonely, and there's no Instagram poll in the world that can make me feel like I'm surrounded by friends or loved ones. I consider reconnecting with NYU friends but quickly remember how annoying their alternative diets and proclivity for reciting Kerouac prose can be. I give my parents a call in Dubai, but the time difference gets in the way and our schedules refuse to line up. Suddenly, it occurs to me that my only true friend left in the world is Saffron. And are we even friends IRL? If I were to lose *Vinyl*—to get laid off, to quit—would we even stay in touch? The thought of reducing my connection to Saffron to just a single follow button on Twitter takes me to a dark, dark place.

To avoid allowing my eternal dread to descend into a prolonged anxiety attack, I spend more time at the office and take over initiatives that give me a false sense of control. For example, I spend the entirety of Wednesday alphabetizing the beauty closet. Then Saffron walks in and is like, "Girl, how much Adderall did you take?"

But I can't stop and think—if I do, I'll start to panic about losing Leila, and there's no point in allowing my brain to walk down those stairs and linger in the basement. After all, she can't avoid her apartment forever. Her name is on the damn lease.

On Friday morning, I'm in the middle of color coding the archive room, where we store every single *Vinyl* Print edition ever produced—it's basically my Mecca—when Loretta texts me that she's coming in. This takes me by surprise: For the past couple weeks, a Friday appearance from Loretta has been about as likely as getting cast as the next Bachelorette. I run over to my desk to make sure I look consumed in her schedule upon arrival.

"Morning, sweet pea! Give me five then meet me inside," Loretta calls to me as she struts by, entering the padlock code to get past the frosted door.

I hold my breath until she's safely inside then run to the bathroom to clean up. My plaid pleated trousers are looking a bit wrinkled, and my baby hairs appear as if they're attempting to contact extraterrestrials, but other than that, I can work with what I've got. I splash a little cold water on my face, count to ten, then return to her office.

"Take a seat, Noora," Loretta says to me as I enter. She's got an earpiece in that makes her look like a cast member in the latest *Men in Black* revival. I suppress the urge to giggle.

"Everything okay?"

She nods and points to the ear, indicating that she's on the phone. I sit quietly, my legs crossing and uncrossing beneath the table, staring straight ahead at a pile of coffee-table books. Loretta nods emphatically, as if the recipient can see her, and lets out a forced laugh or two. I resist the urge to roll my eyes. Instead, focus on the thin folds of tightened skin around her temples, the bleached hairs above her upper lip.

"Ciao!" she coos, her tongue dripping with snake charm. But the second she hangs up the phone, her tone shifts. She removes her earpiece and looks up at me, her face stoic, before peering around the room, as if we're being watched. I feel a lump forming in the back of my throat.

"This C. Bates business has gotten out of hand," she says, shifting back and forth uncomfortably in her seat.

At the sound of C. Bates's name, every muscle in my body stiffens. I intentionally attempt to relax my face, as to not give me away.

"There's absolutely no trace of this person on the dark web. I even hired a private investigator, and as it turns out, there's no New York residence associated with the name. Very suspicious."

A private investigator? I'm toast. I am a piece of very burnt, inedible, radioactive toast.

"It's obviously an alias, which means I'm turning up squat," she says. "Bates must have some sort of personal connection to Jade. Either that, or a grudge against me. I'm not sure which is worse."

"Um," I stutter, trying to sound casual. "Both?"

Shut up, Noora, you bumbling idiot. Shut. Up.

"Nevertheless, I've contracted an expert to do a little bit more digging into the IP address and location of Bates's emails," Loretta continues, completely ignoring my comment. For once, her self-involved oblivion works in my favor. "Obviously, this is off the record and must be conducted off hours. And I'll need you to stay late tonight and oversee the mission. I'd do it myself, but I can't be liable."

Wait. What? And I can?

"Loretta, I'm not sure that's a good idea," I stammer, avoiding her gaze.

But when I look back up, our gazes lock, and I see her. Like, really see her. The crease marks indented on her forehead, purple veins weaving their way through the tapestry of her hands, which are shaking under the table. Her nail varnish is chipped, and there's a small coffee stain below the lapel of her shirt.

She hunches over and places a hand on my tightly clasped grip. I'm surprised by the sweatiness of her palm. I always assumed Loretta ran ice cold.

"Please, Noora," she whispers. "I'm scared."

She looks away from me then, blinking back tears—not alligator tears, not saline drops, but real, mortal, saltwater tears. And she squeezes my hand as if we aren't assistant and boss, reader and editor, admirer and legend. We're just two people, having a bad day.

Damn. Loretta's humanity is really making it harder to hate her.

"Okay," I hear myself say. "Okay. I'll do it."

The color immediately rushes back into Loretta's cheeks, and she springs back into action, pulling her body away from mine.

"Fabulous!" she exclaims. "Then you can let yourself out. And lock the door behind you."

I stand up, a little bit woozy, surprised by the disappointment clouding my frontal cortex. What was I expecting? A thank-you?

"Oh, and darling?" she says, right before I walk out. I look back over my shoulder, my pulse quickening. "Do be careful. I can't have this traced back to me."

I nod then make my way to my desk. But the second I sit down, the weight of my words crash into me like the skaters at Washington Square Park.

Noora. You fucking idiot. What have you *done*?

If Loretta tracks the IP address, she'll be able to trace the story back to my computer. I cannot let that happen. No, I need to thwart her plan by actively working against this contract hire.

———

The day stretches on with little to do without an issue to work on. Loretta stays squarely put in her office, only leaving to take smoke breaks. When she does, she brings Beth or Daniel with her. She's eerily paranoid. Either that, or afraid of being alone for too long. I mean, who knows the next time Jade might jump out of nowhere and launch another full-on attack?

By the way, there are rumors circulating that Jade passed SPP's internal investigation. But she's still being dragged on Twitter, being called a "lifeless hack" and "Japanese Kylie Jenner." The hate out there is so brutal, I don't know how she's showing up to work every day—but she is. She's been keeping her head held high and her nylon joggers hanging low. I can tell her team respects her tenfold for it. The rest of the staff is just waiting for her to retaliate.

The majority of *Vinyl* heads out around 5:30 p.m., partially because they have so little to work on, and partially because they know no one is watching. It's like shoplifting a single piece of candy or a cigarette lighter—the action is meaningless, but you do it to challenge the system and gain a cheap thrill in the process. Even if you have nowhere to be and nothing to smoke.

Loretta waits until everyone else leaves the office. She pokes her head out from behind the door then looks both ways, like a bandit.

"Hey, doll," she whispers to me. "All clear?"

I nod. Daylight savings was last week and now the entirety of New York blacks out around 4:00 p.m., filling the halls with a dementor-like darkness that activates this awfully bright fluorescent lighting. Being alone in the office in the winter is creepy and yet nostalgic. It feels like camping by a dimly lit fire or searching for the bathroom in the middle of the night while holding a single candlestick.

Loretta runs out of the office like a scared teenager who's been caught going to third base in the back of her Mustang by her overprotective dad. I'm left alone in the dark, waiting for this mystery tech wizard to appear.

I think about the tactics I can use to keep them away from my IP address. Maybe I'll offer them a glass of water and sprinkle enough CBD oil in it to immediately put them to sleep. I could trip them as they walk toward Loretta's office and then call 911 and claim it was an accident. Perhaps I'll just lock them out of Loretta's office and claim it was a misunderstanding? And then there's always subtle seduction to take your mind off super sleuthing.

I hear a rustle in the darkness then the sound of someone accidentally walking into a desk followed by a suspicious, "Oh shit." The dark figure moves like a shadow from one end of the office to the other until he emerges into my desk light and is standing right in front of me.

"Long time no see," Cal says. "Well, I actually can't see you. It's hella dark in here."

Of course, Loretta's secret agent is Cal. She probably doesn't know anyone else who can properly navigate a computer.

We haven't spoken since the night of *Vinyl* Sleighs. Not that he hasn't been reaching out, I've just been ignoring his texts. There's just so much I can't tell him. So much I wish I could say. But doing so—explaining the so-called war, whose side I'm on—would be so much harder than just keeping it to myself and dying from the loneliness of it all. Confronting Cal would mean confronting myself, and to be perfectly honest, I'm not sure what I want. To some extent, Leila was right. Don't tell her I said that.

But how am I going to explain why I've been ghosting him?

"So you're Loretta's lackey, huh?" I admire his all-black ensemble. "Welcome to the club!"

He lets out a small laugh, and I immediately shush him. No one can know we're here, not even the custodians. Instead, I grab his hand and swiftly escort him into Loretta's lockbox. When I reach the padlock, I have to gesture to get him to look away from the combination. After typing in the code, we enter the lair and I lead him to the safe beneath her desk.

"These safety measures are intense," he whispers as I begin typing the crypto key into the pad. "What is this, a U.S. naval base?"

"You can never be too careful. There are also, like, three security cameras and a tape recorder in here, but I disabled them before you arrived. Loretta doesn't want this on the record. I'm sure you can understand why."

The lock clicks into place, and the safe door opens. I reach inside and grab Loretta's work laptop and hand it to Cal. He glances down at it then pulls a pair of gloves out of his pocket—the kind used for science experiments. Once he's squeezed each of his fingers into the latex, he cautiously takes the computer off my hands.

"I don't want this to trace back to me," he explains. "Like you said, you can never be too careful."

"So Loretta wants you to get access to as much information as you can on this 'C. Bates' and leave it in an unidentifiable, password-protected folder on her desktop." My bottom lip begins to quiver as I relay the paper note's instructions. "Of course, I understand if that's impossible and super outside of your job description."

Cal gives me a cocky smile. His teeth are so white.

"I studied software engineering, remember?" he says. "Don't worry, this will be a piece of cake."

I clench my fist down hard, burrowing my nails into my skin. When I reopen my hand, there are tiny little indents in my palm beginning to bleed. I take a seat on the couch and begin scrolling through my phone, checking *NoorYorkCity's* engagement, while Cal pops a squat on Loretta's desk and begins plugging away at her keyboard. Somehow, sitting in the darkness under the glow of the laptop screen feels oddly romantic. I glance over to look at Cal, but he's laser-focused on his mission. The second I turn away, I can feel his gaze on me, hot, like a klieg light.

I try to savor these last few moments together before he finds out the truth and inevitably turns on me. Not to mention turns me in.

"So how's your start-up coming along?" I ask, both making conversation and attempting to take his focus off the work. I'm great at multitasking.

"Okay." He hesitates for a second, before continuing. "We just wrapped up our series-A funding, but it's been a difficult round. Honestly, it's been hard convincing a bunch of rich old white dudes to invest in a cannabis delivery company run by a Black guy. But we've made a little venture capitalist noise, so I guess we'll see."

I nod then realize he probably can't see my head move in the dark. Duh.

"Why go into cannabis at all? Why not invest in something that's a little bit safer?" I offer.

That gets Cal's attention. He breathes heavily, stops whatever it is he's doing, and looks up at me. His shadow looms large behind him.

"Well, it's complicated," he says. "Did you know CBD is a twenty-five-billion-dollar industry?"

"Yeah." I actually read about it in an article that Saffron published on *Vinyl*.

"And do you know the percentage of cannabis business owners that are Black?"

"No, I don't." I'm ashamed to admit it.

"Four point three percent. Let that sink in. You don't think it's a little upsetting, considering Black people still face harsher drug sentencing and mass incarceration for marijuana usage and traffic than any other community?"

I stir in silence. He's 100 percent right. I'd never considered that before.

"It's completely fucked up."

"Right, so that's why I'm getting into the industry," he explains. "No matter how hard it is to break in as a Black man. The community deserves better."

I look over at him hunched over Loretta's desk. Are his eyes watering, or is that just a glare coming off the screen's reflection?

I want to run over to him and give him a hug. To hold him. To tell him I'm here for him. But I know that wouldn't be fair, because I'm not ready to be honest with him. So, instead, I sit still and try to find the right words.

"I understand," I finally say.

"You don't, but that's okay. My older brother was locked up for three years just because he was caught carrying."

"I'm so sorry, Cal."

"It's okay, Little Light. It's just the way the world spins. And I'm not alone in this. I've got friends. I have people who are helping me."

Too often, I get caught up thinking about my family's trauma—Islamophobia, the Muslim ban, xenophobic remarks—that I forget to confront my own privilege. Sure, I've worried about my parents' phone line being tapped, but I rarely feel anxiety passing a cop car, at least not in Brooklyn. The truth is, I can sympathize with Cal's experience as much as I like, but I'll never empathize with him. He's right—I'll never actually understand. But I can give him the space and support he needs. Not as his girlfriend or anything. But as a friend. As a human being.

"I've got it!"

Cal breaks me out of my aside. I immediately shush him. I'm afraid he's woken up all of South Street Seaport.

"Got what?" I whisper.

"The IP address! I cracked the code easily. Strange, it says the signal is coming from a laptop on this floor."

Oh my God. I completely forgot: I brought my personal laptop in today to sneak in some blog maintenance between meetings.

I'm so, so dead.

"You don't think it's someone on Digital, do you?" Cal asks. "Maybe Jade herself is moonlighting as C. Bates? You know, to protect the integrity of the work while her character is under so much scrutiny. Kind of a genius play, if you ask me."

I dig back into my palms but find the marks have already rendered my hands numb. I switch to anxiously itching my inner elbows.

"I don't think it's her, Cal."

"But think about it, it makes sense. SPP just finished investigating her, Twitter hates her, Loretta is clearly out to get her, so in order to get *Vinyl* Digital a little good press, she concocts a scheme to mask her identity so she can—"

"It's me."

Cal's eyes shift from my face to Loretta's laptop, then back to me. His eyes narrow, like he's trying to focus on one image in his head at a time.

"I don't understand."

"It's me, Cal. I'm C. Bates."

Chapter Twenty

Cal is sitting on Loretta's couch, his face in his hands, saying nothing. I rub his back in a circular motion, waiting for him to react. Thus far, he's weirdly silent. I was expecting him to scream, to strut around the office throwing random shit around, sliding all of Loretta's knickknacks off the desk before flipping the table entirely, like they do on CW shows.

Before I had opened my mouth, this felt like a giant secret looming over me like a moving crane. I assumed he'd blame me for lying to him and wasting his time. Instead, he burrows his head further into his hands, flexing his left bicep in the process. Did I misread the situation? Is this entire disaster somehow no big deal?

I hear a sort of moan coming from out of Cal's mouth, but it's muffled by his hands.

"What was that?" I ask gently.

"I'm going to have to tell her it's you."

My throat seizes. He's referring to Loretta, his bona fide crime boss.

"You don't have to do that." There's a tremor in my voice. Cal groans, and I feel like a soggy pretzel. I hate that I've put him in this position.

"Tell me why you did it." He looks up from his hands

and directly into my soul. Without warning, he puts his arm around my right shoulder and squeezes. Every muscle in my body tenses.

"Because Saffron needed someone," I tell him.

He squeezes me again, this time harder. "Try again. The truth, this time."

I take a deep breath, and the words spill out uncontrollably.

"Because Loretta banned me from writing, which is the one thing I came here to do, and Jade is using me like a fucking tug-of-war rope and not a human being, and I have no idea who is right and who is wrong—all I know is that I felt powerless—and I wanted to be in control again, so I agreed to write the piece under a pseudonym because I couldn't get fired for breaking the rules since my sister got blacklisted from her job and has basically no savings and needed my help paying our rent, and our parents are in Dubai and can barely even visit us, but then she got a job anyway, but I had already published the story under C. Bates, so the damage was done, and I wasn't expecting for the piece to do so well, but it has, and Jade's talking about giving me a column, only she's not giving it to me, she's giving it to C. Bates, and she might take it back if she knew who I really am, and all I want to do in the entire world is write about something meaningful, so I lied to everyone and I lied to you, and I'm just fucking exhausted and sorry."

I catch my breath, recovering from the words I just puked out into the open.

I didn't mean to be so honest, it just kind of happened. But I meant what I said: I am tired. All the sneaking around, the deceit, the competition has been slowly killing me. It feels nice to admit that to someone. It feels good to confront the truth out loud.

Cal is staring at me with an intensity I've never seen before. It's as if he skipped lunch and I'm the last packet of

Easy Mac in the kitchen. He's about to devour me whole, I just know it.

"I don't blame you," he says. "I get why you did what you did."

I raise a single eyebrow.

"Yeah?" I respond, a little bit coy. "And why is that?"

Cal inches a little closer to me. I can feel his breath on my left cheek.

"Because you're just like me. You're ambitious. You care about getting what you want, no matter the cost."

He takes his right hand and cups my chin, letting the inside of his thumb trace my lower lip.

"That's not true," I say faintly, forgetting what I'm talking about.

"I think it is," he whispers in my ear then gently bites it, nibbling on the lobe. I let out a quiet moan. "I think you're up to no good."

"So you won't tell anyone?" I ask. Instead of answering, he begins to kiss my neck. His lips linger, sucking slightly on the skin. I close my eyes, taking in how good the tip of his tongue feels against my collarbone. When I open them again, I suddenly fixate on the camera sitting in the corner, pointing down at where we're seated. Am I going crazy, or is there a tiny, blinking red light coming straight at me from that direction? I could have sworn I turned off all the cameras before Cal got here.

It's fine. Everything's fine.

From where the camera sits, it'll just look like Cal was whispering something into my ear. Just as these thoughts cross my mind, I feel Cal's right hand begin to wander down my shirt and toward the zipper of my jeans.

"Not here," I whimper. Cal's still breathing heavily on my neck. "Not in Loretta's office. Follow me."

I take Cal's hand and lead him to Saffron's desk, opening the bottom drawer where they keep the beauty closet keys next to all the sex toys people send them. I grab one of those too.

We walk to the other end of the office, keeping our heads down and hidden from the building security cameras. Although, I doubt anyone checks those. Who could be watching? Superman?

We enter the closet. I turn on the light switch, but Cal shakes his head and flips it back off. He immediately grabs me and begins kissing me. My tongue tickles his, like two teenagers grinding at a middle school dance. He pushes me to the floor, tracing his lips down my body with little flowery kisses, unbuttoning the vintage Prada cardigan I'm wearing as a top. He lets out a little groan, pleased to find I'm not wearing a bra underneath. His hands begin to massage my breasts as he sucks gently on my nipples. My body is growing heavier and heavier. I feel something hard brush against my thigh and let out a little giggle.

"What's so funny?" Cal asks, coming up for air.

Once again, I shush him. "Just keep going."

He obeys, moving downstream on my torso, kissing every patch of skin his lips can uncover, like he's on an imperial quest. When he reaches the waistband of my jeans, he struggles with getting the buttons undone.

Is there a sexy way to get a pair of pants off? Let me know if you find one.

When he finally wrestles my jeans past my thighs and pools them at my ankles, I sit up and place my hand over his bulge. But he playfully pushes me away instead.

"I'm good," he says. "I don't need it."

I shrug and lie back down. Cal pulls my thong (which literally has DTF written on it), to one side and slowly slips a single finger in. A small yelp slips out of my mouth.

"You're so wet." He grins.

Using his thumb, he rubs me in a circular motion while his index finger ventures inside me, exploring. My chest clenches, and my hands begin to shake. My body involuntarily flexes and contorts, as if Cal is holding an exorcism and I'm about to cry out when suddenly, it all stops.

"Keep going," I beg.

But Cal is already undoing his pants and pulling down his boxers. He climbs on top of me, using his hand to guide himself inside. I'm tight, but that comes as no surprise; I haven't had sex since I started my job at *Vinyl*. Maybe even, now that I think about it, since graduating. To be fair, sleeping in a living room isn't really conducive to steamy one-night stands.

Cal thrusts himself forward, and my entire spine jolts. I wrap my legs around his middle back, and he pushes in and out of me at lightning speed, pulling me closer and deeper into his body. When I attempt to meet his eyes, they shift away, wandering instead to the shelves of products, surrounding us like Mount Rushmore. As his speed accelerates, I grow tired of the constant prodding and dissociate. My mind flips through memories from the past week like a picture book—my fight with Leila at Bar Pitti, hiding from Jade at Saffron's desk. Seconds later, Cal growls like a behemoth and collapses on top of me, panting and sticky. He was only inside me for about a total of four minutes. I roll over to one side in an attempt to shake him off.

"Okay." I turn to face him, resting the side of my face in my palm and my elbow on the ground. "My turn."

Cal, who is still writhing around on the floor like a sweaty toddler, furrows his brow and unintentionally flexes his pecs.

"What do you mean?" he asks, wiping his forehead. I realize his hand is still covered in his own semen and cringe.

Using my right foot, I kick over the crying tissues so he can clean himself up. "I'm done. That was *really* great."

"Sure, for you maybe." I hand him the new vibrator I stole from Saffron's desk. "But when I have sex, I don't stop until I finish."

He stares down at the toy in his hands as if he were holding a dead rat.

"I've never used one of these before," he admits. "I'm not sure what to do with it."

"That's okay," I tell him, grabbing the vibrator back from his hands. "I'll show you."

Cal sits upright, naked, legs stretched out in front of him like an observant kindergarten student. I lie back down, propping my upper back up on a few unopened packages. Then, I spread my legs, raise the toy as close it can get to my vagina without actually making contact, and press the power button. The waves of vibration tickle my lips, and my body immediately tenses in anticipation. I slowly lower the tip of the toy to the bottom left side of my clit, pressing it into my body in a rhythmic cycle. The second I make contact, I let out a moan.

"Play with my boobs," I command. Cal crawls over to me, excited, and starts caressing my breasts. I up the intensity of the vibrations by one degree. My volume immediately grows louder and more intense. Cal responds by grabbing the vibrator out of my hands and taking control of the vibration patterns. Every muscle in my body constricts then, after a beat, relaxes.

"Fuck, that was amazing," he says, his head popping up from between my legs. "I think I came again. Does that always happen with these things?"

I roll my eyes, wishing Cal would just let me enjoy this moment. For a split second, my world felt worry-free and simple. I want to hold on to that feeling for just a little longer.

"Have you ever seen a woman orgasm before?" I ask.

"I thought I had," he confesses. "But I guess I not. Unless you count porn?"

All splayed out in the dark of the beauty closet, quivering as if he's seen a ghost, I'm struck by how innocent Cal appears. Stripped of his clothes and his cocky attitude, he looks less like the man of the hour and more like a little boy. He glances at me with his big, goofy dimpled smile, and I feel empty.

For months, I've been starving for even the smallest slice of Cal's attention. Now, I've tasted too much. My stomach hurts.

Cal gets up and shifts toward me. He wraps his arms around me, and my body conforms to his. He spoons me from the left side, and I feel like a bag of skin and bones inside of his marble frame. We tangle our limbs like a marionette and create a single silhouette. My eyelids flutter shut, and I feel his breath grazing the back of my neck, hot and wet, like the fountain in Washington Square Park in mid-July.

"You know this doesn't mean anything, right?" he whispers into my ear.

Out of my periphery, I watch as a couple of unopened products fall from the top shelf, knocking into the next and the one after that, like a stack of dominoes. The noise is unsettling, and although I'm technically watching the chaos unravel, I'm somehow powerless to get up and stop it.

"I know," I whisper back.

The samples avalanche onto the ground. I can see an eye shadow palette explode, adding a shimmer to the carpet. It's a beautiful disaster. One I'm dreading cleaning up.

Chapter Twenty-One

The next day, I'm sitting at an outdoor table at the Butcher's Daughter, a health-food hub in Nolita, overlooking a quiet Kenmare Street. It's close to 50 degrees, which means the only table for one without a wait inevitably brought me outdoors. But I decided to go through with it, because the people watching at Butcher's is truly phenomenal, even if the healthy-ish food isn't. It's full of well-to-do vegans and sustainability Soho-ists who spit in the face of single-use plastic but have no problem taking a private jet to Paris. I'm bundled up in my warmest faux fur and typing quickly on my laptop keyboard. It's around 4:00 p.m., and I've finally settled in for a late afternoon of Saturday brunch and blogging.

Normally I like to get an early start on my B&B, but I got home super late after last night's, ahem, activities and let myself sleep in way past noon. I feel like I'm in high school again, illegally drunk on attention, sneaking around an eternally absent Leila. I'm trying so hard to focus on scheduling my outfit posts for the upcoming week, but my mind is wandering as far as Jersey. I keep replaying yesterday's tryst in the beauty closet over and over.

The thing about Cal is I'm extremely attracted to him, and not just because of his crater-sized dimples or freakishly

Hulk-like biceps. I'm drawn to his ambition, to the fact he truly does seem to have an answer to everything. I admire his hustle—I love that he's passionate about making the world a better place, that he aims to not only give a voice to his community but improve it. They're qualities I hope someone sees in me one day.

Which takes me to my next point: I don't know if I like the person I am when I'm with Cal. The way he sees right through me is scary; it's as if he's bypassed Noora and gone straight to Shabnam. But I don't want to believe that person is my true essence. That, if given the opportunity, I would step on others' toes until they bleed in order to get what I want. Whatever darkness apparently beckons to him from within me, I want no part in it. I am a *good* person. I want to believe that.

And I know I can't trust Cal. After fucking for approximately four point five seconds and giving him a cute lesson on the female anatomy, I asked him once again if he'd consider protecting my secret and not telling Loretta what he now knows. Then he said, with his semen *still inside of me* (FYI, I have an IUD, but reminder to self to ask him the last time he was tested):

"I don't know yet."

Excuse me?

He doesn't *know* if he's going to betray my confidence by telling my boss a secret that could ruin my career and possibly my life? Once those words were out in the open, we lay there, panting in the dark, naked and surrounded by fallen beauty products and empty packaging. The things we left unsaid seemed to suck the remaining air out of the windowless vacuum of a room. Eventually, I sat up and began getting dressed. Cal watched me closely, his eyes never leaving my collarbones.

"Can you help clean this up?" I said, gesturing to all the goods scattered around the carpeted floor.

"Hey," he responded playfully. "You clean up your own mess."

Keeping my frustration to myself, I hastily started grabbing lipsticks and empty bottles off the floor and throwing them into nearby bins.

Finally coming to a stand, he reached over and placed his hand on my shoulder. I immediately flinched. We just stood there, two outlines in an unlit room, surrounded by negative space.

"I'll text you," I said, before grabbing the remainder of my things and booking it out of there.

I rode the six train home, a little later than I'd like. There was a woman wearing large, thin hoop earrings, crying into the phone in a language I didn't recognize, seated on my left. A mysterious substance with an even more intriguing smell lined the corner floor. I closed my eyes, held my nostrils, and imagined I was somewhere else. Maybe far, far way, with my parents in Dubai. And my maman was cooking *khoresht*, a single serving just for me.

You know this doesn't mean anything, right?

By virtue of being a woman in the world, I've learned not to equate sexual intimacy with emotional intimacy. I don't think that just because a person from the opposite sex wants my body it means they'll also value my thoughts and opinions. And they shouldn't have to—I've learned from Leila that as long as two people are on the same page before peeling back the layers, there's nothing wrong with casually getting serious. But something about the way Cal chose to communicate how he felt to me, the nonchalant way he painted his words, felt personally cutting. I begin to itch my arms just thinking about it.

Maybe it's because what he said resonates in every other area of my life too. Do I mean anything to Loretta? To Jade?

Even Saffron is benefiting from their "friendship" with me. Is there anybody in my life who likes me for who I am, whoever I am, not because of what I can do for them?

I woke up this morning (okay, fine—it was the afternoon) to a single message from Loretta. My heart sank, but at least my breathing was stable. I knew this was coming.

Loretta (12:13 PM): What were you able to find out?

For a split second, I considered being honest with her. Coming clean about the whole thing and hoping she'd just forgive me for picking the wrong side. Maybe Jade would step in defend me. I could get promoted, become an actual editor, work remotely whenever I want. All of *Vinyl* would respect me. Superman would give me a high five every time I walked through the door.

Fat fucking chance.

Noora (12:14 PM): No luck. IP address encrypted. Totally in the dark.

Okay, so I lied. But she didn't really leave me a choice. A few seconds later, my phone loudly pinged. I looked around the apartment to see if the sound woke up Leila, but of course, she slept over at Willow's. Fantastic.

Loretta (12:14 PM): That is NOT what I needed to hear, my dear. This is very bad news.

I don't know what that means, and I don't want to find out. I'd rather spiral in a public place, all by my myself, surrounded by influencers with no real jobs who somehow make ten times more money in a day than I do in a year.

Out of the corner of my eye, I watch the woman sitting on my right, a certified pick-me girl, tear apart her avocado toast with a fork and disdain. She attempts to cut it up into sections—never once looking away from her rugged, bearded date—with both her fork and her knife. It's as if she thinks she's about to gnaw on a filet of steak. Slowly, she stabs the smallest piece, raises it to her lips, and gives it a good sniff. She hesitantly takes a bite, chewing it like a Starburst that might magically change flavors halfway through consumption. When she thinks he's not looking, she spits it out into her napkin and places it beneath her plate.

I sift through all my work for the day within the next hour—preparing my posts for the next week, penning the prose that goes alongside it. I write what I believe to be a funny yet harrowing rendition of what can only be described as a performance review of ten swanky old Manhattan restaurants. But I use political language, as if they were physically debating each other on the DNC stage. When I'm done, I can't tell if what I've created is pure satire or pure garbage. But at the very least, it's on the page. Ever since writing my covert, critically acclaimed debut column, I've been feeling a little bit creatively stagnant.

"Actually, I *do* consider myself a feminist," Avo Chick's lumberjack manages to say. "Don't forget I voted for Hillary. It's not *my* fault the rest of Pennsylvania didn't."

When I hear those words fly out of his mouth, I take it as my cue that it's time to go. I pay the check, gather my belongings, and retreat to Leila's.

But first, I make a pit stop at Petrosino Square. It's a little past 6:00 p.m. now, which means the sky has somehow gotten darker than my thoughts. I take a seat on my favorite park bench, directly facing trendy eatery Jack's Wife Freda. I have made many important calls on this bench. It's where

I placed a cowardly call to my high school boyfriend on Indigenous People's Day (then referred to as Columbus Day) in order to tell him I needed to take a pause from our relationship, which then turned into a break, which somehow transformed into our breakup. It's the same bench I sat on when I received my NYU acceptance email, then immediately called Leila, who was at college at the time, with the good news. "BIIIIIIITCH," her shrill voice had screamed into the phone.

I miss her so much.

This evening, I'm cuddling up alone on this tiny park bench—next to an adorable Pomeranian and an equally cute little old lady reading the *Times* with a flashlight—in order to call my parents. They'll be just waking up on their tiny slice of the universe, opening their eyes to the possibility of a new day or some other heinously clichéd bullshit. Here's what no one ever tells you about adulthood: The older you get, the more comforting corny can be.

Maman answers on the first ring, as she always does. I can hear her calling Baba to come to the phone in the background.

"I thought you had forgotten about us," she scolds me, her accent thick, caught deep in her throat.

"I know and I'm sorry," I admit. "Work has been really busy, but I know that's no excuse."

There's silence on the other end of the line. My family is a lot of things, but quiet isn't normally one of them.

"We heard you did something to upset your sister?" my father asks.

His accent weighs heavily on every syllable, causing him to add an *eh* sound before every letter *S* and turn his *W*s into *V*s. *Something* becomes *ehsomething*. *Sister*? *Ehsister*. EhStarbucks, and so on and so forth. It used to embarrass me, his accent. His voice was just another reminder of our otherness, a dead giveaway that we were foreigners. That was a long time ago. Now, his Fenglish (a Farsi-English hybrid) just makes me realize how much I miss him.

Oh, wait a second. Leila narked on me. Uncool.

"We just had a little argument, that's all," I lie. "Also, about work. It'll be fine, she just needs to get over herself."

"As long as it's resolved by Thanksgiving," Maman says. "I know you girls love your little tradition."

I gulp—in all the chaos, I totally forgot that Thanksgiving, is like, a week and a half away. "I promise." I'm not sure whether or not I mean it.

"We have to go—Saeed is coming over for *chayee* in an hour or so."

I can hear my father start walking away from the phone, checked out, his mind moving on to his next task of the day. My mother remains on the line.

"What's wrong, *jeegaram*? I can hear it on your voice. You are not yourself."

I feel myself start to sniffle a bit. I will myself to cry, just for the sake of feeling the release. But the tears don't come.

"Nothing, just work," I tell her for the third time. She sighs. My mother gave up prying for details years ago, after an accidental encounter with my diary sent her running for the hills—and to CVS to buy several dozen pregnancy tests.

"Well, promise me you'll apologize to Leila," she says. "*Joonie joonam*, family is all we have got in this world."

With that, she hangs up the phone. I stay seated on the bench, giving my tear ducts one last chance to do their thing. After a few seconds of squeezing my eyes shut and thinking about dead puppies, I give up and walk home defeated.

As I tread the stairs of Leila's walk-up, I notice that even though she's not present, her scent is. Her aroma lingers

190

throughout our tiny shared apartment, spreading like venereal disease. She's clearly coming by whenever I'm out of the house in order to change her clothes and grab necessities. I even notice that this time, she had a spare minute to wipe down the shower and clean my hair out of the drain.

I take out my phone and turn off the Find My Friends feature then stop sharing my location on Snapchat Maps. I'm not giving her the satisfaction of being able to see me when I can't see her.

When I was younger, staying home alone on a Saturday night would give me a lot of anxiety. I'd think about all the rooms in all the apartments in all the buildings in New York City, lit up by the laughter and a promise that only other people can fulfill. I'd pity myself for having no one, loved by no one but my mother. Back then, the only sources of comfort I had were reading, writing, and watching *Saturday Night Live*.

For my family, *SNL* was the equivalent of Sunday football. We'd gather around the TV as if we were a cult and the cable box, our prophet. My parents were both foreigners who, at best, spoke muddled English. But they still laughed at all the right jokes and booed all the right people. *SNL* made us feel like we belonged and, as a consequence, made me feel like I fit in.

Do you know that inexplicable feeling of body-radiating warmth that can only come from laughing *so* hard for *so* long with another person that you start to wonder if, before this very moment, you were ever truly happy?

Only two outlets have provided me with that kind of belly-aching completeness: *SNL* and Leila. So, tonight, I don't text Cal after one too many glasses of wine and invite him to come over. Nor do I call Saffron and admit I have no one to spend my weekends with. Instead, I snuggle up alone and allow the words *live from New York, it's Saturday night* to move through me like a bad piece of sushi.

The host is none other than Donald Glover. The musical guest? Childish Gambino. I google to see if Donald Glover is a Leo. He's not; he's a Libra. *Damn.*

The next hour and a half go by quickly, like a Jet Blue flight filled with zero turbulence and only the hottest new releases. I laugh at the political cold open (Kate McKinnon is chef's kiss), talk back a little bit during Weekend Update, and find myself dozing off after the second musical number. By the time I wake up, the entire cast is on the main stage, hugging, and taking their final bows. I smile widely along with them, as if we're all together at 30 Rock, sweating under the spotlight and owing Lorne Michaels our careers.

But then the screen goes black before switching over to NBC's next segment on the Hulu app: the late late-night show with *SNL* alum Seth Meyers. I keep my eyes locked on the TV, too lazy to get up and grab the remote to switch it off.

Seth starts with his usual spiel by recapping the week in news, entertainment, yada yada. I begin yawning again, absent-mindedly feeling my face and trying to remember if I put on any makeup this morning that I should probably take off.

Then I hear a familiar shrieking voice right in my very apartment. I literally jump off the pull-out couch.

"I am now joined by Loretta James, editor in chief of *Vinyl*, millennials' favorite fashion magazine," Seth announces.

"Culture magazine," I correct him.

I rub my eyes, closing and opening them again, in disbelief of what's happening in front of me. Loretta saunters onto the stage, dressed sharply in a tailored red men's suit, which matches her hair to perfection, and her signature boots.

"What the actual fuck?" I ask my empty apartment.

Loretta's arrival is met with applause from the studio

audience. I reluctantly applaud along with them. Loretta smiles and does a cheeky bow before taking a seat on the couch opposite Seth's news desk.

"Now, Loretta, *Vinyl* is infamous for publishing some prolific work over the years," Seth continues. "But your recent Beauty Politics column debuted just last week and caused quite an uproar, the likes of which we haven't seen since that exposé on music streaming rights. In fact, within hours of the article going live, #ReduceHairiffs was trending on Twitter."

Loretta produces a girlish giggle, as if she has even the slightest clue what *trending* means. I'm worried my eyes are going to get stuck staring at back of my head.

"Well, Seth, what can I say? At *Vinyl*, we don't just care about the 'what' of the story. We care about the 'why.' Why does this matter? And why should readers care?"

This time, the studio audience whistles, and Seth joins in with a slow clap. I grit my teeth.

"And this mysterious writer? Where on earth did you find C. Bates? Isn't this her first time being published? Or his? Or their?"

Loretta let's out a hardy har har, because pronouns are *so* hilarious. So this was why she was willing to go above and beyond to identify C. Bates.

My arms feel like they're on fire. I give them a good scratch.

"Well, I can't reveal my sources," she says, wiping tears from her eyes. "But let's just say this one hit very, very close to home."

Seth and I both sit up in our seats.

"Are you saying the mystery writer in question might even, in fact, be sitting here in this room with me tonight?" he asks. I itch faster and harder.

"I'm not *not* saying that, Seth."

Chapter Twenty-Two

If I murdered Loretta in cold blood but out of self-defense, would it be considered justifiable homicide or manslaughter?

For the first time ever, I almost call in sick to work. Mondays are always god-awful, but the idea of seeing that smug smile on Loretta's face as she calls me *sweetheart* and stomps all over my hopes and dreams might actually destroy me.

I kept replaying the Seth Meyers segment on a loop over and over again, all Sunday long. At first, I thought maybe I was getting sick (it is flu season, after all). But when getting up and walking over to the bathroom in order to hurl felt like too much effort, I know I was really just overwhelmed with anxiety. So, instead of fighting it, I submitted by barely moving all day long. The sun rose and set without me ever leaving Leila's couch, until it was Monday. Now I'm sitting on the subway, dressed in cozy coordinating knits, trying to figure out how I'll be able to avoid Loretta's eye contact all day long.

I mean, who *does* that? Steal another person's idea and take credit for it as if it's a loaf of bread? SHE'S NOT EVEN HAIRY!!! I imagine this is what Jade has been experiencing the past six months. Poor, poor Jade. I can't believe I ever judged her for crossing the line, for fighting Loretta in open battle. I know now that all her actions were coming from a place of pain. She was swinging her sword with an open and heavy heart, which was always in the right place.

And what if C. had been someone else? Wouldn't she be scared of being sued right now? Maybe she actually believes the writer's anonymity will protect her ambiguity, but that's a pretty naive assumption to make. If I were her, I'd be very nervous right now. She's treading on thin ice, and I can hear it crackle beneath her combat boots.

I walk into the office around 10:00 a.m., my hands shaking with rage, and pass Saffron's empty desk. They texted me this morning to let me know they were taking a desk-side coffee meeting before work, that they would see me later to discuss the segment, and that they were "furious" for me. Honestly, I'm pretty fucking furious too.

When I arrive at my desk, I have to resist the urge to enter the safety code to Loretta's office and manically begin tearing it apart—throwing files all over the room, tossing the plant out of the thirty-second-story window. But instead, I sit calmly and seethe in private. Around me, I can hear the few Print editors that came in congratulating each other on Loretta's victory. It's nauseating.

"Did *you* know she was C. Bates?" I hear Raquelle, the Print Beauty editor, whisper across the room. It's the kind of sound that's halfway between silence and a scream.

"No clue, but I'm not surprised. She's always one step ahead!"

I shut my eyes and try to slow down my breathing. My fists are clenched, my fingers agitated, hungry for release. I scratch rapidly in an attempt to soothe my mind, but I'm furious. Loretta couldn't be further behind the curve. Her brand of woke is frozen in 2003. Why would a rich white woman write about capitalism and body hair? How could anyone possibly believe that she's behind Beauty Politics? It's a sick joke.

And then, on cue, the devil herself strolls through the double doors—passing all the whispering Digital editors, pausing to high-five a few Print editors—before parking herself right in front of my desk. She smiles widely at me. I stare down at my computer and count to three.

After about thirty seconds of waiting for me to congratulate her, Loretta gets bored and moves on.

"What's my first appointment of the day, my darling?" she asks, as if she doesn't have access to her own calendar.

"I'm not your darling," I grunt into my desk table.

"What was that?"

"Nothing."

I fish open her schedule and recite her entire day without breaking eye contact with whoever is hacked into my laptop camera. She's got a few internal meetings—Beth, Art, nothing major. Then around 3:00 p.m., there's an off-site coffee with what looks like a team of investors (note to self: Call a very early Lyft). Finally, she'll cap off her Monday with a regularly scheduled blackout meeting.

Loretta half listens, scrolling through her phone, grinning like a goblin.

"Do I have any messages?" she asks, leering over my shoulder at the phone.

"Yup, I already forwarded them to your office line."

She frowns, clearly frustrated that I haven't given her the opportunity to gloat about her interview yet.

"What about flowers?"

"Whatever's come in is already sitting on your office table. I arranged them myself this morning."

Loretta narrows her eyes, her frown lines indented with

irritation. Her lips are pursed, ready to thank me, but I won't give her the satisfaction. I won't bring up this weekend's cameo even if my job depends on it—and, like, it might.

I spend the day basically avoiding talking to Loretta for longer than a minute, out of fear that I might pull out her extensions. Everyone is pissing me off today. Kelsea keeps messaging me every hour, on the hour, asking if we can meet remotely and talk. About what? She won't say, but I assume it has to do with the weekend's festivities. She probably wants to confirm that Loretta didn't actually write Digital's Beauty Politics column under a pseudonym (although, wouldn't that be kind of epic? I can't imagine anything that would get under Jade's skin more). Or she discovered that I'm the one behind the column and she's planning on extorting or exposing me. Maybe both.

Can you believe I'm living my dream job?

When I finally get Loretta into a Lyft after attempting to pull her out of her office closet for approximately fifteen minutes—thank God I called that poor driver in advance and warned him about who he was dealing with—I take a break from scratching my scatterplot stress rash and go visit Saffron.

The second I approach their desk, I can see from beneath the weighted blanket they're hiding under that they have been crying. Their makeup is blotchy, and their eyes are bloodshot. I've never seen them looking messy; Saffron is always the pinnacle of put together.

"Who did this to you?!" I ask, forgetting all about my own rage for the first time in two days. "Should we go to the beauty closet and debrief?"

"I can't leave my desk," Saffron says coldly. "Kelsea is watching me like a fucking CIA operative for Jade."

I follow their gaze. Sure enough, Kelsea is staring at us and taking notes. When she sees us seeing her, she quickly pulls up Safari and pretends to be shopping for snakeskin boots on Etsy.

How perfect for her.

"Oh, okay."

Saffron looks around, paranoid, then gestures for me to lean in closer. I oblige.

"I'm getting torn apart for Loretta's interview," they mumble. "Jade either thinks I knew it was Loretta and was complicit or believes I didn't know anything about it and was negligent. Either way, I'm a traitor or an idiot. I can't win. I'm in so much trouble, Noora."

Their eyes start to well back up with tears, and my heart sinks. I clutch their hand.

"What can I do to help?" I ask them.

They look up at me, wrestle their hand away from mine, and wipe their eyes. "Confess. Come forward. Tell everyone it was you—that you're C. Bates."

I watch Saffron latch on to my reaction, and I gulp. "You know I can't do that," I say slowly.

"Why? Why can't you do that? Because you'll lose your job? If you don't, I could lose mine!"

I stir anxiously, backing away slowly.

"I should go back to my desk," I finally respond. "Loretta should be back soon."

"I'm so fucked," I hear them mutter as I walk away.

Great. There goes my last friend in the world.

Loretta arrives back in the office after her off-site around 4:30 p.m. She struts down the halls with gusto, as if she's running for president. Her enthusiasm makes the entire sleek, millennial-pink space look bleak in comparison. It's as if someone pumped her up with happy pills or took a needle filled with adrenaline straight to her spine.

"My face hurts from smiling so much!" she exclaims as she

reaches my desk. I say nothing and continue to stare at my computer screen.

Loretta stands there, tapping her combat boot. I can feel her gawking at my indifference.

"Okay, I've had enough of whatever this is," she says. "In my office, now."

I sigh and reluctantly get up and follow her. I know that if my goal is to remain employed, I probably should have behaved less like a toddler today. And, yes, I'm about to get my ass handed to me, but I can't help it. I know I'm not in the position to tell Loretta the truth, but I also can't look at her stupid grin without imagining clawing her eyes out with acrylics. If I'm a three-year-old, she's the childhood bully peeing all over my sandbox.

Deep breaths, Noora.

Once I'm seated in the desk chair across from her, Loretta drops the niceties and cuts to the chase.

"Why aren't you happy for me?" she asks pointedly. "We won!"

I stare off into space. "I am happy for you," I say to the wall behind her head.

"You've been in a bad mood all day, dear. Spit it out."

I scratch my inner elbows.

"Is it a family problem?" she pesters. I shake my head.

"Boy troubles? Or girl troubles? He, she, it troubles?"

I stay quiet, refusing to engage in this ridiculous line of questioning. Of course, my strike has the opposite of the desired effect. Loretta grows more and more impatient, like a toddler.

"Or maybe you're just jealous! Oh, that's it, isn't it? Little miss Noora, mediocre fashion blogger, is angry she isn't getting all the praise! She wishes *she* had written the Beauty Politics column instead of me! Maybe then *she'd* be getting all the attention!"

"You didn't write it!"

Loretta's exaggerated, mocking expression shifts as the color drains from her face. She looks back at me, dumbstruck.

"And how could you possibly know that? You told me Cal couldn't find the source."

"Because I wrote it! I'M C. BATES," I snap.

My words slap her across the face. She looks as if I just told her that her grandfather hadn't actually died of old age—he was murdered.

"What did you just say?"

"I'm C. Bates."

Our awkward silence is suddenly interrupted by the sound of a Destiny's Child ringtone. Whose phone is that? Who would have the *audacity* to interrupt this very uncomfortable moment with such a rude, unconscionable—

Oh. It's mine.

"It must be time for my meeting," Loretta says, her eyes misty. Her voice sounds foggy, as if she's waking up from a coma. As my adrenaline and anger start to wear off, the gravity of what I've done hits me like a random burst of Twitter followers. I didn't mean to lose my temper; it just came out. She was provoking me, baiting me. And I fell for it, like the fool that I am.

"Loretta..."

"We'll talk about this later."

"But—"

"Later, Noora."

Loretta stands up and composes herself, pulling her shoulders back and arching her spine slightly. She takes one last, quick look at me and sighs. But not a light, slightly annoyed sigh. Her sigh is heavy, weighted by disappointment. I've really let her down. She walks out the door without another word.

As soon as she's gone, I book it to Saffron's desk. Their chair is empty; they must be in a Design meeting or something. I open the bottom drawer and grab the keys to the beauty closet, tears spilling down my cheeks like the waterfall in Singapore's Changi Airport (as seen in *Crazy Rich Asians*).

You ruined everything. You ruined everything. You ruined everything.

I throw the door open and hear it lock behind me then pace back and forth. The small space feels like it's closing in as I berate myself for my foolishness. *You idiot. You fucking idiot.* My brain attempts to wrap itself around the facts, but I keep running into roadblocks. I can't quite comprehend how, after everything I risked—relationships with my friends and family—I could have wasted it all on a single, childish outburst.

My hands are shaking, so I scratch myself harder and faster to keep them busy. I try to catch up to my inhales and exhales, but my throat starts to close, so I clutch on to my neck instead. My palms feel clammy against my skin.

When I was five years old, I used to cry myself to sleep. Not over anything in particular; nothing was wrong, so to speak. But I'd spend my last waking moments of every night thinking about inevitability—the fact I'd one day die, that the world might never know I even existed to begin with—and lull myself with tears. Some people find the finality of death comforting, a great equalizer. They see the fact we are all just specks on an unspeakably magnanimous canvas as soothing as a mother's hug. But this truth filled me with the fear of something greater than God: insignificance. The cold, isolating reality that your thoughts, your body, your dreams, might never even matter. That's my big bad. And I've been running from it ever since.

Did I remember to eat today? I can't recall.

My mother likes to sing me a French song in broken English, her thick Arabic accent reverberating out of her mouth. "*Que sera sera*." Whatever will be, will be. I always burrow my head in her bosom and fight back tears. I wanted to fight against fate, to control the end of my story. I'd beat death and the never-ending darkness that came with it using something so powerful, so cliché, that it might actually make the smallest of differences: light.

My feet go cold. I lose feeling in the left side of my body first. Then it all goes black.

Chapter Twenty-Three

I hear a door creaking slowly, like a long yawn, followed by footsteps—heeled boots, I think. Their clacking is muted against the carpet, but then again, all sounds are faint and far-away, existing on a different plane, like rain pitter-pattering on the other side of a plexiglass window.

Then there's a scream.

"Oh my God," I hear a voice say, distant and disgruntled. Then there's that slow and steady yawn again, followed by silence. The earth stops rotating.

The door's pulled open. This sounds less like a yawn and more like a quick grunt, the kind you hear exclusively in porn. The muffled steps are accompanied by a new shoe. Loafers. Maybe ballet flats.

"How long has she been like this?" a quiet voice asks. There's a whimpering followed by a tiny cracking sound, like a fork grinding against a plate.

"I-I don't know. I just found her here, lifeless like this. She took the keys right out of my desk drawer when I was in the bathroom. Fifteen minutes ago, maybe twenty. I'm not sure. I had to ask the custodial staff for the spare. Is she...is she breathing?"

I feel something cold graze my wrist, a dog tickling my skin with its tongue.

"She's got a pulse. But look at these scars all over her inner arms. What are those from?" A warm fog passes over me. It smells of peppermint.

"Noora, can you hear me?"

The whimpering grows louder, like storm clouds rolling in over the ocean. Then lightning strikes—the moaning door turns into a full-stop screech, and all different kinds of footsteps outline the night sky. A pair of worn-soled sneakers. Chelsea boots, if I'm not mistaken. A silent poke of a stiletto.

My eyelids flutter open to find a mascara-stained Saffron, a forehead-wrinkled Beth, Dickhead Daniel, Lola, and Kelsea all hovering over me, staring down with feigned concern. I scan Saffron's eyes for meaning; the second we make contact, they break into big, heavy sobs.

"Where am I?" I ask, the alarm bells ringing in my brain. "What's going on?"

The door opens again, and about five more people flood in, two of whom I don't think I've ever seen before in my life. They all cram into the tight space. I try to lift my neck to sneak a peek, but maneuvering my head feels like trying to operate heavy machinery. I quickly give up the fight.

"You're in the beauty closet," Beth says, her calm vocal tone wavering slightly. "What's the last thing you remember?"

The beauty closet.

I'm in the beauty closet. Right. But what time is it? Did I make it to my meeting with Loretta? Has an entire week passed? I feel a hopeless, nonsensical lapse of time.

"Um, well." I rack my brain for answers. "It was Monday. I...Loretta had an off-site. I went to check on Saffron. Loretta came back and called me into her office."

Everything I said to Loretta comes free-falling back into

my brain. Every single word, each hateful syllable. I gulp and shut my eyes. Maybe it was all a dream.

"She had to run to a meeting, but we scheduled a touch-base for later. Then, I came to the beauty closet to touch up my makeup, and now I'm here talking to you."

I look around the room, at all the people whispering and staring at me with pity.

"What's going on?"

I can feel a sharp pain in my chest, as my breath quickens. My eyes feel itchy. Beth takes a deep breath and leans forward so she can rub my back.

"Don't panic, Noora," she says firmly. I try my best to listen, but everything around me is moving so slowly. "You fainted. I'm not sure how long you've been out. Saffron found you in here about five minutes ago."

I start to cry like a toddler whose ice cream cone has been unexpectedly slapped out of her hand by a bully. All my coworkers—my peers, my mentors, my enemies (hi, Kelsea!)—crowding around me is too much for me to take. The tiny walls of the closet begin to close in until I can no longer breathe and begin to hallucinate building security walking in.

"Someone walk me through the incident," the ghost of Superman says. He places a sturdy hand on my shoulder, as if trying to comfort me. Somehow, I feel the gravity of his touch.

This may all be real.

"She fainted in here, that's all we know," Beth says. Saffron sobs like their life depends on it.

"Did she hit her head?" he asks, looking down at me. I shake my head.

"Well, we don't know that," Beth jumps in. "Her last memory was entering the closet."

Superman exhales, shaking his head. He gives my arm a fatherly pat.

"Then we're going to have to call the EMT in here. She might have a concussion."

"What? No!"

The reality of the situation finally dawns on me: The entire SPP office is about to be crowding the beauty closet. Everyone will know I fainted. Loretta will know.

"P-p-p-please," I stutter, taking big gasps between my blubbering bawling. "Please don't tell Looooreeeeeettaaaaa!" I try hard to control my breathing, but my entire body is shaking.

"Loretta?" Superman looks confused. He reaches inside his front pocket and hands me a handkerchief to blow my snot into. I muster up a third of a smile to give him. "Listen, if the EMT is coming, we'll have to contact the police. This happened on company property. You could try to sue."

"I'm not going to sue!" I cry out. Kelsea laughs. Saffron looks up at her and practically spits in her direction.

"You're over the age of eighteen, right?" Superman asks.

I shake my head for a second then remember that I am, in fact, twenty-two. I nod.

"Do you want to contact your parents?"

"They live in Dubai." I sniffle.

"Do you have any other family in the city?"

I think of Leila. I imagine being wrapped up in one of her hugs at this very moment, smelling her signature musk, feeling her fingers run through my hair. It's what I want most. I'd do anything to be with her right now, to take back our pointless fight. To tell her she was right. She was right about everything.

"No, I don't," I tell Superman. He frowns and scribbles something on his clipboard.

Suddenly, a cop bursts into the tiny space, a couple of EMT nurses in tow behind them. Every SPP employee in the closet jumps in unison.

"Okay, everybody out," the cop yells. Daniel, Kelsea, Lola, and all the other randoms immediately evacuate. Saffron doesn't leave my side. "Who's in charge here?"

Beth takes a step forward.

"I am."

"Are you this girl's supervisor?" Mr. Cop asks, taking in the organized rows of makeup around him.

"No, but I am responsible for her," Beth says. "I'm the managing editor of *Vinyl*."

"The fashion magazine?"

"The *culture* magazine," I say from my comatose position. Upon hearing me speak, the EMTs flock to my side. The cop looks down at me and gives me a little wave. I wave back.

"Her vitals look good," one nurse says to the other. "Her heart rate is a little fast, though." They strap a pressurized plastic band around one of my arms. It cuts into my flesh.

"Are you dehydrated?" the first one asks.

"No, ma'am," I respond. I had, like, three bottles of water today. "Sorry, I didn't mean to assume your gender."

"That's all right," they say with a laugh. "Did you eat?"

"Yes. I had a little bit of granola from the free table."

"That's not enough," the EMT jumps in.

They turn to the other and not-so-subtly mouth, *This could be an anorexia thing.*

"It's not," I cut them off. "I know what happened."

The room goes silent. Saffron stops crying and pays attention, and Superman ceases scribbling on his board. Beth takes a step closer.

Why do I always have to open my fucking mouth?

"Well, what is it then?" Mr. Cop asks.

I go to scratch my inner arms, but one of the EMTs slaps it away.

"Stop it! You have cuts all over your arms! You'll bleed yourself dry," the EMT commands. I stop itching. The other EMT, the one playing good nurse, leans down to examine my arms.

"Is it a stress rash?" she softly asks. "Do you struggle with anxiety?"

I look around the room at Saffron and Beth then back up at the nurse. I nod. She sighs.

"I know what happened," the medic announces to the room. "She had a panic attack. Have you had panic attacks before, young lady?"

Saffron and I exchange a look. I hate being called a "little girl" or "young lady." It brings me back to years of being talked down to, treated with condescension. But I'm too freaked out to say anything.

"Yes," I admit, refusing to make eye contact with Saffron or Beth. "But never to the point that I've passed out."

"Did something triggering happen?"

I refuse to answer. There's no way I'm coming out as C. Bates while lying horizontal on the floor of a closet. Please, allow me to maintain *some* semblance of pride.

Besides, they'll all find out soon enough.

"Fine," she says, giving up. "Do you want to go to the hospital and have your brain monitored? In case you do have a concussion?"

I shake my head. Despite the massive amount of humiliation swelling in my brain, I feel relatively fine. A little sore, but the carpet really cushioned the fall.

"All right, then, I'm going to have someone escort you home."

"I'll do it!" Saffron volunteers. They sit down next to me, and I collapse into their arms, crying into their shoulder. They rub my back in a circular motion, just like Leila always does. It feels like listening to a remix of your favorite song—not the real thing, but it'll do.

"I'm sorry about earlier," I whisper to Saffron. "I have something to tell you."

"It can wait." They cut me off. "I'm just glad you're okay."

"What in God's name is going on in here?"

I hear a bellowing voice from outside the closet. My hands clam up. With the force of a natural disaster, Loretta James throws open the door to the beauty closet and marches right in. When she sees me, her face goes pale.

"Jesus, sweet pea, you look awful," she says to me. "What's going on in here? Why are you on the ground?"

She stops to take in the medics, police, and building security, as if suddenly noticing their presence.

"Hello, Officer," she says coolly.

"This young lady experienced a traumatic event," Mr. Cop explains. "I'm sending her home."

I cringe. There it is again.

At the sound of the word *home*, Loretta's ears perk up. She turns to the cop, red in the face.

"Traumatic event? What traumatic event? You can't just *take* my assistant away. I need her here! We have important business to discuss!"

Superman steps between the cop and Loretta, a solid five inches taller than both. He towers over them, quietly seething. Then, he turns around and offers me his hand. I take it, and he pulls me up onto my feet. I feel my knees slightly buckle. Superman seemingly notices and offers his arm. I grab on.

"She's coming with me," he says to Loretta, before walking

me out the beauty closet door. Saffron trails behind us, still sniffling.

"Thank you," I whisper to Superman.

He grunts back. "Just come with me."

We parade through the office—a sea of security, police-men, emergency responders, and *Vinyl* staffers. The rest of the floor gawks at me, whispering. Their eyes are lined with thick, clumpy pity.

"I hear she tried to kill herself," I hear someone mumble. I look down and try to imagine myself asleep, lucidly dreaming.

When we arrive at the elevators, Superman hands me to Saffron.

"Promise me you'll rest tonight, little lady," the nice EMT says. I nod, and we get on to the elevator. As the doors are closing, I see Cal walk into the hall. He takes in the scene then locks eyes with me, a horrified expression on his face. The elevator shuts just as he's about to say something.

And then we all go down.

Chapter Twenty-Four

I'm lying in my bunk bed, listening to Leila snore above me.
Her breathing is rhythmic and consistent, like a samba or a
waltz. Every once in a while, she lets out a little sigh then
switches her sleeping position from one side to the next.
I can hear the rustling of her sheets and comforter from
beneath her mattress. I can't stop thinking about how her
floor is my ceiling and how in some ways, everyone's floor
is someone else's ceiling, isn't it? Maybe even the deepest
depths of our sky create a sidewalk for a passing giant who
lives among the stars, and now I can't fall asleep. I'm clutching a book in my arms, the way some would a stuffed animal.
I look down at it.

Beauty Politics, the title reads. *By C. Bates.*

I immediately sit upright, startled.

Leila, I whisper to her body. She doesn't wake up. I use the
top of my foot to give the bottom of her bed a baby kick—
just enough to stir her awake without bruising her body. But
she remains knocked out and buzzing, like an alarm clock.

Lei, wake up, I call out again, slightly louder this time. The
buzzing continues, a slow, wonky hum.

Annoyed, I climb out of bed, leaving my book nestled
beneath the sheets. My childhood bedroom has a ceiling

covered in glow-in-the-dark stars. Leila always makes me wish on one before going to sleep. I pick the one closest to the door, near the right-hand corner, by the bathroom, because its light is beginning to dim. It's the underdog of all the stars; not the North star, but *my* North star, if that makes sense.

What did you wish for? Leila always asks.

As if I'd ever tell you. Then it would never come true.

There's a small desk facing our bunk beds, covered in loose papers and gel pens, with a *Powerpuff Girls* backpack slung across it. My baba built it for us when I was ten so I can come home and do my schoolwork, study for tests, and write papers in peace. Leila is allowed to use it too—we were meant to share it—but she hardly ever brings her work home with her. She prefers to sit on her top bunk and watch me scribble away below. She says she finds the sound of my pencil quickly scraping away against the page to be relaxing. Like ASMR, she says. I don't get it, but to each their own.

The chair parked at the desk is *covered* in clothing, mostly Leila's. Even though we're only five years apart (I'm in the seventh grade, and she's a senior in high school), the gap feels as massive as a moon crater. It creates a barrier that might as well be a galaxy's distance away.

We barely have anything in common, my sister and I, other than our shared room and overwhelming amount of body hair. She's kissed both boys and girls; my only friends exist inside the books that line my shelves. Lately, she's been fighting nonstop with Maman. She says she doesn't want to go to college, that she'd prefer to enter the real world and get a job, do something to actually contribute to society instead of wasting money on an education that will teach her nothing but how to shotgun a beer. She would prefer to work at a package-free shop or move to DC so she can get arrested while protesting on the National Mall. Like Jane Fonda, she says.

My parents will hear nothing of it. They say the only reason they risked everything by hauling ass all the way to the United States was to see us go to good schools. Leila says this is "projection," a concept I don't fully understand yet. But I pretend to.

We just want what's best for you, Maman says.

You just want what's best for you.

I just lie in my bed, the covers of a freshly opened hardcover pressed to my cheeks, reading a single sentence over and over until something registers.

There's that buzzing again.

Leila must be twitching in her sleep. She once told me she sleepwalked all the way to the lobby of our building, that she came to just as she was about to enter a busy Brooklyn street, most likely about to get hit by a car. A physical manifestation of a nightmare.

I should really organize all the clothes on the chair, though. Most of the items sprawled all over still have yellow price tags on them, with $5 written in cursive Sharpie. They're all left over from this Saturday. Leila took me thrift shopping and taught me how to run one finger over all the racks with my eyes closed, to feel for the fabrics. Polyester was an instant pass. Cotton, linen, silk are all fair game. She showed me how to stop when I felt the difference in caliber, to pick the pieces that would last me the longest, not make the flashiest statement.

It's all about strategy. Don't go for quantity. Go for quality.

I watched her, mesmerized, taking mental notes to review before bed.

The bunk bed ladder has always scared me, mostly because it's a little bit loose and I've fallen off it so many times before. But as my body grew bigger, the floor rose so much closer to my feet, rendering the fall somewhat obsolete. It's nuts the difference a few years can make.

I reach the top of the stairs and find Leila shaking uncontrollably beneath her comforter, as if she had jumped headfirst into a frozen lake in the middle of February. Concerned, I throw the covers back at once, prepared to take her in my arms and huddle for warmth.

"Good morning, Little Light," Cal says.

"AAAaAAAaH!!!!" I scream, my entire body shaking. My hands and feet look like they've grown three sizes.

How old am I? What year is this?

I jump off the ladder, barely landing on my feet, and make a run for the door.

"You know this doesn't mean anything, right?" he calls behind me.

The incessant buzzing continues in the background, swelling like a symphony. I reach the door, turn the knob, and throw it wide open.

I'm in my high school auditorium.

This is the catalyst. It's also where we host weekly assemblies and the fall and spring plays, usually Shakespeare or something like it. The chairs are stitched in a dark-red velvet and fold up like movie theater seats when unattached to a buttock. There's a small tech booth, a glass box resembling a model Apple store, that sits in the very back, atop all the velvet folding chairs, which cascade down toward the stage at an angle, like a county fair slide. I can see Mr. Dailey, the head of tech, messing around with the lighting from afar. Golden framed portraits of our past principals line the walls, all brazen-looking white women over the age of seventy wearing stern expressions. The frames are robust and hand-carved, but the canvases are nothing. Each painting alone is worthless without the right frame.

Every single seat in the auditorium is empty yet warm. I can hear voices, whispering and cackling. I squint, looking for a culprit, but I find none.

Tsk tsk tsk, one sneers.

You look like a Lucha Libre, another shouts.

But you're really just a terrorist, a third chimes in.

The voices are cut off by a drumroll from the loudspeaker above the stage.

The curtains are drawn open. A single spotlight shines at the podium. I hear the clacking of heels approaching from the green room beneath the stairs. A figure moves in the shadows, crossing the stage floor. When they step into the spotlight, I let out a gasp.

It's Leila, dressed in her old school uniform: khaki pants and a crisp, white button-down. There are a pair of black combat boots strapped to her feet; they look just like you-know-who's. She taps on the microphone twice to test if it's on. The tapping creates a glare, which reactivates the buzzing noise. This time, it's so loud that I have no choice but to plug my ears with my pointer fingers.

"My name is Leila," she begins, speaking into the empty auditorium as if every seat in the house is packed. I let out a small cheer, but she doesn't hear me. Instead, she remains laser-focused on the piece of paper in her hand.

"I'm going to be reading an excerpt from my award-winning college essay about the monetization of hair removal. It's titled, 'Hairmerica.' I hope you enjoy."

The room breaks out into a sea of applause. I crane my neck and scan every inch of the theater space, looking for the source of the noise. But it still appears to be oddly empty.

Onstage, Leila clears her throat and starts her reading. The first few sentences are incredibly well-written, her lede dripping with nuance and satirical prose. Her beats even feel oddly familiar, as if I've heard them somewhere before.

Hey, wait a minute.

"I wrote this!" I call out to Leila on stage. But she still

can't hear me. I try waving at her from where I'm sitting in the front row, but she doesn't look down.

"I wrote this!" I shout a little louder.

A ghost in the audience whistles up at Leila, and she smiles and nods into the abyss.

I feel a quick, sharp pain in my chest. They should be cheering for me! These are my whistles. She doesn't deserve the praise. It's just not fair. It's not right!

Someone, a real human body made of blood and bones, sits down in the folding chair next to me.

"What's wrong, *joonam*?" my maman asks.

I throw my arms around her, and she pulls me in close, kissing the top of my head. She smells of turmeric, sumac, and a house full of party guests. I've never been so happy to see her. I've missed her more than I realized.

"Maman, I wrote the essay that Leila's reading! She stole it from me."

My mother scratches my scalp and plays with my hair, just like she used to do when I was a kid.

"I thought you only wanted for people to hear your words, to read your work. So that your stories could help them, to touch their lives. And Leila reading them aloud is doing just that, isn't it? Why should it matter who's driving the car if you ultimately reach your destination?"

I roll my eyes.

"I guess you're right," I say, conceding to her point. "But I still want people to know it was me. Can't I care about the reader *and* myself? Why do I have to pick just one when I could so easily have both?"

My maman picks my head up off her lap and places her hands under my chin so that our eyes are leveled. I can hear the buzzing in the background booming, now pouring down from the loudspeakers.

"Do not let your ego get the best of you," she says. "You're here on a mission to do good. This isn't about you."

I close my eyes, trying to internalize her words and block out the buzzing. This isn't about me. It was never about me.

"Or is it, darling?"

My eyes fly open to find that my mother is gone. Loretta James now keeps her seat warm and holds my head in her hands. I jolt away from her, and she lets out a delicious cackle.

"It's not! I'm not doing this for myself! I'm doing it for the reader! For the magazine!"

"Sure, doll," she says. "Face it: You're a two-faced, cold-blooded bitch. Just like me."

Loretta grins and leans in, as if she's going to kiss me. I slap her away, and she squawks like a seagull, but the buzzing drowns out her wailing. I look up at the stage. Leila hasn't flinched or stuttered once. She continues to read my column out loud with an empty expression on her face.

I look for the exit, in need of a quick escape. But the auditorium has no doors or windows. Was the black box always like this? So literal? I bang on the walls, begging for someone to let me out.

Loretta slowly inches toward me. The closer she gets, the more deafening the buzzing. I see a hooded figure enter stage left and sneak up behind Leila, placing a black gloved hand over her mouth and holding it there until her eyes roll in the back of her head and she collapses into a puddle onstage.

"LEILA!" I cry out. The hooded figure takes a step forward into Leila's spotlight, checks the microphone, pulls back its hood, then looks directly at me. It's—

PING.

I sit upright, covered in sweat, my wet T-shirt clinging to my body and sending a cold shiver down my spine. I'm in Leila's apartment, in my pull-out couch bed. The room

217

is dark, meaning it's most likely still the middle of the night. Not too much time could have passed between now and what went down at *Vinyl*.

It was a dream. I was dreaming.

I exhale, a sigh of relief, detecting a muffled sound in the dark. Using my phone flashlight, I identify the culprit: It's Leila, fast asleep in the armchair next to me. She must have finally come home when she heard what happened to me. I bet Saffron called her.

I know the past twenty-four hours have been, well, definitively *the worst*. But still, I can't help but smile. She looks so peaceful when she sleeps, like a newborn puppy or a little old man.

PING.

The phone in my hand vibrates. I squint down at the fluorescent bright light of my screen and attempt to focus my eyes.

I have thirty-two missed calls from Loretta. Thirty-fucking-two.

I literally *passed out* in a closet less than twenty-four hours ago, and she harasses me the second I leave. Are you kidding me? There are texts too. Dozens of them.

> **Loretta (11:17 PM):** CALL ME!!! IT'S AN EMERGENCY.
> **Loretta (12:35 AM):** WHERE ARE YOU? CALL ME. 911!
> **Loretta (1:12 AM):** SWEET PEA, I NEED YOU. PLEASE GIVE ME A RING.
> **Loretta (2:24 AM):** NOORA IF YOU DON'T CALL ME WITHIN THE NEXT MINUTE YOU ARE FIRED.
> **Loretta (3:43 AM):** IGNORE THAT LAST MESSAGE. SORRY LOVE. GOT CARRIED AWAY.
> **Loretta (3:43 AM):** BUT CALL ME WHEN YOU CAN.

I look down at my phone, stunned. Was it so silly to

believe that something as serious as a health scare would convince Loretta I could spend twenty-four hours off duty? She probably needs to add another off-site meeting to the schedule and can't figure out how to edit her calendar. How could she possibly give me my space when there's so much important work to tend to?

My phone buzzes again. I don't even look down to read the message.

Instead, I power off the battery and bury it in a crevice of the couch. Then I lean over and squeeze Leila's hand three times before falling back asleep.

Chapter Twenty-Five

I wake up to the smell of butter melting and Norah Jones blasting from a phone speaker.

At first, I think I'm still dreaming. This is exactly how I used to wake up on Sundays as a child: music, usually Patti Smith or Bob Dylan, blaring out into the living room while my Baba got started on family breakfast.

I'd float out of my bedroom in my pajamas and sleepily take a seat on the couch, watching him crush herbs into a potion. He's the silent type—kind, but reserved, quiet kindness. Every once in a while, he'd look over at me and wink. I'd attempt to wink back, but my wink was more of blink. He'd let out the kind of laugh that sounds more like a cough and resume cooking.

"*Sobekher*, crazy lady," Leila sings to me, and my eyelashes flutter open.

She's standing in the kitchenette in her bra and panties, an apron with the *Birth of Venus* etched over it, which I happen to know she bought at the Met gift shop approximately six months ago. She's holding a pan in one hand and an uncracked organic egg (I can tell it's free-range by its undead color) in the other. Her hair is unbrushed.

"I'm making eggs," she announces. "Scrambled."

Now I'm sure I'm dreaming. The smell wafts past me and fills the living room as the sun peeks in behind the curtains, flirting with the wallpaper. I lie back and stretch my arms above my head, my face settling into a yawning smile.

And then I remember.

"So," I stutter slightly, trying to choose the right words. "I'm assuming you heard."

Leila doesn't look up from the yolk, she is so aggressively whipping. But I see a small smile creep onto her face.

"I told you that you needed to see a therapist."

"You were right."

"I always am."

She looks up and holds my gaze for a few seconds. Concern radiates out of her like a space heater. Then she breaks eye contact and goes back to cooking.

I don't know whether to laugh or cry, so both sensations get caught in my throat and I burp instead. The last week was the longest year of my life. Everything has changed, and at the same time, nothing. I feel like I'm twelve years old again, and Leila is going to take care of me—she'll tie my shoelaces and make my lunch and brainwash all of SPP into forgetting the last twenty-four hours.

Speaking of which.

"Where's my phone?" I ask Leila, as she meticulously shakes the pan, effectively scrambling the heck out of our eggs. Her head bobs to the music, her body slowly swaying like a wind chime. She seems relaxed for the first time in months.

"Not sure," she replies, melting more butter. "Why do you ask?"

"Well, I'll need to let Loretta know I'll be late for work."

Leila puts down the pan, the color draining from her face. Outside, an ambulance siren rolls down our block.

"You don't seriously think I'm going to let you go back there, do you?"

I pat around the couch-bed, searching for my phone. I could have sworn I stuffed it in here sometime in the middle of the night, unless that was all a part of my terrors. Entirely possible; I was definitely lucid throughout the hour.

"Seriously, Lei, where is it? What time is it?"

I'm digging my fingernails under each cushion and crevice, searching for the device. Leila clicks her tongue and sighs.

"It's 8:00 a.m.," she says. "Don't worry, you haven't missed a thing."

She reaches inside her apron and pulls out the phone, extending her arm to me. I get out of bed and walk over to her, but the second I go to grab it from her palm, she yanks her hand away, like a snapping turtle.

"Promise me you'll call in sick," she pleads. "At the very least for today. Promise me!"

To Leila's point, I was almost just hospitalized for a panic attack. That's definitely not "normal behavior."

But if I don't go into work today, who will prevent Loretta from telling the world that I'm C. Bates? Or worse, firing me?

I snatch the phone out of Leila's hand, laughing maniacally like a four-year-old, then race around the apartment clapping my hands. I feel a huge rush to my head then a bit woozy. I sit down on the floor and hold down the power button.

Sixty-five missed calls. Twenty-four texts. Eighty-seven emails. One Google alert.

My head starts pounding. I should've just listened to Leila and kept the phone off. I could have lied to Loretta and told her I dropped it down the elevator shaft. Or that I tragically died in a car crash.

I absentmindedly click into the Google alert, hoping to avoid responding to my messages for one minute longer. I set up Google alerts for Loretta's name, so I can flag down any bad press to Dickhead Daniel before it gets picked up by larger media outlets. There was once an issue with Popsugar, a paparazzi photo, and a zit the size of Jimmy Neutron's hair. I don't really want to get into it.

The Google alert redirects me to a *Women's Wear Daily* link, a fashion site that usually covers industry news.

Shifter & Pearce to Fold *Vinyl*'s Print Magazine after 20+ Years
The brand will live on as a digital-only platform

I drop the phone.

My hands are shaking, and my mouth feels dry.

"Water," I croak to Leila.

She looks down to find me seizing on the floor and promptly puts down her spatula.

"Jesus fucking Christ!" She runs over with a glass and starts force-feeding it to me then picks up the phone off the hardwood and zooms in on the screen. She lets out a small *oh shit.*

"I'm so, so, sorry," she musters up. But I can barely hear her. I'm too busy trying to make sense of this tangled-up mess in my mind.

All the blackout meetings. The weekly secret strategy roundtables. The discretion taken with the calendar locations and invite list. They must have all been P&L meetings with SPP's upper crust. Budget must have been in trouble for a long time; cuts could have started before I did.

Every single one of Loretta's feigned attempts at personal branding. The horrible Instagram takeover video, the hours we spent filming, cutting, and reshooting each take. The Experiences event. They were attempts at modernizing her profile, to churn her into a more sellable product. She knew the brand was failing. I have to believe she tried every last-ditch effort to save it.

Which brings me to the war with Digital. This is where the water gets a little murky. There's no doubt in my mind that Loretta knew that if *Vinyl* wasn't profitable in 2019, the print edition would surely become the sacrificial lamb. So she did everything in her power to make sure the magazine's buzziest pieces were published in the physical magazine, not online—or at the very least, the credit went to her. Jade's music streaming rights piece. My Beauty Politics column.

That in no way excuses her behavior over the past six months (or Jade's), but it does, at least, add a little color. She was fighting for survival. Loretta knew it was going to be us or them, and she was willing to protect her own. Even if it meant burning bridges and doing dirty deeds.

Or did she do it all to protect herself?

If *Vinyl* Print is kaput, existing solely as the carcass of the site, who will dig its grave? I have no clue whether or not SPP would trust Jade to continue overseeing the entirety of the brand on her own, especially after the offensive tweets debacle (which Loretta must have known. Damn). But Loretta has literally zero understanding of how to work on the internet, how to run a digital media company. Sure, she's a marquee name. Loretta James is synonymous with *Vinyl* magazine; she brings prestige to the table. But I wouldn't trust her more than five seconds with my touch pad. Why should an entire audience of readers, who have turned to us for answers every month for the past two decades?

Then I'm hit by a pang of unparalleled sadness. Actually,

it's grief—it spills out of my head and into my body like a carton of milk.

I find myself mourning for *Vinyl*. Not the place I've worked for the past five months. Not the wounds of warfare scarring my arms and legs, or the hours I've been over-worked with no overtime pay. Not the deceit or the rumor mill, Loretta's condescending "sweetie" remarks, or Jade's lethal side-eye. I'm bogged down by the space that will be left in *Vinyl*'s absence, a hollow melancholy for the magazine I grew up with. The glossy pages and witty profiles and the hundreds of forgettable ads. The photographers and writers and editors who poured themselves onto every single piece of paper. And the readers who slurped it up like ramen.

They deserve better. *We* deserve better.

I feel a lump in my throat. Seconds later, it's the size of a New York City bus.

"Lei, I love you, but I have to go."

We lock eyes, and she silently nods, taking my hand and squeezing it three times. I blink back tears.

It takes me five minutes to get dressed. I opt for a nod to the early 2000s, the years that *Vinyl* was at its prime, when Loretta had just begun to steer the ship. I cover my entire head in colorful butterfly clips and douse my lips in a shimmery gloss.

I'm ready for *Vinyl*'s funeral.

As I ride the six train, it occurs to me that I had momentarily forgotten about what went down yesterday evening. I had been so consumed by own career that I'd failed to see the bigger picture. I'd been more self-involved than Kim K. on her way to drop Khloé off at jail.

An older woman wearing a large shawl and glasses pushed to the tip of her nose looks up at me. In her sixties, if I had to guess. Jewish. She's wandered far from home—this specific flock of art film–loving, sheep farm–breeding, *New York Times* crossword puzzle–obsessed folks usually don't venture too far from the romantic prewar town houses of the Upper West Side. Unless, of course, they're taking a field trip to Katz's Delicatessen or Russ & Daughters.

The woman looks at me, then down at her phone, then back up at me again. As the train pulls into the Brooklyn Bridge station, she cranes her neck in alarm, double-checking she's on track to her destination. I take this opportunity to lean over and sneak a peek at whatever she's been squinting at on her iPad.

Just as I suspected, she has the *Women's Wear Daily* article open on her screen. It's out there, floating through the stratosphere. Everyone knows. I think guiltily back to all the unread messages, emails, texts, and missed calls that continue to blow up my own phone. I'm likely about to walk into the zombie apocalypse, but with more Gucci belts and less vomit. Oh, and far more terrifying.

When I arrive at SPP Tower, Superman can't even make eye contact with me. Instead, he looks down at his desk as I pass, his chin pressed to his chest. He must have heard the news. It's had about three hours to spread like the swine flu, infecting everyone it touches. And I was *this close* to remaining quarantined.

The second the elevator doors fly open on the thirty-second floor, I can hear chatter. I turn the corner then stop in my tracks.

The bullpen is *packed* with people.

Everyone is whispering with an overtly loud flashiness. It looks like every single Print and Digital editor came into work for the first time in *Vinyl's* recent history. They've set aside their differences to bond over one commonality, an equalizer greater than hatred: fear. Some are crying quietly at their desks. Others are preemptively decluttering their work spaces. A few look up at me and scoff, as if I'm the Grim Reaper, here to carry them all over into the hellfire.

"What are you doing here?!" Saffron exclaims, running toward me and throwing their arms around my neck. "Shouldn't you be horizontal being fed fluids through a tube?"

I can't even laugh. It's all too horrible.

"I had to be with everyone," I tell them. "I had to be with my family."

They take my hand and lead me into the wreckage. Everyone stops whispering and stares at me. One Print editor—Margie, in charge of home and finance content—runs toward me and grabs both my hands.

"Is SPP putting us up for sale?" she asks frantically.

"I bet we're getting acquired," another editor chimes in. "I bet *Bustle* is buying us. Or *Vice*."

"Are we all getting laid off?" someone from Art asks.

"Will we get severance?"

"Is SPP going to reallocate some of us to Digital?"

"Who's leading the site now?"

Every single person speaks out on top of each other until all I can hear is the humming sound of white noise, angry like a wasp. I take a deep breath and clear my throat. The crowd shushes.

"I don't have the answers you're looking for," I say. "But I will go talk to Loretta right now and let you know shortly."

Kelsea lets out a choked laugh and rolls her eyes.

"You don't know, do you?"

I study her face for clues as my face flushes. Feeling like a fool, I scan the room once more then shake my head.

"Noora, Loretta didn't bother to come in today. She's missing."

Chapter Twenty-Six

Noora (12:37 PM): Hey Loretta, where r u????
Everyone is kind of freaking out… are you planning
on coming in today?
Noora (1:05 PM): Hi! People are sort of panicking
over here. I think it would really help if I knew what to
say? Please call me!
Noora (2:27 PM): Loretta, SPP's HR rep has taken
over your office. She made me give her the code
to the padlock! What's going on? I'm getting really
worried…

I check Loretta's email for clues about what's about to
go down, but it appears that someone wiped her hard drive
clean.

At first, I assume the worst: *Loretta was the first to get laid
off and no one bothered to tell me.* The remains of her body and
her ego are slowly floating down the East River right now,
consecrated before God herself.

But then I refresh the page and realize I no longer have
access to her inbox. It would appear she actually changed the
password, locking me out altogether.

This brings me to my second theory: Separate from the

magazine folding, Loretta fired me yesterday, after the beauty closet debacle. And once again, HR neglected to give me notice. I am just another schmuck, a fall guy for the rest of my team. Everyone will assume I was laid off because of the news, when in actuality, my fate was sealed long before word got out.

Vinyl's lead HR liaison, Margaret Hader, struts right past me, her tightly wound top bun pulling back the skin on her face as if it's a Botox-induced Halloween mask. She barely bats an eye in my direction, and I take that as a sign I have not, in fact, been let go. Her black pinstriped skirt suit says real estate agent, but her recently shined Louboutin sling-backs say, *I killed my ex-husband for the insurance money.* If she asked me to jump, I'd fucking dive into the Hudson.

"Open this door," she commands. It takes me a split second to realize she's talking to me.

"Um, Loretta really doesn't like anyone in her office without her consent," I yammer away, avoiding meeting her eyes. Margaret Hader glares at me, her thick-framed glasses pressed against her eye sockets.

"Noora, I'm not going to ask again," she responds, clenching her fists. "Open this door right now before I call someone from the Tech Hub to come break into the keypad."

My stomach churns. The last thing I need right now is to see Cal. I inch toward the door and enter the password (Sarah's birthday). It clicks right open, and Margaret Hader pokes her head in, then her entire body. She makes herself at home at Loretta's desk, spreading a series of documents over the table, manila folders stacked behind her. I gulp.

"Very well, then," she says. "Now we can begin."

"Begin what?"

She glances down at the piece of paper in her hand, clicking her tongue like a beetle. I stare out the window, watching the fog roll into Lower Manhattan.

Thanksgiving is days away, which means the city has been oddly vacant, like a department store right before closing. Manhattan residents have fled to their hometowns to celebrate with their families, and NYC locals have flocked to their country houses in the Hamptons, Connecticut, and Cape Cod. The only onlookers that remain are tourists, here to stand in the 5:00 a.m. cold and freeze their asses off while waiting to see the Garfield balloon float in the flesh.

Maman and Baba never understood Thanksgiving. They always said every day should be spent sending praise and giving thanks and couldn't wrap their heads around the holiday. So, growing up, we barely celebrated. Sometimes, we took a walk in Prospect Park as a family, but that was the extent of it. Since they left for Dubai and I, for school, Leila and I have made our own tradition of going out to dinner and drinking a little bit too much mulled cider. If the cocktails are strong enough, we'll end up in Hell, also known as Times Square, and catch whatever show couldn't sell enough tickets. Last year, we saw *Mean Girls* on Broadway. The snacks are always overpriced, so we snuck in our own *Lavashak*.

Margaret Hader clears her throat.

"Send in the first one. A miss Philippa Potters."

I nod and exit the room. Outside, Print and Digital are united and waiting for me—or rather, for answers.

"What did she say?" Seb asks.

"What does she want?" Lola chimes in.

I inhale for three counts then exhale four.

"Philippa, she wants to speak to you."

All heads turn to the back of the bullpen to stare at Philippa Potters, a visionary. One of the best sartorial eyes of our time. A legend in her own right, who, until this very moment, has been wrapped in an oversize shearling coat by the Row, typing furiously into her Blackberry as if it's still 2011.

"Me?" she asks, confused.

I shrug my shoulders. As she rises from her desk, a lingering darkness hangs over the office space. The lights in the room practically flicker.

"Good luck," I whisper as she passes me, but she's already gone.

The rest of the team murmurs, speculating about what's going down behind Loretta's frosted door. I secretly check my phone for texts. Zero new messages. Loretta has gone dark on the worst possible day. I keep a low profile, listening to whispers circulating around the bullpen.

"Maybe she's getting promoted to director."

"Wouldn't Loretta be the one promoting her?"

"Unless she's replacing Loretta…"

I close my eyes and try to concentrate on my breathing. Four in, six out. Six in, eight out.

Not even five minutes later, the door swings open, and Philippa Potters stands in the doorway sniffling into her fur collar. She walks toward me and hands me her SPP security badge, then struts to her desk with her bowl-cut bobbed head held high. She stops in front of her enclave, grabbing her Celine purse before walking out the door without saying another word to anyone. She leaves her laptop behind.

"Send in Devika Wilder," Margaret Hader calls out behind me before returning to the office and shutting the door.

Devika stands up, already in tears, and creeps toward the office. Gwen from Social squeezes her shoulder as she passes the Digital desks. Up until a few days ago, Gwen would have sooner lost a tooth than console her publicly, in front of the entire team.

As soon as Devika enters Loretta's office, the room goes berserk.

"Surely they can't fire every single one of us?" Alex asks,

panicking. "I mean, I've been with the company for three years. That must count for something?"

"Noora." Saffron comes up to me quietly and places an arm around my shoulder. I rest my head on their chest and try not to cry. "Where is Loretta? She should be here, fighting for us."

"Where's Jade?" I counter. "Shouldn't she be here, fighting for *her* team too?"

Saffron blinks.

"I don't know."

We stand there in silence, holding each other tightly as Print editors get called into Loretta's office, one by one, then run out in tears. Some exit with fury, screaming horrific things about Shifter & Pearce. Others can barely utter a single word, their bodies shaking with each giant sob. But the majority just look scared. They glance up at me, hoping for some sort of explanation. I still have none to give them. Loretta appears to have turned off her phone. For all I know, she was the first to go.

"Beth Bennett? Beth Bennett, you're up."

No.

Beth emerges from her office and walks calmly toward her. I want to run to her, to throw my body in between her and the chopping block and offer myself up for the slaughter. Instead, I stand frozen in place, silent. Beth gives me a soft smile as she passes. Minutes later, she comes back out and nods to the team.

"It's done," she says. I can no longer control my emotions. A single teardrop slithers out of my right eye and onto my cheek.

"They can't do this to you!" I wail. "You've been here longer than anyone. You created *Vinyl*! They at least owe you a reassignment, somewhere else in the company. We can fight against this, Beth! I know we can. We can fight it together."

"No," she says firmly. I wait for her to follow up, but she doesn't. She just stares at the clock on the wall.

"But you have a family," I whisper. "Kids."

"We all have responsibilities. At the end of the day, this is a business. There are no exceptions, no special cases. And besides, I am so much more than what I do." Beth looks directly at me, taking my hand in hers. "And so are you, Noora."

"I'm so sorry, Beth," I cry, getting snot all over her perfectly manicured hand. "I'm so, so sorry."

"Stay in touch," she says to the rest of the team, before retreating to her office. Minutes later, she exits the thirty-second floor with all her belongings. Twenty years, two decades worth of groundbreaking work, all wrapped up in a single cardboard box. That's all she has left of the magazine she poured her life into.

She takes one last glance at the remaining members of the Print team, smiles, then steps onto the elevator. As the doors close, I shut my eyes and wait. I keep waiting, for her to come back up and tell us she forgot something, that she wouldn't let it end this way. That, like always, she's got a plan. But she doesn't. The only thing coming back up are the scrambled eggs Leila made me this morning.

Over the next two hours, every single editor who touched the Print magazine is eliminated like *Bachelor* contestants. The bodies in the room grow thinner and frailer, until there are so few of us left that the entire office feels brisk, as if there's cold air floating out of the radiator. After hour one, most of the team has been let go, and the rest of our stomachs are aching in anticipation of whatever's to come. We've all sort of accepted our fates, although no one wants to be the first to admit it. Instead, we try to raise the office spirits with positive affirmations. Crystal even begins to blast "Good as

Hell" on the speaker, and we pretend to enjoy listening to it, even though the mood is a bit more Sarah McLachlan than Lizzo.

And then, without warning, it all stops. The last editor is fired—Lindsey, on Art, who used to be in charge of print illustrations—and no one else is called in. Margaret Hader remains in Loretta's office but doesn't rattle off any more tribute names from her list. The room begins to chatter. I check my phone.

Still no new messages.

"Can you all please join me in the conference room in fifteen minutes?" Margaret Hader announces from the crack of the doorway before looking over to me. "Noora, can you please secure two bottles of champagne."

"Champagne?" I ask incredulously. "Are we celebrating?"

"Yes. Indeed, we are."

I grab my coat, prepared to run to the liquor store and buy two bottles of cheap prosecco.

"Wait!" Saffron calls out to me. "Why don't you use these?" They're holding two unopened bottles of Dom Pérignon in their hands. I feel a knot in the back of my throat. Those look familiar.

"Where did you get those?" I already know the answer.

"Beth's office," Saffron says. "She would want you to have them."

"What if she comes back for them?"

"Noora," Saffron says gently. "I don't think she's coming back."

Reluctantly, I accept the bottles then lead the charge of the remaining staffers into the empty conference room.

Margaret Hader sits at the head of the table. Shockingly, Jade is standing right behind her, smiling like the Cheshire cat.

"Thank you so much for coming," Margaret says, as we flood in. "Today has been a hard day for our family. It's always difficult to lose coworkers and teammates. But it had to be done. Today had to be the day."

A wave of whispers billows down the table.

"This is the team we've decided to move forward with in 2020. Look around this room. If you have a seat at this table, your job is secure. That was the last of the layoffs."

I feel a shiver of sheer disbelief run down my spine. This doesn't make any sense.

"What about Loretta?" Saffron asks what we're all thinking. "Is she still editor in chief?"

Jade frowns.

"We can't comment on that at this time," Margaret Hader says.

"What about *her*?" Kelsea asks, pointing directly at me.

I gulp, shutting my eyes and waiting for the executioner to take off my head.

"Noora stays."

My eyes fly open. Wait, what?

"For now."

Jade hands Margaret Hader a stack of paper cups. She takes one of the bottles of Beth's Dom off the table and pops the cork. Champagne sprays all over the table. Digital editors in the splash zone grimace as the sticky substance slides down their necks. I stare down at my hands in disbelief.

The entire Print team was just laid off. *Beth* was just let go. Why on earth am I still here?

Margaret Hader pours the Dom into cups, and Jade begins passing them around the room. Once we're all holding champagne in our hands, Margaret Hader uses a ballpoint pen to clink against the paper cup.

"A toast," she says. "To *Vinyl* Print, its editors, and all its many accomplishments. The magazine has been priceless to the Shifter & Pearce Publishing family and a beacon of hope to many of its young readers. It was one of the women's lifestyle brands to pair together fashion and politics, social issues and entertainment stories, movements and makeup tips. It was revolutionary at its founding and truly put this company on the map as a cultivator of all things cool. We appreciate all the hard work our fallen comrades have put into the magazine over the past years."

"And to *Vinyl* Digital," Jade bellows loudly, as if reading from her personal manifesto. "The future of the *Vinyl* brand. May we continue to carry out *Vinyl*'s mission statement while modernizing its content to be as inclusive and inter-sectional as possible. We've made it this far, but we still have a long way to go before we're taken as seriously as *Time* or the *Atlantic*. But it's an election year. And we're not just going to put ourselves on the map. We're going to start *redrawing territorial lines!*"

I look around the room. All the editors look slightly ter-rified yet simultaneously riled up.

Jade raises her cup.

"To *Vinyl!*"

"To *Vinyl!*" The room cheers.

"To *Vinyl*," I whisper.

Chapter Twenty-Seven

I used to dread Mondays. I thought of them as the broccoli of weekdays, harsh and bitter, only paying off in the long haul with no immediate rewards. I'd yearn for Fridays, for mornings without choir practice before school, for lazy afternoons that lacked homework or bedtimes.

When I graduated from school and joined the ranks of the adult world, I faced a new reality in which summers melted into one giant season, and Monday offered a reprieve, a fresh start to the monotonous loop of weekly life. The day I had always dreaded became the one to look forward to—a clean slate, a new horizon. Like New Year's and your birthday rolled into one. This was the attitude I adopted during my time at *Vinyl*—focusing on being grateful for another week at my so-called "dream job," for another chance to make something happen, to ensure this week would be *the* week.

But the Monday after *Vinyl* folded and all of Print was laid off does *not* feel like Christmas morning.

I spent the weekend in bed, resting after my brush with death. Okay, not death. But surely fainting is death's cousin. It gives a brief looksie into the other side of the door. And let me tell you, I did *not* like what I saw. If memory serves, limbo looks a little too much like Penn Station.

Leila nursed me back to health like a champion. She brought me *ash*, which is basically Iranian soup, and peppermint tea, just like Maman used to make, with a pinch of lemon and honey. Together we watched hours upon hours of trash TV, from *Southern Charm* to *Million Dollar Matchmaker*. We allowed our butts to sink into the couch until they formed an indentation. We vegetated as if we were in a mutual medically induced coma.

Willow stopped by too. I've discovered she and Leila are actually quite sweet with each other. They held each other gently on one side of the room as Willow scratched Leila's back and played with her hair. She gave me her condolences about the news and made me laugh by reading me some of the funnier headlines I'd been avoiding on Twitter.

Best of all, they both served as a distraction. They helped me kill time by recounting horror stories from the shoots they'd been working on—the outrageous demands and runner lists of the clients, the horrific Photoshop disasters, the secrets spilled on set. I tried my best to hang on to every single word, without letting my mind wander too far in either direction.

And then Sunday came and went, like a series finale, bringing me face-to-face with my supposed blank slate. But for the first time, I have no interest on dabbing my quill in ink and dotting the page.

I called Loretta over twenty times this weekend. I texted her multiple messages each day. But she hasn't responded, not even to an email. I've reached out to all my ex-coworkers to ask if anyone has managed to commiserate with her or received a conciliation text, but no one has heard a peep.

In my tenth hour, I remembered I actually have her active on Find My Friends. Ironically, she had suggested it herself, after agreeing to attend a dinner in Harlem one night and asking if I'd keep a watchful eye on her location, in case any-thing "fishy" went down. According to the app, she's been at home with Sarah this entire time. She just can't be bothered to pick up the phone to tell me that. Or, you know, if I still have a job.

Monday. The first day. A new day. A chance to start over. Who knows, Loretta might even come in today. She'll apolo-gize for her blackout silence, claim Sarah held her hostage. Maybe she'll let me go on the spot because of everything that went down before this drama began and shook up the office like an Etch A Sketch. Your guess is as good as mine. Anything could happen.

As I begin my march to work, I remind myself of one vital, key fact that promises to get me through my day: Thanksgiving is on Thursday, and Wednesday is an SPP company holiday. That means I'm staring down the barrel of a two-day workweek. I can make it through two days. I can do anything for two days.

Cal also texted me a few times over the weekend. Just to check in, he said. He heard all the details of my fainting incident on Thursday, and he wanted to know about the state of my health. He wondered, could he bring me any chicken noodle soup? He also wanted to know if I had heard from Loretta.

Is she staying on as editor in chief? He had texted me. **I don't care or anything, I just wanna know.**

Get in line, buddy. You and everyone's mother. His mes-sages had just made me roll my eyes. His fishing expedition is as transparent as the Chanel PVC quilted mini.

When I arrive at *Vinyl*, I'm surprised to see everyone else bothered to come in on time today too. I guess everybody left is still on edge from last week. But what the fuck are they are they going to do if we're late, fire us?

I know, I know. Too soon.

Instead of sitting *at* their desks, plugging away at stories, the entirety of the Digital team appears to be lounging *on* their desks, gossiping. In fact, the only table surface not covered by an editor's tush belongs to Saffron. There must be issues with the JMZ Subway lines or something. Lest we forget they're traversing all the way from Bushwick. It's less of a sprint, less of a marathon, and more like an eighty-day pilgrimage through the heat of the Sahara desert.

"There she is!" Seb cheers as I walk through the double doors. "Woman of the hour!"

"I told you guys," I say, rolling the purple, puffy bags beneath my eyes. "I don't know anything. Loretta hasn't spoken to me."

Seb and Lola exchange looks, grinning from cheek to cheek. Staci on Social begins to chew on her nails, despite clearly having just gotten a gel manicure.

"Okay," I say, giving in to the suspense. "What did I miss here?"

The team all looks off into different directions. Crystal pretends to read something on her phone, even though I can tell the screen is very clearly blank. Alex scribbles something into his notepad—doodles, most likely.

Enough of this filibustering.

"Okay. Out with it. What's going on here?"

"Do you know, like, why you got to stay on when no one else on Print did?" Lola asks innocently, widening her Brita-water blue eyes. I narrow mine.

"You know as well as I do that it's a mystery."

"Really?" she asks, taking a step toward me.

"Really," I say, taking a step back. December is so close I could snort it, yet somehow, it suddenly feels very hot in here. I fan my face and take off my coat.

"Noora, what caused you to pass out last week?" Seb jumps in.

"I didn't have anything to eat that day. Why do I feel like I'm on trial here?"

"So there were no other stressors you were dealing with that day," Seb pushes further. "Nothing out of the ordinary going on in your day-to-day life."

Okay, am I under investigation or something? It's not *my* fault *Vinyl* Print folded. It's also not my fault all my peers are being let go. I'm a lowly assistant, literally so far down the ladder that I spend most of my days shoveling shit!

"I'm not going to stand here and take this," I tell them. "Either you explain to me what the fuck is going on, or I'm turning around, walking out the door, and working from home for the day."

I'm bluffing, but who's going to call me out on it? My boss literally might be in Witness Protection.

"It entirely depends," Alex says quietly to himself. Without turning my head to look, I can hear in his voice that he's blushing.

"On what?"

"On who we're talking to."

"What?"

"Noora or C. Bates."

Oh.

OH.

The entire room begins to applaud. Seb lets out a hiss. Alex can't help but join in with a whistle.

"I...I'm not sure what you're talking about," I stutter.

Behind my mess of a mouth, my brain is doing cartwheels. How do they know? How did they find out?

"Oh, give it up, Noora!" Crystal laughs. "We all know it was you! We're so proud of you, dude! Guess we all know why you got to keep your job now, huh? Why would the Liberators let go of their Brutus?"

"I didn't betray the Print team, Crystal." My voice is shaking, as are my hands.

"Sure, Noora," Lola says, shaking her head and pursing her lips. "Keep telling yourself that. You're a total Angelina! And here I had you pegged as a Jen."

She scans me up and down, then lets out a *tsk*.

"I guess you *are* a true Gemini. I knew I was right to keep an eye on you."

The crowd stirs, celebrating among themselves. Once the hysteria begins to settle down, the editors slowly start to sit down at their desks and open their laptops. It must feel strange working as if this is any other Monday—assigning stories to freelancers, top-editing pieces from last week, scanning Twitter for news. As if nothing is wrong, and everything didn't change. But they don't have any real direction, no clue who their boss is right now, just like me. So they act as their own managers. They use their better judgment. They make the call.

"Guys, listen to me. It's not what you think. I didn't! I mean, I did. But not for the reasons you *think* I did!"

"Noora," Saffron says quietly, coming up behind me. "Let's go to your desk."

As they put their arm around me and walk me to my little cube outside Loretta's office, I feel my entire body tense up. We walk silently, our limbs tangled together, until we're out of the immediate sight and sound line from the rest of the Digital team. The second I'm in the clear, I pull away from them. They stumble, knocked a bit off balance. When they're back on their cowboy-booted heels, they turned to face me.

"I know you're going through a lot right now," they say. "We all are. But seriously, what the fuck? You do realize you passed out in a closet just a few days ago, right? I *found you there.* Do you know how scary that was for me? I thought you were dead! Then you ignore all my texts checking in you, making sure you're okay. The magazine shutters, half our coworkers get fired, and you never bother to ask me how I'm coping. And the very worst part? You refused to let me tell Jade about your secret identity when it was *my* head on the chopping block, but today, I get to work to find the news circulating faster than DeuxMoi. Noora, I thought we were friends. Not work friends. Real friends. What gives?"

I clench my fists, digging my nails into my palms once more.

"I know what you did, Saffron."

They cock their head to the right, confused.

"Well, that makes one of us. Maybe you can enlighten me?"

I feel my face getting hotter and hotter.

"How could you tell them it was me? Especially at a time like this! They'll never take me seriously now!"

"Whoa, whoa, whoa, you need to chill," they say, resting their right hand upon their heart. "First of all, I did no such thing. Second of all, if I did, would it be such a bad thing? Wouldn't it prove your *loyalty* to the Digital team?"

I shake my head in disbelief.

"Not at the expense of Print. Not when people's jobs are at risk. Their livelihoods. *Beth's* livelihood!" I'm talking so fast that I hawk up too much spit and pause to chuck it into a nearby trash can.

Saffron wrinkles their nose and mouths *ew.*

"You've officially lost it. I know you don't trust anyone right now, but you can always trust *me,* remember? Even when you've been a shitty friend to me, I've been there for you."

"YOU'RE THE ONLY ONE I TOLD!" I scream at the top of my lungs.

There's *no* way the rest of the team didn't hear me. I bet people all the way in *New Jersey* heard me. And I oop—

"Not the only one," Saffron says, before turning on their heels and walking back to their desk.

I stay behind, stirring with fury, choking on their dust.

The only two people who knew that I was C. Bates were me and my editor, aka Saffron. I didn't even tell Leila! And I tell Leila *everything*, including when I accidentally used her retainer as a bracelet in the fifth grade. Well, actually, I guess Loretta knows now too. But she's been on house arrest for four days straight.

But what would she have to gain from that? Admitting she had nothing to do with the column would only make her look even weaker than she already does. And if that were the case, what am I still doing here?

No, it wasn't Loretta. It had to be Saffron. They were the only person privy to the information, the only one with all the facts. The only soul with the power to destr—

And then it dawns on me.

It's like standing right in front of a Chuck Close painting and seeing nothing but a mélange of colored circles, like eyeballs or polka dots, then backing several feet up. Suddenly, you're looking at the full picture. You've never seen so clearly in your life. The image calms into focus, and you have the revelations that what you've been studying is not, in fact, random shapes and arbitrary colors but a face. Eyes, nose, teeth, ears, lips, all belonging to one man. A man you thought you knew but was always a stranger to you.

A man with a dimpled smile and a Howard T-shirt.

Chapter Twenty-Eight

I ask Cal to meet me Tuesday after work, in neutral terri-
tory—at Cafe Select, a tiny enclave off Kenmare and
Lafayette.

When the clock strikes 6:00 p.m., I immediately hightail
it out of the SPP Tower, waving farewell to no one, Saffron
included (I apologized for yesterday, but they left me on
delivered, so the atmosphere is still tense). That's the one nice
thing about not having a boss or any sense of where your life
is headed: No one can tell you where and when you can take
a piss or head out for the day.

The late-November atmosphere in New York is light,
brisk, and irresponsibly brimming with confidence. Sure, it
gets dark now at 4:00 p.m., filling anyone working within an
enclosed office space with a mild form of seasonal depres-
sion. And leaving the building to be immediately greeted
by a slew of pitch-black sky before retreating to your icebox
doesn't exactly inspire or motivate you to make plans with
an old friend, wait alone at a cocktail bar, or haul your ass
to the gym.

But there's something enigmatic about the holidays in
New York. Maybe it lies in the distinction between loneliness and being alone. Because, although you may be feeling a

bit isolated around Thanksgiving and Christmas, you are not, in fact alone. You are going through the motions in solidarity with your fellow city dwellers. Their camaraderie may not always usher in good tidings, but it can certainly fill you with joy if you know where to look.

There are very few shared experiences all New Yorkers can bond over. The beauty of this city is that every individual is so unique that we are inevitably united over so little. In other words, the one thing we have in common is that we have virtually nothing in common. All walks of life diverge drastically from one another, and yet we meld like heavy metals, all existing under a single polluted roof. When we do come together, it's usually through the channel of hatred: a delayed subway line, a tourist who stops in the middle of the street to take a picture, a Chicago transplant complaining about the quality of the pizza. We buy into the same notion of superiority—that we rise above trivial commonalities by way of our suffering.

But then there's that first night in November, when Madison Avenue lights its first snowflake hanging over a traffic light and an empty crosswalk, and the city suddenly feels like home. Perhaps not our home, but home to something. And that something, that sinkhole of sustenance you can't quite place your finger on, sparks the wonder of possibility.

I arrive early at Cafe Select and take a seat at one of its three outdoor tables. The red glow of the heat lamps grazes my neck, radiating a wave of warmth throughout my body. On the other side of the glass window, I can hear the murmur of casual conversation, the clinking of wineglasses at the bar. String lights hang from the ceiling, lighting up the space with an ethereal glimmer, like a scene from *Midsummer Night's Dream*. A large clock—a Rolex, no less—hangs overhead, encouraging patrons to stay out late, to refrain from heading home to their spouses and their toaster ovens. And the combination of tiny Swiss flags, the kind you only find hidden in club sandwiches, and the hot elixir of mulled wine and cheese fondue bubbling over a small portable stove, allows New Yorkers to step out of the tedious monotony of their daily lives and into the extravagance of ski chalets in the Alps.

Cafe Select has always welcomed me with open arms. Although its patrons have deeper pockets and purses than I and speak more languages combined than the entirety of the UN, it feels like a safe space. There's always a table waiting for me as I walk in. That's more than I can say for its upscale neighbors. It's dependable—I always know what I'm going to get.

I wish I could say the same for Cal.

Cal (does it stand for Calvin? Short for Caleb? I guess I'll never know...) arrives about fifteen minutes late, on the dot. He's wearing an olive-green peacoat over a black cashmere turtleneck and looks as dashing as he did the day I met him. He's giving me major zaddy vibes.

He takes a seat at the table across from me, sliding the sleeves of his coat down his arms and delicately tossing it over the back of his chair. He then pushes his turtleneck up his forearms, flexing his biceps with every nip and tug. When he's made himself at home, he finally looks up at me, making glass-shattering eye contact. With one hand on his cup of water and the other reaching toward me, his face breaks into a smile, exposing his impossibly white teeth and Shirley Temple dimples.

I feel my vagina start to pulsate again. This is not going to be easy.

"I'm so glad you texted me, Little Light," he says. "I was starting to think you'd forgotten about me."

"Never." I mean it. "You'd make that too hard. Besides, I thought this is what you wanted?"

Cal cranes his neck slightly and frowns, taking a sip of his water.

"What do you mean by that?"

"*This doesn't mean anything*," I repeat his words back to him.

He winces. "Yeah. Not my finest hour." He offers up a sympathetic smile on a platter but no apology.

I continue in my crusade.

"I know what you did." I lean forward in my seat, never once breaking from his gaze.

"Oh, do you now? And what's that?"

I take a deep breath and brace myself for impact.

"You told the entire Digital team that I'm C. Bates."

Cal lets out a *chuckle*, choking slightly on his last sip of water. My eyes narrow. This is no laughing matter.

"What's so funny?" My hands are shaking. For once, I wish he'd just engage in a serious conversation with me, laying all the cards on the table.

"Correction: I did *not* tell the entire Digital team you were C. Bates," he says. "I told Jade Aki."

I begin to cough. The couple at the neighboring table looks over at us and glares.

"Why?! Why would you do that?"

Cal looks around, clearly embarrassed by my outburst. But after all he's done to me, frankly? I couldn't give less of a *fuck* about his feelings.

"Can you please keep your voice down?"

"WHY?" I scream louder. Nothing like a "hysterical female" to wake someone up and out of the alternative reality they've been living in.

Cal leans back in his chair and folds his arms in front of

his chest. The stress lines in his forehead reappear. They look like a sidewalk crossing.

"Because she asked," he finally says.

"That's not good enough."

"Because she offered to help me."

"Try again."

"Because she's going to introduce me to investors, okay, Noora?" he blurts out. "To grow my business. Aki was the it girl of New York media. She's friends with the Hadids, for fuck's sake. She sat front row at Chromeo this year! An endorsement from her would go a long way. And I'm having a lot of trouble securing funding, if you must know. What's wrong with an educated young Black man trying to secure his bag? So, yes. I told Jade, and maybe she told the rest of her team. She wanted to know who C. Bates was! It was obviously not written by Loretta, and she was desperate to regain the upper hand. So, yeah, she hired me to break into the IP, same as Loretta. You asked me not to tell Loretta. I didn't. And from the sound of it, you left the lid open on that yourself. But you didn't ask me not to tell Jade. So, instead of freaking out at me *in public* in the middle of *Soho*, you can fuck right off."

I shudder, frightened by his sudden cruelty. What he says makes sense, but it's no excuse. I asked him to protect me, and he chose to betray my confidence for his own personal gain instead. No amount of start-ups or dimpled smiles can sully the facts.

And then something else dawns on me.

"Is this the first time?" I ask quietly.

He stops seething in his seat for a split second to look back up at me.

"First time doing what? Telling Jade that you wrote a dumbass column about shaving?"

I let his abrasive words and tone trickle off my skin like holy water.

"Your first time helping one of the higher-ups, on the heels of an empty promise?"

For the first time since taking a seat, Cal gulps, noticeably nervous. He grabs his cup of water and traces the rim with his thumb. The glass around his hand starts to fog.

"Answer the question, Cal."

"I *might* have helped Loretta out with a couple of small tasks on her to-do lists. In exchange for a sizeable donation. You know, just a few basic things, like cleaning out her inbox, editing together a video, setting up security in and around her office space, and—"

"And creating a series of fake tweets then leaking them to the press?"

Cal looks down at his lap, his left knee shaking like crazy. "Maybe something like that."

I look at him and scowl, disgusted. His moral compass is so out of whack that he's headed straight into the Atlantic. Was I so distracted by my horniness for him that I couldn't see what a monumental ethical screw-up he was, is, and always has been?

Cal notices my expression and leaps up out of his seat.

"Don't you dare look at me like that, Noora! I'm not a bad person. I voted for Hillary. I paid for my ex-girlfriend's Plan B, not once but *twice*. I made you come using a fucking dildo!"

I continue to stare at him in disbelief, shaking my head. The role reversal is so comical. It's Dalí-level surreal.

"Like you're so perfect. I know what you did, Noora. I know everything. You abused your power as Loretta's assistant and snooped through her email then told Jade's perky blond assistant who the holiday cover star is. I traced your computer signal, remember? You're the reason the Zendaya issue fell apart. You're the reason we had to have that entire ridiculous Experiences event in the first place! You lied to your boss, betrayed your team, and played both sides like a fucking fiddle, so don't go off on me about loyalty. Because you have none."

He takes a second to catch his breath. I hold mine, shell-shocked. Then, without warning, he reaches across the table and frantically grabs both of my hands. He grips them so tightly, it hurts.

"Don't you see? We're the same, you and me. These people don't give a damn about us, and we couldn't care less about them. We're looking out for number one—ourselves. We have what it takes to not only survive but *thrive* in this turbulent fuckmobile of an industry. That's what brought us together in the first place, and why we can't be kept apart for long. Don't you feel it, Noora? This thing between us? I've tried to fight it. I've *been* fighting it for months! But this energy between us is inescapable. I think we might just be cut from the same cloth."

He takes my face in his hands, clasping my cheeks in his palms. I shut my eyes tightly, refusing to look at him.

"What do you say we finally take this thing to the next level, Little Light? I want to be with you, and I know how badly you want me. So let's do this thing. Let's make our way through this hellhole of an industry together. Our heads combined can outsmart them all. There's nothing we can't accomplish. One day, they'll all be kissing our feet *and* our asses. What do you say?"

My eyes fly open. I take a good, hard look at him. His nose pressed against mine, his hands cupping my chin, his breath hot against my neck. I realize I got it right that first day in the elevator. He really is a boy—a quivering, cowardly little boy.

"Happy Thanksgiving, Cal."

As my lips move, it dawns on me how easy it would be to lean a little bit too forward and kiss him, one last time.

"I don't know about you, but I'm thankful for a lot this year. I'm thankful for this job, which forced me to grow skin thicker than horse leather. I'm thankful for my coworkers, who taught me to trust no one but myself, as people are rarely who they appear to be on the surface. I'm thankful for my sister, who teaches me every day that there is still good in the world, people who genuinely strive to bring even the smallest sliver of kindness into each other's days. And I'm thankful for you, for showing me that tiny little fuckboys don't grow out of their immaturity but instead grow into fuckmen. And for reminding me of exactly who I am not. I am nothing like you, Cal. I don't care about getting my name out there or the fame and notoriety of being a celebrity writer or influencer. I would never purposefully try to hurt anyone for personal gain. And I damn well wouldn't sacrifice the good of the magazine in order to raise my public profile or for a few extra bucks. In layman's terms, I may not be a good person, as you say. But I have good intentions. And you have an empty JUUL pod where your heart used to be. Never contact me again."

I take one last swig of my glass of merlot then pick up my coat, wrapping it around me like a blanket.

Cal sinks into his chair, visibly stunned. He tries to speak—most likely a rebuttal—but finds he can only whistle. I take one last look at his beautiful face, now stoic and strained, then turn around and walk away.

There's a street violinist playing classic versions of contemporary songs at the end of the block. As he lifts his bow, I feel overwhelmed but filled with relief. It's finally over. For the first time in six months, I am free.

"Hey, Cal," I call out to him, whipping my head around. "One last thing: You're bad at sex."

Chapter Twenty-Nine

By the time Thanksgiving descends upon Manhattan like a slow-moving swarm of bees, New York has already begun preparing for Christmas. That's just the way this city rolls: It's always looking forward, moving forward, but never back.

All the shops have begun blasting Christmas classics and decorating their windows with ornate holiday displays and decorations. Madison and Fifth Avenue have basically transformed into pageantry. Walking down either requires pushing through a sea of tourists huddled together in some form of a demented hug, stopping every five seconds to ooh and aah at the twinkling lights and the gold velvet ribbons. It's all a little too camp, just like New York itself.

Central Park, on the other hand, grows widely understated and reserved to the point of sheepish. The trees are naked and frail, blushing as they lower their branches to cover their crotches. The damp slew of mud that lines the Reservoir and the Bridle Path like papier-mâché is covered in fallen leaves, peppering the ground with color and texture. It's larger than life, by far the closest natural habitat to grace the concrete.

In other ways, it's just a collection of quiet moments. An elderly couple sits on a bench in front of a statue of three bronze bears and watches the children play on a nearby swing set. A group of teenage girls picnic on the lawn, giggling to themselves as they pass a single cigarette back and forth like a game of telephone. And a near-invisible photographer, dressed in black leather, captures it all, as he hums the melodies of Leonard Cohen, close enough to his chest that only he can hear.

Central Park is the only location in all of New York where a person can really hear their thoughts echoed back to them. So, naturally, it's where I retreat the morning of Thanksgiving.

Leila and I have plans to treat ourselves to Mr. Chow later tonight, a fancy Chinese restaurant on Fifty-Seventh Street that's filled with tapestries, fancy clientele, and servers wearing bow ties who refuse to take your plate until you've eaten every last bite of the food you ordered. We're going to stuff ourselves until we have to unbutton our jeans and then attempt to sneak into *Dear Evan Hansen*. Attendance will likely be considerably low on Thanksgiving.

I make my way down the park, toward the exit. I pass the tiny gazebo on the top of a mountain made of rock formations and stop briefly at the boat pond filled with tiny, motorized sailboats to stare at the big metal Alice in Wonderland statue I used to attempt to climb as a kid. No matter how many times I'd get close to making it to the top, I'd always slide back down. But for some reason, I'd keep on trying. I never learned. Then I make my way through the Central Park Zoo to wave to the sea lions that populate that tiny roundabout tank.

I check my phone to see what time it is. A quarter to 4:00. I still have a little time before I need to meet Leila at home; she had a few errands to run before our dinner.

Taking a seat on one of the benches lining the zoo walkway, I wait for the clock to hit the hour. When it does, a familiar tune begins to play, slightly squeaking like the sounds of an old jewelry box, the kind beholden to a ballerina. As the melody unfolds, the brass zoo animals that greet pedestrians as they enter and exit the zoo begin to dance in a mechanical circle, as if animating for the very first time.

As a child, I was entranced by their performance, begging my parents to wait, even for a just a few more minutes, so I could watch them jive around. But the clock strikes 4:01 p.m. and the minute passes. It's over. As if it never happened in the first place.

I collect pine cones as I walk. They're scattered all over the grass. Sometimes, if I see a particularly shapely cone, I'll hop a fence or veer a little off course so I can grab it before it gets crushed under the weight of another man's boot. I figure that if I collect enough, I can use it to create a centerpiece or some kind of decor for Leila's home. A small gesture to say, *Thank you for putting up with me over the past six months. Will you except this autumnal offering as an apology?*

Once I place enough in my purse, I notice several of the cones are crawling with tiny critters. I sigh and consider dumping them all out. But a few seconds later, I opt instead to just bring them home with me. Who knows? Maybe they'll prefer Chinatown to the Upper East Side.

I make my way back downtown and up the stairs of Leila's walk-up. I barely make it up two flights before I pause to listen. There's a sound murmuring from a couple floors up; it sounds like Iranian music, the kind my parents would play for us when I was a kid. The inflections of the singers' voices bounce off the walls of the stairwell and fill my chest with warmth, fullness. I run the rest of the steps and burst into the apartment.

Leila is standing in the middle of her kitchen with Willow. They're both cloaked in their matching art history–themed aprons and covered in a white powder I hope to God is flour.

Behind them is a never-ending buffet of American foods: yams, mashed potatoes, cranberry sauce, pumpkin pie. There's even a massive turkey, which appears to be accompanied by none other than *fesenjoon*, my favorite *khoresht*.

I feel my eyes begin to well up with tears. It's a Middle Eastern American Thanksgiving hybrid, the first of its kind. And it's beautiful.

"Lei…" My voice trails off as I try to articulate how I'm feeling.

At the sound of her name, Leila looks up from concentrating on her stuffing and breaks out into a ginormous grin. Willow puts her arm around her and gives her a kiss on the cheek.

"Happy Thanksgiving!" Leila yells, running toward me and pulling me tightly into her chest. "I know this isn't really our thing, but I figured that after the past few months, we could both use a little celebrating."

"I also helped convince her," Willow adds, pulling me in for a hug as well. "You know she isn't really all that into tradition, are you, babe?"

They peck quickly, and my heart sings with adoration for my little unconventional family.

"My only complaint is that there's no way we're going to be able to eat all this food."

I take in the feast that they've prepared. There's barely enough room in the apartment for it! Leila's had to open all the windows to let the heat out and has covered each and every surface, from the coffee table to the entryway vanity, in treats. If it weren't for the pungent smell of Chinese cooking, I'm sure I would have sniffed it from the sidewalk.

"Maybe we can donate the leftovers to a soup kitchen or a shelter?"

"Oh, I don't think that'll be necessary," Leila says, a flicker of mischief in her eyes. I watch as her gaze moves from coy to confused as she spots the dents in my purse. "What have you got there?"

"This?" I suddenly feeling like a total loser. Leila spent this entire day cooking for me, and I thought a couple of pine cones could make up for what a massive bonehead I've been. "I went for a walk in Central Park, and, um, thought it might be nice to collect some pine cones. I thought I could make, like, a festive decoration for the apartment and present it to you as a gift. You know, since I've been such a pain in your ass over the past few months."

Leila pokes around in my bag and pulls out the cones. Amused, she begins arranging them in different shapes on the kitchen counter.

"They're perfect!" she says. "We'll make them into little centerpieces for the food. Just like the Pilgrims!"

"I think you might need a little history refresher there," Willow says. "Our weird, wonky Thanksgiving will pay tribute to the Indigenous. We'll all say a prayer before eating our dinner. And include a moment of silence in their honor."

Leila nods in agreement.

Then the doorbell rings. I look up, surprised.

"Did you order takeout or Postmates wine or something?"

Willow shakes her head, and Leila shrugs. Confused, I go to open the door.

"Happy Thanksgiving!!!" Saffron shrieks, handing me a bottle of sparkling cider. Their partner, a skinny, pale, band person dressed in a baseball cap and New Balance sneakers, trails behind them.

I stand still, in shock.

"What are you doing here? I thought you were mad at me!"

"Your sister called and invited me to Thanksgiving, silly." They help themself into the kitchen and start looking for glasses. "I wasn't going to pass up an opportunity to experience a real Iranian American holiday now, was I?"

I inch toward Saffron as they pull out the cork of their cider and begin passing around drinks. They move with so much enthusiasm and charisma, I can't help but smile. Their partner nestles into the couch, pulls out their phone, and begins watching soccer. I shuffle forward until I'm close enough to whisper.

"I've been such a selfish bitch," I tell them.

"I know." They turn around and kiss the top of my forehead.

"And a bad friend."

"I know."

"I ended things with Cal."

They look up at me then, concerned. "Okay, I didn't know that. Good. He was a sack of shit."

"I'm sorry I ever doubted you."

"Let's not focus on regret. There's no amount of regret that can change the past. It's Thanksgiving and we're together, for fucks sake! Let's focus on being thankful in the present."

We clink glasses, link arms, and chug our ciders, before Leila announces that the food is ready. She and Willow have arranged everything buffet style, so participants can help themselves to whatever they'd like from a series of different spots throughout the apartment, including above the toilet and on top of Leila's bedroom dresser.

As we're shoveling food onto our plates, I teach Saffron about the basic principles of *taarof*. It's a concept of civility that doesn't directly translate to English, but the crux of it is this: You must offer someone something three times, and they must decline all three times before you accept their no verbatim. On the receiving end, you must turn down said offer three times before saying what you really mean. It's like a dance, or a game of chicken—the first person to blink has to endure the suffocating hospitality of the other.

I had to save Saffron several times from being forced to eat way, way too much mashed potatoes.

Once we're all seated on Leila's couch—aka, my bed—we go around and perform *Sepasgozarim*, or *Sepas* for short, a round-robin of blessings that entails telling a short story from the past year, listing all that you're grateful for, and saying a short prayer. Leila goes first. She shares that she's most grateful to have found a new job from which she is able to derive purpose, one she looks forward to waking up and going to every morning. She also adds that her lowest point this year was when she was most afraid of losing the apartment and blesses all who helped her to make ends meet during that difficult period. I tear up listening to her talk about asking neighboring restaurants if she could take their leftover food that they would normally throw out, to eat for dinner. I had no idea it had ever gotten that bad. I guess I never really stopped to ask, but I wish I could go back and listen.

Willow goes next. She says she's grateful to have met Leila, who opened her eyes to a world of spontaneity, adventure, and inspiration that had been closed off to her because of her rigid work ethic. (Willow has a rigid work ethic? Wow, I really should have made more of an effort to get to know her better. I guess I've been too focused on *Vinyl* to spend time with her one-on-one.) She blesses her new family, our family, for welcoming her with open arms and teaching her all about a brand-new culture she knew so little about. Her speech ends with her kissing Leila's hand and whispering, "I love you."

Something about the specific shade of red that Leila's face turns tells me this is her first time hearing it—perhaps ever.

Saffron follows suit. They talk about how grateful they

are to still have a job after everything that's happened at SPP over the past six months. Then they go off on a tangent, thanking their partner for agreeing to skip their family's Thanksgiving to be with them instead. Apparently, Saffron's mother's side of the family has banned them from spending holidays at home because they believe their gender identity conflicts with Catholicism and are too concerned the entire house will either burn in hell or be burned down in real time by Satan. So Saffron has been spending holidays with their chosen family for the past five years instead.

I had no clue their relationship with half their family was still so strained. We spent so much time talking about the *Vinyl* family that I guess their own never came up. As I sink into the couch, listening, I think about all I still don't know about Saffron. Everything I still want to find out, all the questions I have yet to ask, all the stories I'm dying to hear—if they'll let me.

And then it's my turn. I think long and hard about my own *Sepas*.

I'm obviously grateful for Leila, for putting a roof over my head and a bed to crawl into when my anxiety is keeping me up at night and haunting each shadow in the walls.

I couldn't have gotten through the past few months without Saffron, who talked me through so many decisions, both good and bad. Who literally found me sprawled out in a closet and brought me back to consciousness. Who literally saved my life.

As the words of my blessing begin to pour out of me, I realize there's still one person left to thank, for every opportunity I've been given. The person who took a chance on me, who helped me to force my foot in the door. I wouldn't be a published columnist right now—C. Bates wouldn't even exist—if not for her. I have to face it: She made my dreams come true, even if the reality of that dream looked more like a nightmare.

Now she's in hiding. Her phone is turned off, and her email passwords have been changed. Meanwhile, the rumor mill continues to circulate daily headlines—she's committed suicide. No, she's run away and moved to Australia! Actually, I heard a pretty convincing tale that she'd been the target of an intervention and forced to attend a rehabilitative retreat in Arizona, the kind that lasts a month and requires completely cutting yourself off from the outside world.

I laugh, thinking of Loretta in a robe and slippers instead of combat boots, her white roots peeking out beneath her firecracker-red hair.

Then it hits me: I know what I have to do.

"Guys, I need to run out, but I promise I'll be back by dessert," I tell the table. "There's somewhere I need to be."

Chapter Thirty

All the houses on Loretta James's block in Park Slope have been abandoned for the holidays. The windows are dark and empty; the wind whistles as it blows empty plastic shopping bags down the street, getting caught on the outstretched limbs of trees and lampposts.

Loretta's own town house is lit up brighter than the Rockefeller Center tree or a couple of drunk teenagers sneaking vodka in water bottles into a BYOB karaoke bar. Now that the sun sets so early and dusk engulfs all the colors that easily catch the light, the blue of her front door appears more melancholy than magnificent. It evokes sadness. I feel sad.

I walk up the stairs of her stoop. I'm about to let myself in when I hesitate.

I close my eyes and try to picture Loretta and Sarah sitting at their long, marble dining room table, at either head. In my mind's eye, they're both dressed to the nines—Loretta is in a taffeta, hot-pink ball gown and her signature combat boots, whereas Sarah is in a sleek suit the same color as her off-duty scrubs. And they're eating in silence, so quiet that you can hear the sound of forks clanking against plates, knives cutting into white turkey breast.

Then I try to insert myself into the space and find I can't

even imagine how I would proceed. I don't fit into my own daydream. What would I say? Where would I sit? I watch as Loretta looks up from the cranberry sauce she's moving around on her plate—a far cry from bone broth, if I may say so myself—and stares directly at me. How can she see me?

Alarmed, my eyes fly open, and I'm back in front of her big, blue door.

I count to five then knock three times with a loud, steady fist. I hear footsteps scrambling on the other side. They sound muted, like the scraping of a chunky sneaker.

"Who is it?" I hear Loretta's voice faintly call from somewhere else inside the house.

"Not sure," Sarah replies. "It's too late for trick-or-treaters and too early for carolers, right?"

I can hear someone laugh, a melodic lighthearted chuckle. Who was that? It couldn't possibly have come from Loretta, could it?

"Maybe it's another Jehovah's Witness," Sarah says. "Only one way to find out."

The door flies open, and I come face-to-face with Sarah, who looks up at me, mouth agape.

She's dressed in a pair of plaid pajamas, the kind American Girl dolls wear. Her hair is in a loose braid that falls down her back, and she doesn't have a drop of makeup on. Once the shock settles, she smiles at me.

"Noora, what a pleasant surprise! Please come in," she says, gesturing for me to follow her inside. "Honey, Noora's here!"

"What?!" I hear Loretta's voice call out from down the hall.

As I remove my shoes, I notice how different the house looks with two people occupying it. The fireplace is lit, creating a warm glow in an otherwise cold, manicured environment. The smell of Chinese food wafts in from the kitchen. And as I turn the corner, I'm surprised to find Loretta not seated with her back straight, at her dining room table, but curled up on the couch, covered by a knitted blanket. She's holding a white takeout box in her left hand and using her right to pick out dumplings and plop them in her open mouth. It would appear she's put her chopsticks to work, holding together a messy bun that's sitting on top of her head. Her signature red hair is visibly graying; it's clear she hasn't been to the salon in at least a week—so, I guess SPP isn't the only place she's been avoiding. Perhaps most surprising is the fact she's in sweatpants. Okay, a cashmere sweat suit, but still!

The image of Loretta James vegging out on her sofa, watching a rerun of the National Dog Show, is one I'll never be able to get out of my head.

"Darling, what in God's name are you doing here?"

She stands up and throws her arms around me, pulling me in for a tight embrace. I stand perfectly still, listening to the judges rate a Yorkshire terrier on the TV behind me.

"Why aren't you celebrating Thanksgiving with your family? Oh, right, your parents are back in Afghanistan or wherever, aren't they? But don't you have a sister? You two must have had some sort of falling-out, eh? Well, it's no matter. You can join us here. Although I must apologize, neither of us were expecting company. We've both been feeling so exhausted you see, Sarah with her night shifts and myself with, well, you know. So we didn't feel up to cooking and chose to cheat Turkey Day a bit by doing as our Hasidic neighbors do and ordering Chinese food!"

I'm about to correct her but decide not to bother. I have bigger items on my agenda.

"Loretta, where have you been?"

Sarah gets up and slips into another room, probably sensing what's to come. Loretta looks up wistfully at the fire.

I decide to try again.

"I've been worried sick, Loretta. We all are. You haven't been returning our calls or texts, your email password has been changed, you're not even posting Instagram stories. You went totally AWOL at a time when everyone's desperate for answers."

I pause and study Loretta's facial expression. She looks stoic, sculpted out of fine marble. I continue.

"It was absolutely terrible, Loretta. Margaret Hader, she fired everyone on Print. Your entire team. Even Beth. She was let go, just like that! And then we had this weird champagne toast thing to 'cheers' the end of *Vinyl*. Jade was there, but there was no formal announcement that she was taking over as editor in chief. Everyone wants to know if you're still in charge—if you'll be taking over as the new head of Digital and restructuring the team. They all suspect you might be, for one reason and one reason only: me. I'm still here. I wasn't laid off with the rest of them. But then you stopped coming in, and everyone started to panic."

Loretta says nothing and plays with her wedding ring.

"What's going on, Loretta? Are you coming back? Am I out of a job?"

Loretta sighs deeply. She uses her thumb and pointer finger to shove another dumpling into her mouth, then chews slowly and swallows with dramatic flair. Then she looks up to meet my eyes.

"I'm sorry I scared you, love," she says, locking eyes with me. "The truth is, I've been scared myself. You see, I found out the night before the announcement that *Vinyl* was kaput. The night of your little fall, remember?"

Little fall is an interesting way of describing fainting, but okay.

"That night, the head of SPP offered me Jade's position

with my current title: I'd stay on as editor in chief but oversee the website instead. And I just didn't know what to say or what to do, so I asked for time to consider my options. I called you a million times to discuss, but you didn't pick up!"

I was sleeping off my *little fall*, but I digress.

"The next morning, I just couldn't bring myself to face my team, especially when I didn't have any concrete answers myself. So I just decided to escape, to unplug. To make my digital footprint as close to invisible as possible until I had figured out what I was going to do next. I didn't know HR was going to lay off my entire team without me there. I figured they'd wait! I thought I'd bought everyone a little more time. But I should have known better. That company can be so ruthless, so heartless sometimes. Truly, can you imagine being that self-absorbed?"

No comment.

"So did you figure out what you're going to do next?" I ask. "Have you concocted the perfect plan to get us all out of this mess? Because I'm all ears."

Loretta smiles and takes my hand, holding it tightly. Behind me, a golden retriever makes its grand entrance.

"Over the past few weeks, I took some time to meditate, to go on long walks around the city—incognito, of course— with no real destination in mind but in search of some sort of greater truth. And you know what I stumbled upon, just yesterday, in the West Village?"

I shake my head.

"A protest of hundreds of queer people, of all colors and ages. They were sitting peacefully on the sidewalk, lining the walkway to Stonewall, singing songs and passing around signs. I stopped and asked one for a light. I didn't want to admit this to you, but I have a bit of a smoking problem. It really is such a nasty habit."

I can't help but roll my eyes at that one. Loretta doesn't seem to notice.

"Anyhow, we struck up a conversation. He explained to me, this little transgender African American boy from Alabama, that they were all out there to ask for better working conditions and protections for gay folks in the workplace. Isn't that something? Decades after I protested at Stonewall, these kids were out there singing for the same supper. I sat down next to him, and he was telling me about all his pronouns and all that, which to be quite frank, confuses the bejesus out of me. This child is yammering on and on about social justice and intersectionality and privilege and all that stuff, when I finally cut him off. And you know what I asked him, sweet pea?"

"No, Loretta. What did you ask him?" Her speech is so insensitive (but so is Loretta) that I'm struggling to keep a straight face.

"I said, 'You ever read *Vinyl* magazine?' And he just gushed! It was adorable! He realized who he was talking to and began profusely apologizing for ranting for so long, thanking me for my work with the magazine and the movement and everything. As it turns out, he's a big fan. Get this: He told me that when he was little, before starting to transition, he used to use the money from his after-school job to *buy copies of Vinyl* and study the spreads. Can you believe? He felt inspired because of the pages of *my* magazine. I was just pleased as punch."

I try to imagine Loretta James, sitting on a dirty sidewalk corner, talking to a trans, Black protestor from a flyover state. For some reason, the image won't compute.

"Anyway, our conversation led me to my ultimate realization. I got into this world because I wanted to make a difference. I thought I could create real institutional change for young people, and goddammit, I was right! For a little while, at least. But I was only able to take care of others because I was taking care of myself. I knew print magazines inside and out, Noora. I could put together an ROS in my sleep. But digital? I can hardly tell you where the mouse button is. I can't think as fast as the internet! I don't understand the internet. And what's more is, I don't understand what your generation wants. I don't get what fires you up in the morning, what gets you out of bed. What matters to you people? As far as I can see, it's all viral trash, soundboards, and clickbait. So I have decided to turn SPP's generous offer down. I will hand in my resignation in the morning then email the staff to inform them of my departure."

I swallow back tears. I find my own emotions confusing. I didn't expect this to hurt so much. "Where will you go?"

Loretta looks into the fire. I watch as the flames dance around in her eyes, like two flamenco dancers.

"I'm not sure yet. I think I'll rest for a long while, spend some time with Sarah. We're thinking of adopting, you know. Me, a mother! Can you imagine that?"

Loretta's face lights up as she talks about Sarah and their family, and I feel the first of many tears slide down my cheek.

"Don't cry, honey! You'll land on your feet. I know you will. Don't take this the wrong way—you were kind of a shitty assistant, but you're a wonderful writer. And this industry is full of talented people who will never get recognized because they don't have the balls to stand up for themselves and mediocre people who get to throw around fancy titles because they have giant egos and zero skill. You're neither of those things. That's why I know you'll be all right."

I wipe my face with the back of my right hand then extend it forward. She takes it in hers, and we share a firm handshake.

"It was an honor to work for you."

"For *Vinyl*," she corrects me. "For the reader."

"For the reader."

I smile then take one last look at Loretta James. This is how I'd like to remember her: cuddled up on the couch, hand-feeding herself noodles, her head on her wife's chest, laughing at a miniature poodle.

As I turn around and retreat to that blue front door for the very last time, I hear someone call my name.

"Wait, Noora," Sarah says, catching up to me. "I made you a doggie bag of food to take home."

She hands me a brown paper bag full of sweet-and-sour chicken, and I graciously accept. I don't have the heart to tell her I live in Chinatown.

"And I also wanted to thank you," she adds.

"Thank me? For what?"

"For everything you did for Loretta. I know she probably didn't always make it easy for you, what with her crazy temper and compulsive smoking that she somehow thinks she can hide from me. But I know she cares a great deal for you. She's grateful, Noora. You did a great job."

Her words echo loudly in my ear, and I let out a big sigh of relief. Until this very moment, I didn't realize how badly I needed to hear them.

"Thank you. That means more than you know."

She smiles and asks me to stay in touch. I know I won't, so I say nothing back. Instead, I walk out of that pretty, blue door, and never look back.

Chapter Thirty-One

When I walk onto the thirty-second floor of SPP Tower Monday morning, after a weekend of recounting my trip to Park Slope over and over again to Leila and Willow and shoveling turkey and cranberry sauce sandwiches down my throat, I'm not sure what to expect.

Loretta's staff-wide email went out this morning, as expected. To my surprise, it was much more emotional than I had given her credit for. I could practically hear her erratic sniffling through the lettering on the page.

Dear Vinyl *family,*

It is with great sadness and chagrin that I must inform you that as of today, I am stepping down as editor in chief of Vinyl *magazine, effective immediately. This brand has been my home for over a decade and working here has taught me everything I know about being a good writer, editor, and peer. I am so proud of all the work we have accomplished together, from our coverage of the 2016 election to our trend reporting during New York Fashion Week. Since its conception,* Vinyl *has always been the premier destination for women's culture content. I have no doubt that this will continue under the leadership of my successor, Jade Aki. She has an exquisite vision for the digital site, and I am comforted by the fact that I will be leaving my beloved in very good, finely manicured hands.*

It was such an honor to work with each and every one of you. I have no doubt that I am better for knowing you, learning from you, and growing alongside you. I can't wait to watch as every single of one of you steps into the limelight and changes the earth's gravitational pull, one groundbreaking piece of journalism at a time.

Good-bye for now, my kitties! Please do stay in touch.

Ms. Loretta James

So that's it then. Just like that, an era ends. And while I have yet to receive an email from Margaret Hader informing me my services are no longer needed and that I can collect my things and be gone by the end of the day, I have no doubt there's one sitting in her drafts, just waiting to be sent. But I've come prepared, armed with two giant tote bags and a stack of thank-you notes. I plan to write every single person on staff a handwritten goodbye note, with my personal email attached. If I'm going out, I'm going out in style. I refuse to burn a single bridge.

I'll miss Saffron, of course. But I know we'll stay in touch. They've transcended work-friend status. We've become forever friends, and we'll continue to thrive outside the confines of SPP's ceiling-to-floor windows. We'll be just fine.

Honestly, I'm looking forward to having a little bit of time to refocus my thoughts and figure out what I actually want to do with my life.

Well, I know some things: I want to write for a publication that cares about its content, not just its clicks. And I want to be with someone who cares about me—all of me—not just what I can do for their career. And for the first time, I don't think that's too much to ask. I'm putting myself, my physical and mental health, first. Like Loretta said, I can't serve others if I don't serve myself first, right?

I refuse to settle.

But the industry is fundamentally flawed. Every single media company is struggling to figure out how to make money off clicks and clicks alone. Is it selling ad space? Running branded content alongside its daily features? Throwing sponsored events? No one has the answers, but everyone's vying for solutions, fighting each other for the best resources and personnel in order to ensure their survival. Print magazines are as good as extinct; newspapers are growing archaic. Online portals are pivoting to video, then podcasts, then newsletters—all to no avail.

So, instead, they're forced to lay people off. To freeze hiring. To acquire smaller companies or let larger conglomerates acquire them. To unionize in fear of being let go after years of humble service, just like Beth. We keep fighting yet feeding off one another, consuming each of us whole, until there are no individual brand identities. We'll all just become one big internet black hole.

But then what becomes of the reader? Surely that big black hole will swallow the reader alive. There's no shot they stand of staying alive navigating the ether, all alone. How will they learn to insert a tampon or register to vote? Where will they get their information, curate their taste, and formulate their opinions? What becomes of integrity, of free will?

The truth is, for far too long, the reader has been standing on a chipped star, one that's slowly burning out and dying. If they don't venture out, in search of a whole new universe, they're headed for an inevitable collision.

I want to offer them refuge. I want to come up with the solution, to protect them by giving them a space in my shuttle. I just have to figure out where I'll get my fuel.

Now that money is no longer an issue (Leila says business is good, and I choose to believe her), I think I'll take some time to really put more thought into the content I'm curating. For the first time in six months, I can really sit down and write a meaningful discourse for *NoorYorkCity*. I'll freelance to make ends meet, pitching stories that are timely and potent. In fact, Saffron already said I can pitch them whenever an idea comes to mind.

So I guess Beth was right. I will be okay. I am more than where I work.

The first thing I hear is the sound of laughter and shouting, followed by vintage Britney Spears.

When I turn the corner, I find the entirety of *Vinyl*'s Digital team clinking red SOLO cups filled with black coffee and mimosas and munching on bagels and lox as "Lucky" blares in the background.

I stand back, taking in the scene. They appear to be *celebrating* the announcement of Loretta's departure, as if she had waved the white flag of surrender and the war were finally won. *Vinyl* Digital is victorious, once and for all. Jade Aki actually defeated all her enemies.

Seb spots me hiding in the corner and runs up to me, cheeks flushed from the alcohol.

"Did you hear? Ding-dong, the bitch is dead!" he declares cheerfully, grabbing my hand and pulling me into the group. Lola offers me a smile and a hit of her vape, but I politely decline.

I take a seat next to Saffron, who gives my shoulder a

squeeze to let me know they're here if I need anything before joining in on the fun. I sink into their desk chair and listen as they chatter away with excitement about what their jobs will look like now that they're the only *Vinyl* editors on staff.

"I bet we'll all be given raises," Gwen says. "How could we not? We'll be pulling double the weight."

"Or even promotions," Crystal adds. "I mean, think about it. If I was the Digital Fashion editor, and there was a Print Fashion editor, but now I'm absorbing her writers and publishing all the content she normally did, I'm basically two people in one body! How does that not make me the senior Fashion editor, at the very least?"

"You don't manage anyone," Alex says curtly.

Crystal rolls her eyes. "Whatever," she says. "The title is *symbolic*."

Everyone starts talking on top of one another again, trying to envision what an editorial restructure and a magazine run entirely by Jade would look like. Would we swap out all our marquee photographers for young, queer, up-and-comers? Maybe we'd finally stop partnering with old haute couture fashion houses and collaborate with designers who are passionate about sustainability and inclusion, like Jeremy Scott or Patrick Church. As my coworkers hypothesize, I zone out while staring at the padlock on Loretta's door.

It occurs to me that Loretta never told me what I should do with all her things. I think about the framed photo of Sarah she has sitting on her desk. Should I box it all up and ship it to her town house in Park Slope? Should I donate what's left of her overflowing comp table to charity or my local homeless shelter? Or should I leave it all to be turned in with my security badge?

"What was that?" Alex asks.

Oops. I didn't realize I had been speaking out loud that entire time.

"Sorry, I was trying to figure out what I should do with all the shit left behind in Loretta's office."

Lola snorts.

"Who the fuck cares? Loretta's an elitist reptile who never gave a single shit about a single person in this office." She exhales, blowing out a thick cloud of smoke. "God, it feels good to be able to say that out loud."

"That's not true. She cared about me. And the magazine."

"Don't be such an idiot, Noora," Seb says. "It's not cute. Loretta used you just like she used everyone else. Stop defending her! There's no need to give two shits about her opinion. Don't wish her well! Be like me. I hope she gets hit by the L train! Or gets bitten by a rat and contracts some new strain of the bubonic plague!"

"Seb," Saffron interrupts, narrowing their eyes. "Too soon. Too far."

I sit in silence and watch the team crack up over Seb's machinations, before moving on to gossiping about members of the Print team's layoff announcements and job searches. They whisper and gasp in a repetitive pattern, as if tossing a ball back and forth, spreading rumors instead of kindness.

I can't believe this is the group of people I once idolized, the "good guys" I wanted so badly to be a part of. I guess you can't really be a hero without making a caricature of the villain. Most people aren't "good" or "bad," "woke" or "bigoted." The majority of us just exist in a gray area, trying to make the right decisions and to cover our tracks when we make the wrong ones. It's survival of the fittest, really. And sometimes, the most socially aware can be the most problematic of them all.

"Well, I'm going to go pack up my things." I say, interrupting their celebratory chugging competition. "I'll be at my desk if anyone needs me until the end of the day."

"And where exactly do you think you're going?" Kelsea asks, emerging from behind me. She's dressed in a long Canada Goose jacket and a cashmere beanie with a pompom sprouting from the top like a sunflower. If I were a betting man, I'd wager it's made of real fur.

"If Loretta's out, that means there's no room for me here anymore."

Kelsea rolls her eyes and gestures for me to walk with her.

"Well, do you have a minute before your big concession speech? Because Jade wants a minute alone with you."

I raise my eyebrows, and she shrugs. We continue to inch toward Jade's office.

"If I had to guess, she wants you to pass on a message to Loretta? Maybe you can kindly tell her where she can stick it," she says with a defiant smirk.

"Sure, Kelsea," I say, smiling. She clearly has no idea corporate offered Loretta the opportunity to stay on and that Jade was handed her job on a platter. It feels nice to know something she doesn't, for a change. "I bet that's it."

We arrive at Jade's door. Kelsea knocks slowly then leans her ear against the door.

"J, I have Noora here for you."

"Great, send her in!" Jade calls from inside.

Kelsea turns to me and flips her hair off from her shoulders. "Good luck!"

I've never been in Jade's office before, but it's exactly what I'd expect. It's smaller than Loretta's and doesn't have a single window. In fact, it's more like a glorified closet space with a few cabinets, a desk, and a rolling chair. I'm sure she's just itching to get her hands on Loretta's kingdom. The walls are covered with framed Basquiat prints, and there's a thick, red Supreme sticker on the back of her laptop. Instead of a second desk chair, she opted for a plush green couch. On second thought, I think it's actually the color jade.

"Hey, Noora! Or should, I say *C. Bates*?"

She playfully nudges my arm, and I breathe out a sigh of relief. In all the excitement, I had totally forgotten about my column. Of course, this is what Jade wants to talk to me about.

"I'm so sorry I didn't tell you. I had made an agreement with Loretta that I wouldn't do any writing for the Digital team and didn't want to break my promise to her. I was afraid of losing my job. But Saffron and I are tight, and when they needed a writer in a crunch, I didn't want to let them down. It was never my intention to lie to you or anyone else on the team. I never expected the article to get picked up, and it all spun out of control."

I finish my rant and catch my breath as Jade watches me. She's practically licking her lips in anticipation of jumping in.

"Girl, why didn't you just tell me? I totally admire your guts. You remind me of a young me, except much more badass. Did anyone ever tell you I started as Loretta's assistant?"

I nod slowly, curious as to what she's getting at.

"I know what a royal pain in the ass she can be. She's basically Hitler in a skirt. But she's gone now, and I'm going to take care of you. I think you've got real talent, Noora. And I'm so impressed with your dedication to inclusive, diverse, intersectional storytelling. It really shines through in your work. Thank you for your service!"

My body stings at the insensitive Hitler reference, but I brush it off.

"Wow, thank you," I say, taken aback. "I mean, you're welcome."

"Which is why I'd like to offer you a full-time position here on the *Vinyl* Digital team, as the new associate Features editor. You'd be responsible for overseeing a handful of staff writers and writing one to two op-eds a week. You'll also be working closely with our Wellness, Politics, and Fashion editors on profiles and editorial shoots. What do you say?"

I can't believe this is actually happening to me.

I've spent years dreaming of this exact moment, and now that I'm in it, it feels like I'm wearing someone else's skin.

"I–I'd like that very much," I reply, my voice quivering.

I'll have to call Leila right away to give her the news. Then Maman and Baba in Dubai. Jade claps with delight.

"Amazing! The next step will be bringing HR in to negotiate the official offer, but there were a few things I wanted to discuss with you first. I'd love for your Beauty Politics to remain an official *Vinyl* series, with you as the face behind it. That would mean coming out to the world as C. Bates, perhaps even doing a bit of press to explain Loretta was never behind the writing to begin with. I know that may seem daunting to you, or perhaps a little awkward, but I can ask Daniel to work with you on the prep so you aren't surprised by any of the questions that come up. Obviously, a little Loretta-bashing is okay, but too much will be total overkill. Use your better judgment."

"I, um—"

"There's one other thing I wanted to talk to you about. Now, I'm sure you're already aware of this, but you would be our only Middle Eastern editor on staff. In the coming year, I'd love for *Vinyl* to really lean into identity storytelling so we're at the forefront of every social justice conversation happening in the media landscape. So, with that being said, how do you feel about playing up your heritage for the column? Would you feel comfortable wearing a hijab in your author photo? I think it could be really controversial, great for driving traffic. You'd inspire so many hate-clicks!"

My jaw drops.

There it is.

There's the truth. The truth behind all the hashtags and viral videos.

Jade doesn't care about inclusive storytelling any more than Loretta did. She cares about starting controversy. She isn't interested in what I have to say as a writer; she only seeks to tokenize me.

My identity is just another commodity that can be packaged, repurposed, and used to drive traffic.

The Digital team is no better than the Print team. How profoundly disappointing.

I don't even take a beat to think.

"Jade, thank you so much for your offer," I wrinkle my nose. "But unfortunately, I'm going to decline."

"What? Why?" Jade jumps out of her seat in a panic. "Was it the Loretta-bashing thing? Because I was only half serious about her being Hitler!"

I stand up to meet her at eye level. As I do, my remaining anxiety melts off my body, down my legs, and into the floor. I feel calm and levelheaded for the first time in months.

I am wielding my own power.

"Respectfully, a hijab is not a prop. And neither am I."

Chapter Thirty-Two

It's the first week of December, and walking through lower Manhattan feels like being trapped inside a chaotic snow globe.

Every street corner is covered with Christmas tree vendors selling wrapped-up evergreens and wreaths, creating miniature forests in the heart of the urban jungle. The smell of pine overpowers the scent of piss, and the twinkling lights bleeding into the red blinking glow of police sirens make me feel a little more at home.

But New York is a city that's always propelling forward, powering full speed ahead. So, alongside the makeshift woodlands and ethereal campgrounds, you can find sparklers, and glitter hats and glasses that spell out the coming year—2020—or perhaps the tidings of the future, a happy New Year to you, and you, and you.

In this city, your true self can always be more authentic. Your best year can always be better, beat out by the what's yet to come.

I've heard people, outsiders mostly, critique this attitude. They wish New York would slow down and exhale. Settle for what it has, for what it is right now, in this moment. But like me, the city refuses to settle for less. It's too ambitious to pause for a please and thank you.

Instead, it remains hopeful. It knows that power lies in possibility.

As I step out of the SPP Tower for the very last time and onto the cobblestoned streets of South Street Seaport, I feel the light inklings of a December hailstorm graze against my cheek. As I look up toward the sky, hundreds of tiny little white flecks of winter dust begin to descend upon the city, like birds migrating south for the season. I wipe one off my cheek then make the decision to walk home in the squall, instead of taking the six train. A long trek, or perhaps even a frolic, is exactly what I need to clear my head and my lungs.

The first part of my body I ever waxed was my upper lip. I was eight years old. Leila was twelve, but a self-pronounced big girl. She had already been waxing for four years and was thus in charge of taking me to my first appointment.

We went to a Korean spa in Midtown Manhattan, a long subway ride away from our apartment in Crown Heights. Tightly clutching Leila's hand, I bravely marched into the establishment and announced to the receptionist that I was ready to be beautiful. The woman behind the register had cocked her head.

You're already beautiful, she had said. *On the inside.*

I thought was so silly—what's the point of being beautiful if others can't see it?

I followed her into the dimly lit stall in the far back, right corner. I asked if Leila could come with me but was told the space was too small for three. She had to wait outside.

The room smelled of cucumber and was painted lime green. There was classical music playing in the background. The woman—I think her name was Kim—asked me to lie down with my head facing the wall and my feet closest to the door. She twirled the hot wax around on a thick Popsicle stick then slowly lowered it onto my face, spreading it over my philtrum like peanut butter.

I was surprised by how good it felt—warm and soothing, like standing a little too close to an open fire and drinking in the heat.

Is it going to hurt?

She smiled down at me, like Zeus from the top of Mount Olympus or a bird about to shit some good luck on top of your head.

Yes. But then it will be over. And you'll look like the person you truly are.

It was then that I was overwhelmed with a paralyzing fear—of pain, of the moment my hair follicles were ripped out from under my skin like a child from its mother's arms.

For the first time in my life, I felt my hands begin to shake and my lips quiver. My heart raced a mile a minute, and I found my nose couldn't keep up with the pace, so I began breathing in and out of my mouth. Kim noticed instantly and took a step back.

What happens if I back out?

Then you'll stay like this forever.

Kim gestured to the wax that had already hardened into the moldings of my face.

So my choices are to stay and get hurt, or leave and hate myself for it?

Tough decision.

Kim sat down on the parlor bed next to me, swinging the Skechers on her feet back and forth.

Life is full of tough decisions. Making a choice and sticking with it shows strength of character.

Even when both options suck?

Even then.

I shut my eyes tightly, made peace with my resolution, and awaited judgment day.

Seconds later, I screamed. The sting of the wax seared my skin, causing my eyes to well up. But my heartbeat slowed its cadence, and my hands folded into my chest.

Kim handed me the mirror, and I peered at my reflection with the curiosity of a newborn. What greeted me stung even more than the wax.

For the first time, I looked a little more like myself. Or, at the very least, the image I've always had in my head. I realized, then and there, how deeply I'd internalized the Western idealization of beauty, the time and energy and I had wasted feeling trapped inside of my bag of skin. But the fat, the blood, the bones—none of it mattered. Appearances are easy to fake. I could mold myself into whatever I wanted to look like. I could become anyone I wanted to be. But first, I had to figure out what *feeling* like myself meant. That would be the real challenge.

From that day forward, I, too, promised to never look back, only forward.

As I make my way up Pearl Street and toward Bowery, I begin to skip. One foot in front of the other, my body jiving to a tune that's unseen, unheard, and unspoken. I haven't moved this way since I was a child, and it feels liberating, like taking off your bra at the tail end of the day.

I kick up my ankles, moving faster and faster, brushing off looks of confusion and pity from onlooking New Yorkers who don't agree with the practice. As I fly by bakeries and bodegas, I people watch my fellow NYC locals. I skip across red streetlights and into oncoming holiday traffic, past honking cabdrivers and Uber Pool passengers crying about their latest breakup to a sympathetic stranger. I skip past dog shit and carolers; men running down St. James Place with a bouquet of flowers in their arms and a smile smacked upon their faces; and women hunched over benches, wiping away tears and wailing without a care for who can see them. I skip with preschool children in yellow traffic vests, all lined up like ducks in row, being walked toward the Tenement Museum for a midday field trip. I skip away from the last six months and toward the rest of my life.

"Excuse me!"

A short, young girl with big brown eyes, bleached white hair, and roots the color of mine catches up to me. She speaks with a hint of an accent, the kind that peeks out from behind the blinds at the very end of a syllable or in the mispronunciation of a word. I recognize that glitch in vowels—it's the kind of stutter you aren't born with but grow into by hearing a Middle Eastern parent repeat it over and over.

I smile at her, and she looks back at me with a startling familiarity.

"*Salam*, so sorry to bother you, but are you Noora?" Her eyes wrinkle in the corners, and her baby hairs fly in the December wind.

A tiny snowflake catches her eyelashes, and she just leaves it there, without pausing to brush it off.

"Yes, *baleh*! My apologies, remind me of your name?" I'm embarrassed that I can't place her face.

The girl laughs.

"We've never met," she explains. "My name is Fatimeh, and I'm a huge *NoorYorkCity* fan. I've been following you since you first started blogging in 2015—I just love your style. Like, that thrifted brown corduroy suit you wore last Monday? Such a vibe. Even your bright-yellow puffer you're wearing right now is serious goals."

"Thank you!" I clutch my heart, taken aback by the flattery. I've never met a reader in the wild before.

"No, thank you. For writing about being young and a woman and Middle Eastern and American. I always felt like every single part of my identity was at odds with the other, tugged in different directions, close to being torn apart. No matter how much I messed with myself, I could never make the pieces fit together. And then I discovered your blog. For the first time, I realized it was okay to feel like an ever-evolving mess, to live in a space that's neither here nor there. To have multiple homes and no real homeland. To believe so many conflicting things and nothing at all."

She opens her arms wide, and I reach down and give her a hug. Our two bodies meld together.

A sense of purpose washes over me. Every muscle and bone in my body both relaxes and reenergizes at once.

"Thank you for reading," I say wholeheartedly. I mean every word.

"Of course. I'd follow your writing anywhere."

And then she's gone, as quickly as she appeared. I'm left smiling like a sap, alone on a New York City street corner.

I reach Chatham Square and turn left onto Mott Street. The red lights from the Chinese open-air markets flood the street and reflect off the white sheets lining the tops of garbage cans. Peking duck wafts past me and into Lower Manhattan, like the exhaust of a parked car with the engine still running. The snowing has stopped, turning to a pale, graying slush beneath my feet.

I take another step forward, and the melting water vapors below me explode upward into my face, like a piñata. I let out a childlike giggle and take another step.

Blam.

Another sludge puddle detonates beneath the bottom of my boot. My walking turns to marching, big, grandiose steps like a soldier or a Radio City Rockette. I'm having so much fun playing in the gunk of what once was metropolitan snow that I don't even notice a pedestrian behind me.

Without thinking, I leap into another shallow pool with both feet, causing an eruption the size of Staten Island.

The dirty ice sprays all over my face, hands, and clothes, creating a tie-dye pattern that can only be procured from playing in the mud. Unfortunately, my fellow passerby gets hit by the debris too. They let out a small yelp, as if I'd hit them with my car.

Wiping the slush from off their face, they turn to look at me.

It's a man in his early thirties. He's wearing a long, cushioned coat that looks like a sleeping bag and suede boots. His hair is slicked back with so much gel, he resembles a broker, but his long, neon-pink acrylic nails suggest he's never signed on the dotted line a day in his life.

Has he wandered all the way here from the gallery district in Chelsea, where he owns a small one-bedroom with his boyfriend of five years and three cats? Or perhaps he's from Queens, and lost his way back to Astoria somewhere along the W train, and now refuses to take the L. He could be born and raised in Harlem, a Midtown maverick, or a complete anomaly by way of Boerum Hill. Honestly, your guess would be as good as mine; I'm struggling to place him. He's difficult to define, to put in a box.

We lock eyes, and he sneers at me. I smile back. I know a fellow local when I see one.

"Hey, watch it, lady!" he screeches. "This is *New York City*, not Minnesota or wherever the hell you're from. We don't play in the snow here. We walk as quickly and as quietly as we can, without drawing too much attention to ourselves, because we've got places to be and people to see. And if you get one more speck of dirt on my brand-new Burberry coat,

I'm going to make you Venmo me the full price of my dry cleaning. Got it?"

I nod my head, a mischievous grin spreading from cheek to cheek.

Then I take a deep breath and jump.

New Yorkers are fucking crazy—myself included.

Reading Group Guide

1. Noora is quick to accept her job offer from *Vinyl*, even after seeing some glaring red flags during her interview (like the box of tissues in the beauty closet). If you were in her shoes, would these red flags be enough to deter you from your dream job?

2. Even though the *Vinyl* Digital team is young and progressive, microaggressions still run rampant in the office. What microaggressions did you notice throughout the novel? Have you seen similar behaviors in your own experiences in an office?

3. This novel was written by an industry insider. How do you feel about her take on the media industry? Does this align with your own expectations of what it's like to work for a major publication?

4. Noora does her best to be a decent person, free of biases and problematic behaviors. However, she is only human. Despite her best efforts, her narrative is still flawed and not always self-aware. Where did you notice Noora failing to

meet her own standards of political correctness? Do you think her narration ever strays from her own values?

5. Cal is swoon-worthy at first, but he eventually reveals himself to be quite the opposite. Did you see any red flags in Cal's character before his final confrontation with Noora?

6. What do you think of Loretta's intentions in her feud with the Digital team? Do you admire her desire to keep the Print team alive, or do you think her motivations were more malicious?

7. One of the biggest dilemmas Noora faces is her decision to pick sides in the war between Print and Digital. If you were Noora, what would you do? Would you stay loyal to the Print team or act as a spy for the Digital team? Do you think Noora made the right call?

8. In the world of *A Hundred Other Girls*, Loretta is famous as a feminist icon, but her actions in the novel don't often feel very feminist. How do you think her old-school mentality fails in the modern age? Would you consider her a feminist by today's standards?

9. What was your reaction when Jade's tweets were leaked to the media? How does your own perception of cancel culture affect your reaction?

10. What does the title *A Hundred Other Girls* mean to you after finishing the book?

A Conversation
with the Author

How did your own experiences in the media industry influence your decision to write this book?

I've worked at every level in print and digital media, from entry-level assistant to deputy editor. In order to write this book, I drew inspiration from each and every position—*Vinyl* is no one magazine but rather an amalgamation of the industry. Over the years, I've watched passionate employees grow disillusioned with their "dream roles" as they fight for job security. I came to realize that the true pulse of their content—the reader—was getting lost. I wanted to write a story dedicated to finding it again.

The feud between the Print and Digital teams at *Vinyl* is a key component in the plot. Do you think print and digital media are at war in reality? Have you seen this same tension in your career?

Between print magazines trying to appeal to advertisers targeting a Gen Z audience and digital newsrooms attempting to balance meeting traffic goals with producing clickbait, I've definitely seen this tension play out in real life. But I actually believe that both teams are united in their fight for survival, with print brands facing the threat of folding and digital platforms living in fear of layoffs. Although the two are often pitted against each other, they're both struggling to create sellable content without compromising their integrity.

What's your writing process like? What was your process for writing *A Hundred Other Girls*?

In many ways, I've been writing this book in my head since I was a little girl. I've always been obsessed with coming-of-age novels but felt like I never had access to heroines who looked like me or had families like mine. I wanted to write a novel that was both fun and insightful, with a completely diverse cast of characters whose identities were integral to who they were without being key to the plot. In other words, representation without tokenization. And ever since I began my career in media and saw how different—and diverse—the industry has grown since *The Devil Wears Prada*, I knew it was high time for an updated depiction.

I still work full-time as a writer and editor, so I wrote this book after-hours, drawing on all the industry drama that I had been privy to, both first- and secondhand. In order to paint a full picture, I interviewed a lot of my former colleagues, read articles published in *Business of Fashion* and *Women's Wear Daily*, and digested more pop culture than I care to admit. I wanted this book to feel as timely in 2022 as it did when I wrote in 2019. I never could have predicted that it would feel even *more* urgent and topical today than it did three years ago!

What was your favorite scene to write?

Oh my God, this is so tough because I had *so* much fun delving into all of the scandal, gossip, and intrigue surrounding the world of *Vinyl*. Selfishly, I'm going to have to go with Noora and Cal's romp in the beauty closet. As a former sex and relationships editor, I've always dreamed of writing a spicy scene that featured a young woman who was unabashed about chasing her own pleasure, taking control of her sexual agency. From her incorporation of a sex toy to her disappointment in Cal's, er, performance, I really loved exploring what sex can look like when women clearly communicate their needs. It felt so true to life and unlike anything else I've ever read in the genre.

Which character was the most challenging to write?

All of the characters are morally gray and therefore, were a challenge to write, but I found Loretta to be the most nuanced. On the one hand, she's clearly a narcissist who has zero awareness of how her actions and words impact the people around her. But she's also obviously driven by her insecurities and has had to overcome so much in order to thrive in a patriarchal environment—she's earned her icon status. Navigating Noora's push and gravitational pull to Loretta often toed the line because I wanted readers to understand why, after everything is said and done, Noora is still torn about where her loyalties lie.

What's the most important thing you hope readers take from *A Hundred Other Girls*?

The title of the book alludes to an old-guard, toxic, "lucky to be here" mentality that permeates many industries and encourages burnout culture, a mentality that pits women against other women and belittles their self-worth. I hope that, by reading this, readers are encouraged to draw boundaries and are reminded that they are more than their job descriptions. Your voice can never be reduced to a title, and your identity can never be packaged for clicks. Your perspective is unique and valuable because it's *yours*. You are inherently worthy.

Acknowledgments

There are a lot of people without whom this novel wouldn't be possible, so my sincerest apologies in advance for the Oscars acceptance speech–style rant I'm about to go on.

Taylor Haggerty and the rest of the Root Literary family, thank you so much for immediately understanding and believing in this novel—and me. Without your confidence in the project, strategic thinking, and calming presence, I don't think I could have even gotten through the submission stage. Let's do this forever, 'kay?

Addison Duffy, thank you for falling in love with these characters on the first read. I can't wait to further expand and explore their world with you.

Kate Roddy, thank you for championing this novel, developing its story, and holding my hand through every step of the process. From fielding my 1:00 a.m. food-for-thought emails to leaving insightful edits and kind notes throughout the manuscript, you made every revision fun.

Kathleen Carter, thank you for coming on board with so much enthusiasm and passion for the project, and for truly believing that readers will see themselves in Noora's story.

Cristina Arreola, I'm still in awe of the fact that we're working together again. You were one of the first people I told about this book, and the fact that it reached your inbox again, over a year later, is true kismet. Thank you for your sharp insights, strategic thinking, and pep talks.

You five are the dream team, and I couldn't be more grateful to have you in my corner.

To the rest of the Sourcebooks team—Jessica Thelander, Manu Velasco, Brittany Vibbert, Kelly Lawler, Molly Waxman, Valerie Pierce, and, of course, Todd Stocke and Dominique Raccah—thank you for believing in this book from the get go and giving it every opportunity to succeed. I am so forever grateful to be a part of your family.

Sandra Chiu, thank you for designing the most beautiful cover that perfectly encapsulates the spirit of Noora and the world of *A Hundred Other Girls*.

Bahman Kia, thank you for being my first-ever editor. All I've ever wanted to do is make you proud. I'm sorry I wouldn't let you read this one. Gisue Hariri, thank you for giving me that pen at graduation and reminding me that I'm a writer when I lost sight of it myself. Encouraging me to pursue my creative inclinations at a young age was the greatest gift you two could have given me, and I feel immensely privileged to have you as parents.

Ava Hariri-Kia, thank you for inspiring me with your passion for your own work and motivating me to give my all to this project at a time when I had given up. You are the coolest person I've ever met, and I admire you more than anybody on the planet—even if it took you two years to finally read my manuscript.

Matthew Falkner, I started and finished this novel with you by my side. Your love, support, and patience is injected into every word on every page. Thank you for picking me up off the floor, listening to me read my work aloud, attending my panels, and toasting my victories. I'm sorry I broke that mirror. I couldn't have asked for a better partner, and I love sharing a life with you. I love you.

To my aunt Mojgan Hariri, thank you for being my biggest cheerleader. To my grandparents, thank you for calling me once a week for two years and asking when the book would be available for purchase. And to Angie Tinto, thank you for reading to me when I was little and raising me to be a woman of principle, pleasure, and love.

Ariel Matluck, Simone Rivera, Katie Duncalf, Audrey Ellen, Brooke Yalof, Cora Vasserman, Aidan Macaluso, Hannah Smith, Caitlin Merrell, Alexandra Falkner, Emily Oppenheimer, and Ashlie Williams—thank you for being my beta readers and for diving into Noora's world back when it was simply *CliqueBait*. You are the realest of friends, and I'll never forget it.

Tessa Forrest, Faith Brown, Madeleine Bokan, Maddie Hiatt, Ruby Redstone, Emi Warner, Sydney Goldberger, Yasmine Almaimani, Remy Gwertzman, Mai Morsch, Calvin millien, Tony Pezullo, Ebuka Anakoute, Julia Collins, Veronica Lopez, and Maria Bianculli, thank you so much for all of the cover feedback. I'm sorry for spamming your feed.

Cassidy Sachs, thank you for answering every panicked question I have about the publishing industry and dreaming this up with me in college. Guess what? We did the thing. Very cool!

Amanda Montell and Gabrielle Korn, thank you for being the best group chat a debut author could have ever asked for. You two humble me with your counsel and talent.

Louisiana Mei Gelpi, thank you for taking my beautiful author photo and for your true friendship. I owe you that milkshake.

Willa Bennett and Melanie Mignucci, there simply aren't words. I couldn't get through a single day without you two.

Thank you isn't enough. I love you isn't enough. This book is as much yours as it is mine. WT forever.

To my colleagues at Condé Nast, Bustle Digital Group, and Her Campus Media, thank you for your camaraderie and support. You make this industry better, and I'm so proud of all that you continue to accomplish.

Prof. Fink, Prof. Sugimura, Prof. Lori Merish, Mrs. Frosch, Ms. Jewett, and Ms. Silva, you will probably never read this, but thank you for teaching me how to engage with literature and giving me the tools to one day craft my own.

Meg Cabot and Lisi Harrison, thank you for helping me feel less alone as an adolescent and inspiring me to do the same for others. P.S. Did you ever get my fan mail?

To all the avid YA fans who never saw themselves as protagonists: Noora belongs to you.

And to my readers, from the people who have supported and engaged with my work since my early days at *Teen Vogue*, to those who have followed my journey on BookTok: Thank you for coming along on this adventure with me. We've grown so much together. This novel is for you.

About the Author

© Louisiana Mei Gelpi

Iman Hariri-Kia is a writer and editor born and based in New York City. A nationally acclaimed journalist, she covers sex, relationships, identity, and adolescence. You can often find her writing about her personal life on the internet, much to her parents' dismay.